Kiss Like You Mean It

Louise Harwood is the bestselling author of *Lucy Blue, Where Are You?*, *Six Reasons to Stay a Virgin*, *Calling on Lily* and *Hippy Chick*. She is a full-time writer, and lives in Oxfordshire with her husband and two sons.

Praise for previous Louise Harwood novels

'Refreshing, light-hearted and emotionally intelligent'
The Times

'Louise Harwood's latest novel is hugely compelling, hugely enjoyable and hugely readable'
Heat

'I found this light-hearted, feel-good flight of fancy pretty addictive'
Daily Mail

Louise Harwood

Kiss Like You Mean It

PAN BOOKS

First published 2010 by Pan Books
an imprint of Pan Macmillan, a divison of Macmillan Publishers Limited
Pan Macmillan, 20 New Wharf Road, London N1 9RR
Basingstoke and Oxford
Associated companies throughout the world
www.panmacmillan.com

ISBN 978-0-330-44209-1

1 3 5 7 9 8 6 4 2

A CIP catalogue record for this book is available
from the British Library.

Typeset in Palatino by Royle, London EC1M 4DH
Printed and bound in the UK by CPI Mackays, Chatham ME5 8TD

Visit **www.panmacmillan.com** to read more about all our books
and to buy them. You will also find features, author interviews and
news of any author events, and you can sign up for e-newsletters
so that you're always first to hear about our new releases.

For Tom and Jack Harwood

Prologue

Carey stared up at the ceiling and willed Anton Klubcic out of her bed. Why couldn't his PA call him? Or surely there was a minion to be fired, or a plane to be caught, or a multi-million dollar movie holding its breath for his go-ahead? She felt his weight shift above her and she closed her eyes and held her breath in hope, but Anton had other things on his mind. He caught a red ringlet of her hair around his finger and she felt him tug it insistently.

'Open your eyes and kiss me.'

Anton liked girls to do as they were told. She could feel his breath on her face as he waited for her and her eyes really didn't want to open at all, she had to drag them apart, then force out a little smile for him, as if he truly was the only man for her. She let him pull her closer until her lips met his and he could catch her in another bristly kiss. It was 10.15 in the morning, why couldn't a chambermaid burst through the door? His tongue twisted with hers and she bore it gracefully, even managed a little sigh.

'What will I do when you're gone?' He touched her cheek with a stubby finger.

She looked up at the sweat beading at the edges of his Botoxed forehead, at his thick white hair, parting still in place, at his large bulbous nose.

'Draw me up a ten-million-dollar contract?'

For a moment she thought she'd blown it. He looked back at her completely stunned, and then let out a hoot of laughter and she giggled in relief as he collapsed against her, pinning her down on the mattress and kissing her again.

'I see I've met an honest girl at last.'

'Anton, I swear I was joking!' she protested, winding her hands around his neck, thinking I've blown it, fuck, fuck, fuck.

'Of course you were.' He looked at her appraisingly. 'So do you have an audition today?'

She'd told him over and over again and still he'd forgotten, and she realized this was the first time she'd properly got his attention since they'd met the evening before. He probably didn't even remember her name.

'It's the casting at Hyatt Adonis. I'm Carey Sloan,' she added for good measure.

'I'm sure you'll do very well.' He looked at his watch and she saw him flinch at what he saw.

'Are you okay?' She stroked his face.

'Time's up, baby.'

She pouted at him. 'Oh please don't go.'

'I'm not.' He laughed. 'You are.'

'I don't think so,' she stammered. 'This is my room.'

'So?' He rolled away and turned off the bedside light, returning the room to a gloomy dusk.

So she had pissed him off. Adrenalin pumped through her. Don't cross him, don't challenge him. All the warning bells were ringing but still she couldn't stop herself. 'This is *my* room, Anton.'

'But you keep me awake and now I need to sleep. In four hours I catch a plane to Japan. You can come back when I have gone.'

He found a blackout mask on her bedside table and put it on, then turned his back on her, pulling the covers high around him, shuffling himself comfortable.

She ripped back her sheets and jumped out of bed. It was 10.15 and at a quarter to one she'd be walking into her casting at the Hyatt Adonis Agency, 1965–1703 Sunset Boulevard, LA 90716. What the hell was he playing at? In precisely two and a half hours she would be walking into the most important moment of her life and this fat fuck under her sheets was giving her no time to prepare. In fact, she wanted to cry. He was completely ruining everything by not getting out of her bed and giving her back her room.

She'd been going to order room service and eat croissants in bed and then do some yoga to keep herself calm. She'd been going to groom and pamper herself for as long as she wanted, with no flatmate banging on the bathroom door. Did Anton know just how often she got the chance to spend time in a room like this? Did he realize how badly she wanted that part? Just how much he was ruining her life?

From his stillness she wondered if he was already asleep, and she knew there was nothing she could do but what she'd been told. She walked naked through the room to her cupboards. She'd wanted to think about what to wear for the casting and here she was having to make the decision in the dark.

She looked at her clothes. The part she was up for was of a young French farm girl caught up in the First World War, and she couldn't see much in her cupboard to help convince the casting director she was the one. But then, as the girl spent most of her scenes naked in a hay barn with a doomed British soldier, she guessed it was probably the body under the clothes that mattered more. She wondered if that was why she'd ended up in Anton's bed in the first place. Perhaps she'd already auditioned without even realizing it.

In the gloomy light she chose a pair of tiny cut-off jean-shorts, a jewelled leather belt she'd bought in Las Vegas, a shocking pink vest top that went with her nail polish and clashed with her hair, and a pair of high wedge-heeled sandals. She took them into her bathroom, then moved quickly into the shower, washed, dressed and put on some mascara and lip-gloss.

From the doorway she looked back at the fat little gremlin lying in her beautiful king-size bed, polluting her beautiful room. What a waste of time, she mouthed at him. And then she remembered how hard he'd come on to her the evening before, and how although sleeping with him had probably not kick-started her career, not sleeping with him would certainly have ended it.

At the lifts she caught a glimpse of herself in the huge hotel mirror and immediately felt better. She had to admit those Vita-Tan pills had worked brilliantly – even in the unforgiving Los Angeles sunlight her usually pale skin had a beautiful Hollywood glow. She turned to check the backs of her legs.

4

Eat your heart out Rory Defoe, she whispered at the mirror.

Rory Defoe was playing the lead, the British soldier in the film. No, he wasn't a soldier, she remembered, he was something else, something odd, a cameraman, that was it. She didn't know cameras had even been invented then. Perhaps it wasn't the First World War but the Second? She leaned forwards to check her mascara. Much more importantly, whoever got the part would have a love scene with Rory Defoe in a hay barn. Enter Carey Sloan.

The lift had still not arrived. She hit the button for a second time and wondered whether to take the stairs, but the mirror was just too tempting to leave right away. She stepped back a pace and looked at herself appreciatively. She tossed back her ringlets, then tried a sad look for the mirror, gave her reflection a little wave as she imagined herself standing at the door to the hay barn, saying goodbye to her soldier. She had to get the part. The film was called *To End All War*, and although she'd been given the script she hadn't read it all yet, couldn't even say what the movie was about, beyond the scenes between the farm girl and the soldier-cameraman. But what she did know was that it was produced by Anton Klubcic, financed by Anton Klubcic, distributed by Anton Klubcic, bankrolled by Anton Klubcic. Don't cross Anton Klubcic, that much she did know.

She wondered if she'd upset him.

Carey Sloan.

She imagined him wagging his fat finger as he shouted out her name to his secretary, telling her to write down the name Carey Sloan in his book of girls *never to work in this town again*. And that would be it. Her career over just like that. And Anton had done just that before, finished small-time players who had done no more than cough in a key moment at one of his premieres. And then, other times he'd done the opposite, plucked his Eliza Doolittles out of the gutters and into his beds, making them stars. The actress Liberty Boyd, co-star of *To End All War*, was only the most recent. Carey had allowed herself to fantasize she might be next.

She straightened to her full six foot, pouted a little at her reflection and tried to wipe the look of worry off her face. Why had she made that stupid joke? Men like him, para-noid, unstable men with egos the size of the Beverly Hills Hotel, shouldn't be teased. She should have known better.

She was still at the mirror, still deep in thought, when finally the lift doors opened behind her. And so quietly that she wasn't even aware it was happening, a man stepped out behind her, so that where once there had just been her, now there were two. It was as if by the power of her thoughts alone she'd conjured him out of thin air. Rory Defoe, surely the sexiest man on the planet, standing right behind her, barefoot, with wet hair and a skimpy towel, looking as if he'd just stepped out of the shower.

With the knowledge came a great rush of elation and she found she was unable to make a sound, could only stand there beside him, and look at him look at her, and then it was all too much and she only had time to think, briefly, I'm going to faint, before she sank down on the floor of the hotel corridor, literally collapsed at his feet.

Rory thought it was very funny, she fell so tidily and carefully. When she didn't move he dropped beside her and touched her forehead with his hand, and after a few seconds more her eyes fluttered open.

'You need to lie down.'

'I am lying down.'

'Somewhere more comfortable than a cold marble floor. Where's your room?'

'I don't want to go there. Help me to a chair.'

She felt a wonderfully strong Rory Defoe hand clasp her arm and help her to her feet and then gently push her down again into an ornate gold-painted armchair positioned beside the lifts.

'Do you want me to fetch you some water?'

'No,' she shook her head. 'I'll be fine in a moment.' She laughed at herself, shaking her head. 'I cannot believe I just did that. How embarrassing. Although I guess you're always having girls falling at your feet.'

'Never ones as pretty as you.'

She went to stand up again, then paused and sat abruptly back down.

'Are you in a hurry? Is there someone I should call for you?'

She couldn't believe he was there, crouched at her side, so close she could hardly stop herself from resting her cheek against his beautiful chest. 'I don't know anybody here.' She leaned forwards and let her long red curls fall around her face. 'But please don't worry about me, you surely have better things to do.'

Carey wasn't to know that girls had tried this trick on Rory more times than he could remember, ugly ones, pretty ones, tall ones, short ones, all of them thinking they were the first to come up with such an ingenious ruse. Usually he left them to it, but something about Carey caught his interest.

'Where's your room?'

'Just down there. First one on the left. But I told you we . . . I . . .' she corrected herself hurriedly. 'I don't want to go there.'

'Then you'd better come to my room. I don't think you should be left on your own until you're sure you're feeling better. I've got a script to read. We'll share a brandy and I can keep an eye on you. Half an hour, that's all. Then I'll let you go.'

At that moment a hotel porter smartly dressed in a black and gold suit came scooting swiftly around the corner.

'Mr Defoe, I don't think . . . '

Rory waved him away. 'She's fine.'

'Please, Mr Defoe, you'll surely understand we can't have our guests behave like this.'

'She fainted,' Rory said.

'Oh, I am sorry. Please forgive me, sir. I heard you laughing and I saw her on the floor and you were there above her and I thought . . .'

'What did you think?' Rory asked.

The man dropped his gaze and looked hurriedly away. 'I'm real sorry, Mr Defoe, I thought nothing, nothing at all.' Then he looked beseechingly back at Rory. 'Please, sir, you know I did not mean any offence. It's just, after last night . . . '

'Ah, yes, last night,' said Rory. 'Of course.'

'What happened?' asked Carey.

'None of your business,' said Rory, and she saw for the

first time how pale he looked, and how his hand, still holding on to her arm, was shaking.

'And we've had other guests, not like you, sir, no, not like you at all. Guests who do not know when to stop, who have no sense of what should only be done behind closed doors.'

Rory nodded. 'You thought that you were seeing it all over again.'

The porter sighed. 'Sir, yes. You could say so.'

'Then I will take this young lady.' Rory turned back to Carey. 'What's your name?' She told him. 'I shall take Carey to my room. I will look after her carefully and when she is fit to travel I shall send her on her way.'

Carey rose eagerly to her feet.

'What floor are we on?' Rory demanded, re-tucking in his towel, bashing at the lift buttons, and for the first time Carey found herself wondering why that was all he was wearing.

'Where were you going?' she asked him.

'You know what? I don't remember.'

'Don't worry about us,' she told the porter, feeling rather sorry for him. 'We're off now.'

As the doors opened she saw the relief on his face that they were no longer his problem. Of course, with Rory dressed like he was, and with such a bad-boy image as he had, no wonder the poor guy had leapt to such conclusions.

She turned back to Rory, her finger hovering at the floor numbers.

'Do you want to go up or down?'

He came towards her and took her in his arms. 'I think both,' he replied.

*

Anton's temper held for all of the ten feet from his hotel door to the lift but was lost completely when a hotel porter told him exactly what had happened to the tall red-headed girl that he'd seen at the lifts.

'I thought I heard his fucking voice. Would know it anywhere. What room's he in?'

'I don't think I can tell you that, sir.'

'Look here, you little shit.' Anton spun around looking for something to throw and saw a blue glass jug full of flowers.

'Please don't do that, sir.' The porter moved like lightning and lifted the vase to safety.

'Tell me his room number. Jesus Christ, if you don't tell me, my secretary will. She booked all the fucking rooms in the first place. You realize why he's here, do you? That sex-addicted, drug-addicted snake? He's here because of me. Because of me and my film and if I find he's done anything, if he's laid even a finger on Carey Sloan, he will never work in this town again. Never, do you hear me?'

The porter nodded nervously. Anton took a deep sigh. 'Okay, it's not your fault. I know that. Just doing your job, I understand. I respect that, In fact I like that. I'm sorry. I get angry. I'll give you a job, you know what. I'm going to give you a fucking job, make you more money in a month than you make in this place in a year. Wait, don't move. Wait right there . . . Sofia . . .' he bellowed into his mobile phone. 'What floor is Rory's suite? And where is that?' He nodded at the porter. 'First floor, the entire fucking first floor, can you believe we've given him that? Who the fuck does he think he is?' He turned back to his PA. 'And Sofia, got a guy here, I want to give him a job. He's right here. Listen to him and fix something up for him, will you?' He handed the porter his mobile phone. 'Hand it in to reception when you've finished and I'll pick it up later. Right now I need to find Carey Sloan.'

Anton wanted to kill Rory. He'd felt it the very first time he'd met him, two months before, when they'd met to talk about the film. Anton had looked into Rory's indigo blue eyes and could almost see the beautiful girls reflected there. Rory had slept with more beautiful women than anyone else he knew, women who Anton knew would not look twice at him, even for the part of a lifetime. And he hated Rory for it, hated his dark good looks and his body that stayed so perfect despite the partying, and his height and his youth and his wealth and his talent. Hated the way he could drink and take drugs all night long and still break your heart on set the next morning. At times Rory's talent made Anton feel as if everything he'd achieved was second rate, but now, finally, Anton was the one on top because his company, Studio X, was backing Rory's next film, *To End All War*, and for the first time Rory was dependent on him, and although he had a loyal following, and people that counted talked of Oscars one day, he wasn't there yet; he needed this film to work, Rory needed Anton on side.

Outside Rory's suite, Anton hammered on the door, then when nothing happened leaned close to listen. He heard nothing. It was an expensive door, designed not to let out its secrets. Anton waited just five seconds more and then knocked again, and this time Rory answered almost immediately.

He took away Anton's confidence like no one else he

knew and he hadn't even said a word. It was something in the way he looked at him, looked down at him, because for a start he was so tall, but it was also because there was something in his expression that said he found everything about Anton faintly funny.

I want to kill him, Anton thought again, and pushed Rory backwards without saying a word, walked into the room to find Carey sitting demurely in a chair, wrapped in a hotel bathrobe.

He strode over to her, fury meaning he didn't think what he was saying.

'Take it off,' he demanded.

'No!' she cried.

'Take off the bathrobe. I want to see what you're wearing underneath. If you're wearing anything underneath.'

'How dare you?' Rory walked up behind him and shoved Anton so violently that Anton found himself falling sideways into a sofa. 'Don't you dare humiliate her like that.'

'It's okay, Rory.' Carey had seen the purple rage on Anton's face. She stepped up and let the bathrobe drop to the ground. Beneath it she was wearing a large blue shirt.

'I didn't want to wake you,' she told him gently. 'I thought it was better that I slipped away quietly, in my best hotel nightshirt.' She came closer and gave him a little smile. 'I think I might steal it. Do you think they'd notice? I have my clothes here. I was going to find somewhere to dress, perhaps go down to the spa, and then I met Rory and he kindly said I could come here and use his suite.'

She looked beseechingly into Anton's eyes and said it very firmly, so that there was no mistaking the implication in her words. She hadn't slept with Rory. She was telling him that. Of course she hadn't. Now Anton felt a fool even to have thought of such a thing. She'd only just left him, she'd left their room, what, fifteen minutes earlier? Surely even Rory couldn't move that fast. Anton straightened on the sofa. He still couldn't look at Rory but he could nod quietly back at her, covering up his bluster and anger as if it had never been there.

'The porter said you'd been ill. I was worried.'

'And Rory was so kind.' She smiled sweetly. 'All I needed was a quiet few moments sitting here with a glass of water.'

He nodded. 'Go back to your room. Recover there.'

Anton waited but there was no hint of a glance to Rory. 'Of course, Anton. Great idea. But I'm fine, now, promise, completely better.'

Anton waited until Carey was safely out of the room and out of earshot and then turned back to Rory.

'First, I will kick the shit out of you if you ever touch me again. Second, I will crucify you if you go near her on set. If I give her this part she's going to be under your nose and you're not to touch her. And if I find out that you have she's finished, you're finished and the film is finished. Over. Got that? And third, if you don't get your act together soon the film's finished too.' He cast a disgusted look around Rory's suite, at the drawn curtains, the contents of the mini-bar scattered across the tables and floor, the overflowing ashtrays. 'How did that window get broken? Did a woman jump out of it?'

'I don't like threats, Anton. I thought I explained that to you the first time we met.'

'Then you'd better get used to them because you'll find I do like them.'

'Carey is her own boss.'

'No. Carey is a cheap tart who'd sleep with a gorilla if it could help her career.'

One

When you go home, tell them of us and say,
For your tomorrows, these gave their today.

'You should let your moustache dry. If you go outside now it might blow away.'

'So, glue it on tighter.'

Ella prodded it tentatively. 'Okay, keep still. I'm going to get my gun.'

'Jesus, Ella, whatever I did I'm sorry.'

'And stop talking, for God's sake. Let it dry.'

But instead, damn him, Matthew laughed and then spun on his swivel chair so that he could face her. 'What gun?' he asked, forgetting about the dirt that had taken her a good half hour to build so painstakingly across his face. He absentmindedly scratched at his cheek with a fingernail, taking off some more.

She grabbed his wrists in her hands. 'You are so unprofessional.'

'What gun?' he insisted without moving his mouth.

'Glue gun, and if you don't keep still I'll shoot you with it.' She swivelled him around to face the mirror once more and leaned over him, swiftly replacing layers of grime to his face with her stipple sponge, then moved back to consider.

He lay back again and closed his eyes, surrendering happily to her touch.

'Does it shoot real bullets?'

'What do you think?' She quickly changed sponges and pressed across his top lip, making perfect fat droplets of vaseline sweat. She blew on them gently, then stifled a yawn.

Silence but for the steady sound of his breathing.

'Oh God, do that again,' he quietly begged. 'That was heaven.'

She ignored him, concentrating on what she was doing, still not happy with the dirt on his cheek. It was too obvious where he had rubbed at it. She stretched for her trolley with a foot and rolled it closer, then reached across him to look for the colour that she needed, a creamy oil-based powder, Burnt Dawn, third from the right, second row down. In the scene he was shooting today, Matthew's character, William Denman, was caught in a gas attack and lost in no man's land.

Matthew leaned close in to the mirror and studied himself intently, and Ella took a step back to allow him.

'I look heroic,' he breathed, and he was complimenting himself not her.

'Just don't touch your face.'

'Certainly not.'

He said it so reverently she had to smile.

'You think I'm vain, but wouldn't you be?' He still couldn't take his eyes off his reflection. 'James McAvoy eat your heart out.'

'I think that was the Second World War. You're in the First.'

'But who looks cooler in their uniform?' He held up his hand to silence her. 'Don't say anything. You know it's true.' His eyes found hers. 'And I'd have made a brilliant Ambrose March.'

She snorted with laughter. 'Actors, actors, how come your egos grow so big?'

Matthew didn't like that. 'If I didn't think I was any good I wouldn't survive.'

'That's probably true.'

'Absolutely it's true. You don't know what it's like. You sit in here, gossiping with your mates, pouring yourself a coffee, mixing your scar gel, while outside I'm putting my soul into a part and most of the time nobody even notices.' He was watching himself in the mirror again, now transfixed by the emotion on his face. 'Being an actor isn't easy, Ella.'

'I know it's not, Matthew.'

'I live with William Denman's torment every day.'

'It must be very hard.'

'You said I was unprofessional.'

'You were.'

'Want to see how professional I am?'

'No. Why? What do you mean?'

Without a pause he went on. 'I am Lance Bombardier William Denman of the Shropshire Division of the Royal Horse Artillery,' he told the mirror. 'Yesterday my beautiful Irish mare, Culloon, was shot beneath me.'

Great fat tears immediately welled up in the corners of his eyes.

'Don't! Stop! Your face!' Ella leapt for a box of tissues.

'I'm showing you that I don't need some menthol blower to make my tears.'

'You're such a jerk, Matthew.' She dabbed carefully at the corners of his eyes.

'I'm showing you I'm good at my job. I'm saying I carry William's pain with me everywhere. Can you imagine how that feels?'

'And I'm saying I've spent the last three hours working on your make-up so your pain is my pain too, and please hold on to your tears until you get on set, where I'm sure they'll be appreciated.'

He grinned. 'So, don't call me unprofessional. Okay.'

'Loser.' She caught his chin and turned his face towards her, relieved to see that the tears had drained away again with no lasting damage. 'Freak.'

He settled back in his chair. '*Actor*. Did you hear the extras cheer when we wrapped last night?'

'Yes I did.'

'That was such a great feeling.'

'Good.'

'And when I went into Florent yesterday I was stopped four times for autographs.'

'You must be very proud.'

'You'll regret this conversation when I'm a star. When I refuse to have you make me up because of your previous lack of respect.'

But he'd lost her, as usual his face proving far more interesting than his voice. Ella had given him special-effect hand-painted contact lenses, one bloodshot and both with tiny broken capillaries, and she was interested to see that the recent tears had given his eyes an unnatural glow. He was going to cry again once filming began, so he definitely could do with yellowing up – he needed a drop or two of Eye Juice, which just might sting a little (she hoped) as she popped it in. It was a mixture that she'd made for a horror film a couple of years earlier and he needed just the tiniest drop to give a hint of mustard to his corneas. She tipped back his head and held his chin to stop him flinching, then carefully squeezed the bottle and watched as his eyes instantly responded.

'I think you'll find you've been lucky to have me,' she told him, holding his head still for a moment more.

No, she could see he wouldn't believe that. Make-up artists, two-a-penny, that's what Matthew thought. She could tell that he was always slightly thrown by what he saw as her lack of deference and didn't yet have the nerve to confront it. And she knew that if he ever did make it to super-stardom he'd become a self-regarding monster.

He shifted under her hand. 'Let me go. I'll be late.'

'You know Poppy will come and get you when they want you. One minute more. I need your eyes to settle down.'

She let go of his chin, then unscrewed a tube of Blood Gel S7-63 and squeezed a pea-sized blob on to the top of her hand. Immediately he turned to see what she was doing.

'Keep still.'

'Honestly, Ella, you're so predictable.'

'And be quiet or I'll glue your lips shut.' She stirred in a streak of brown. 'Or perhaps I might stick your nostrils together. See how convincing your acting is then.'

'You'd be doing me a favour because it's tough out there today. William's caught in a gas attack.'

'You think I don't know that?' She gave him a hard stare as she mixed her colours, irritated because clearly Matthew thought she *didn't* know. At the end of a full week of film- ing and God knows how many hours in her chair and he still believed there was little more to her job than sticking on his moustache and pushing him out of the door every morning. For a moment she wondered about putting him right, stopping him leaving the trailer until she'd gone to the back and fetched the giant memory boards, showed him how she and the rest of her hair and make-up team knew the script better than almost everybody else, inside out and especially back to front. She could have pointed to the notes and photographs built up around each scene that told them exactly where every new spot of blood had been added or smear of dirt wiped away, how the continuity of the film depended on them getting it right. She could have explained about the months of preparation undertaken by the hair and make-up and the costume departments, track- ing down the photographs that showed the cut of a First World War uniform, the style of hair; the hours and hours watching Ambrose March's original footage of his friends and comrades; the painstaking, perhaps the Oscar-winning lengths her boss Rosalind had gone to to ensure she'd got everything exactly, precisely, wonderfully right.

Instead she decided not to say a word. He'd been a bore and this was his last day under her care. Even if he had to return for re-shooting, with any luck she wouldn't be looking after him. And in any case she knew he wasn't interested. He never questioned whether his moustache was sufficiently 1916 or if the dried blood on his face was sufficiently brown. It never occurred to him to wonder how the stains and stiff dirt had been added to his uniform – by burying it underground for three weeks before filming. To him the costume department and the make-up artist were there to make him look the part; how they did it didn't really bother him.

She reached for a fine flat brush, touched it to the colour on her hand, then added a minute smudge to a blister just below his jawline. For a while there was silence as she worked, then suddenly he spoke again.

'I'm standing beside a gun carriage and I'm staring out across a plain. Ahead of me the land looks as though it has been churned by a mad plough. As far as I can see there is nothing but mud, no trees, not even a blade of grass . . .'

She was aware that the intonation of his voice had changed, so subtly she could hardly say how.

'There are turrets of mud and craters full of water. At some point we're going to have to move forward, and how I'll get this gun carriage across such a quagmire I don't know. But we've done it before, and I don't have to move yet, and for now it's very peaceful and still and the early morning mist is shot through with pink and gold. And you know what? I'm actually thinking it's a beautiful day. I stroke the neck of the horse beside me and I tell us both that this beautiful morning mist is going to hide us and keep us safe. I'm standing there looking at that pink and gold, waiting, half asleep . . . And then I smell pineapples heavy in the air and suddenly all hell breaks loose.'

Ella's hand still hovered next to his cheek. Then she dropped into the chair beside him. He looked different too, his eyes had gone dark and wide and he stared at her with such desperate intensity she felt a strong sense of unease building up inside her. Of course it was Matthew, but it wasn't Matthew, it was William Denman, and again she wanted to tell him to stop because she knew what he said next might be too heart-rending to hear. She knew the script but this wasn't the script. The words he spoke were suddenly, completely real.

'And all around me men are starting to clutch at their throats and shout and even as I'm standing there watching them I can't stop myself taking these deep suicidal breaths. Of course once I knew it was a gas attack the horror and terror made me just like them. I vomited up my guts I was so afraid. But then, before I had a chance to think what to do, the guns started firing, shells exploding and our horses were shrieking, slipping in the mud, trying to bolt free with those great gun carriages holding them back. I don't mind telling you I let go of my rein and ran, but I couldn't see where was forwards and where was back. I remember how hard it was to breathe and how I could look around and hear and see nothing at all. I remember the mist thick as smoke and all around me a sound like the crackle and snap of twigs on a bonfire and then I saw a man running in front of me and I followed him, zig-zagging to dodge the snipers, until suddenly his tin hat was tossed into the air like a spun coin and he fell and I realized the crackling sound was machine-gun fire.

'I was shot in the shoulder. I fell and I lay there and I could hardly cough I was so weak. I closed my eyes and waited to die and when I opened them again I found I was beside Ambrose. I saw that he had a gas mask on and was unconscious or dead.'

'How do you know this?' Ella whispered, even though she didn't want him to answer. She wanted him to go on, to keep talking in William's soft Shropshire burr, a low hypnotic voice that, for all the times she'd watched him, all the times she'd read the script, she'd heard nothing like before.

'There was a shell hole just a few feet away from us and I knew that if I could get Ambrose into it he might survive. I got to my knees and then, I don't know how, I managed to get back on my feet and I stood up for the last time and dragged him in by his ankles and lay back down beside him. But I still couldn't die, could I? Not yet.'

Ella silently shook her head. Now he was back on the script and she knew what happened next.

'Because there was his camera, his Aeroscope, oh yes, we all knew its name. There it was, standing up on that blasted heath, half buried in mud. Once I'd seen it I found I couldn't look away again, couldn't even close my eyes. I'm choking and coughing and crying and dying and that Aeroscope is all I can see. Everyone knows how much I hate that camera. I've told anyone who'd listen and plenty who wouldn't. I'm the last person to be held responsible for it now. And haven't I disliked Ambrose every day that I've known him? And now I've saved his life but Jesus that's still not enough. Dear God, I cry. Don't say I have to fetch that camera. Let me lie here, let me die. And I know that if I leave it where it is nobody will ever find it. It will get buried, forgotten and I want to let it because I happen to think no man should be shown the war that Ambrose March has filmed. But I also know that that camera is as much a part of Ambrose as his heart.'

Ella had thought she knew this part of the story inside out and back to front, better than anyone. She thought she'd read through the script so many times it couldn't still surprise her. And she'd thought Matthew was a flashy know-all without much talent and very little sympathy for his part and clearly that wasn't true either. But this wasn't the script – in the script Matthew barely had a line to say – this was the truth, William Denman speaking out from the grave.

'So I tell myself to crawl out once more but this time I find I cannot move. I'm sinking in a sea of mud, I kick my legs out from under me and the movement forces me back to reality. I cough, curl up in pain, I'm so exhausted, so very weak. And then my eyes open again and the camera is still there and I know I have to reach it. I try to push myself to my feet but this time I only make it to my knees. I move so slowly through the mud and the floating silence and that camera never gets any closer.

'I touch it. I lift it up. And then, one-armed, I carry it all the way back to Ambrose and when I get there I drop it beside him, try to protect it with his greatcoat, and then I fall to the ground. And Ambrose doesn't wake up and he doesn't know that it was me who saved him or me who saved his camera.'

Ella put her brush quietly down on the table beside Matthew.

'You're very good. It's a shame nobody else will get to hear you say that.'

Matthew said in quiet surprise. 'Don't say I made you cry?'

'Something in my eye.'

'Rest In Peace, William Denman.'

'What you said just then . . . I'm sure that must be how it was.'

He nodded. 'Of course it was. It was like that and much worse, every day. But I like to remember that Ambrose *did* know he'd been saved and who saved him. It's well documented that Ambrose recalled being shot and that he woke to find himself in that shell hole with William beside him.'

'And we know what Ambrose March did next too. Got back to his feet and immediately started to film William's dead body. What kind of a man could do that? He'd almost died, he'd woken to find a dead man beside him and even then the first thing he did was reach for his camera.'

'But by filming him he was honouring William in the only way he could. Those stills have become some of the most famous images of the war. That sequence that Ambrose filmed just before he fell – the piece that William saved – it was so shocking he wasn't allowed to show it until after the Armistice, and even then for years only in private cinemas. Now historians say that it is one of the best, most remarkable sequences they have.'

'I've seen it.' Ella nodded. 'It's exactly the same footage Hayden is dropping into the script. Matthew, I'm sorry.'

'For what?'

She smiled. 'Only for having you down as a good-for-nothing actor who hardly realized which war he was in.'

'Phew, proved myself in the nick of time. You know how I like a chance to show off.' He shifted in his chair, looked back at himself again, and she could see he was pleased she'd said it.

Sweet Matthew, she thought, just eighteen and with such unexpected talent. 'I hope you had a chance to show off on set.'

'I hardly have a word to say and what I do say they'll probably cut. You know it's a little part.'

She shrugged. 'It's a little part that packs a big punch. This could make you.'

'No, Rory is the one who will take the glory this time. But one day, one day it will be me.'

In their first few weeks of filming she hadn't seen enough of Rory Defoe's acting to make a judgement. She'd heard people say he was very good on set and very bad off it, holding up the entire cast and crew while he finished a crossword or a cup of coffee and frequently turning up for early morning shooting still drunk from the night before. She'd been on set for a few of the scenes that he'd shot with Matthew – there'd been two covering the first time Ambrose March and William Denman had met at Euston station on their way to the Front – and then a couple of weeks of filming the large battle scenes in no man's land, including the scene where William saved Ambrose's life, but at the time she had been in charge of the hair and make-up of ten extras as well as Matthew's and there'd been no opportunity to stand back and take Rory in.

She picked up her powder brush and dusted Matthew lightly across his face, setting everything in place. He was almost ready to go.

'You haven't met Rory yet, have you?' Matthew asked.

'I've said hello.'

'Did he answer?'

'Very politely.'

'Are you scared?'

'Of what?'

'Come on, Ella, of working with him. This has to be the most monumental break for you. When he asked for you to take over from Melinda you must have been thrilled – surprised, I'm sure, but so excited.'

Instantly she was irritated by him again. Instead of answering straight away she started to pack away the powders, creams and brushes, returning each of them to their rightful place among the hundreds of others.

The head of hair and make-up, Rosalind Lane, was looking after the female lead, Liberty Boyd, and in truth, if Rory hadn't always worked with his own personal make-up artist, Ella would probably have been assigned to him from the start.

She zipped up a sponge bag and closed another box of colours. 'I'm interested to know why you think that.'

Immediately Matthew was on guard. 'Why? What's the matter? What did I say?'

'What is it that makes you think I could be out of my depth?'

He stared her out. 'Because he's a star.'

'And you don't think I've made up stars before?'

He shrugged. 'You're working on people like me and the extras, so no, I don't think you've made up stars before.'

'Then you're wrong. Okay, there's an order, of course: Rosalind at the top. But even Rosalind isn't too grand to make up an extra when she has the time, and I've been looking after you because my main actor, Marat Benjern, isn't due on set for another week. Once he arrives I won't have time to work with anyone else.' Then she remembered that had all changed now. 'Actually, wrong, what am I saying? Of course now I'll be working on Rory, Minnie will be looking after Marat.'

Matthew was clearly surprised. 'I didn't realize you were ever down to look after Marat.'

'That's because you never asked me. And in case you're wondering, no, that won't be a monumental break for Minnie either.'

'Don't say it like that. And it's not that I don't think you'll do a fantastic job on Rory, of course you will. I suppose . . .' He screwed up his face in consternation, clearly desperate not to trip over again. 'It's just you're so fresh and gorgeous.'

She winced. 'Oh shut up, Matthew. That makes me sound like a bunch of flowers.'

'I mean it. You can't have been working for more than a few years, so how come you've got so far?'

'Because I'm good. Because a couple of years ago I was on a horror film with Rosalind called *Skin Tight* and we worked really well together, and then we made *Lorna Doone* last year and Rosalind won an Oscar. But you know I'm only taking over Rory because Melinda had a burst appendix. I'm sure she'll be trying to get back on set as fast as she can.' Actually Ella hoped Melinda would take her time. Once she began working with Rory, she couldn't imagine having to stop again and the chances of there being a seamless and unnoticeable changeover seemed unlikely.

'She didn't get appendicitis, she got pregnant.'

'That's just a rumour.'

'Still. You keep Rory at arm's length.'

'You know I can't do that. Up close and personal. It's in my job description.'

Matthew shook his head. 'Please, Ella. Everybody says he's completely out of control. You don't want him to take you down with him.'

'He's a great actor and honestly, I'll be fine.'

'Give him another week and he'll hit meltdown. If he's not shagging the wardrobe assistant he'll be drunk on set. You know Hayden released him for three days' re-shooting *Life As You Know It* in Kiev? Apparently he got back at five this morning and isn't going to bed at all. He's so unprofessional! How's he supposed to give us all his best shot this afternoon when he hasn't even been to bed?'

Desperate, all-consuming envy, that's what she could hear in Matthew's voice. *He* wanted the chance to rush from a film set in Kiev straight to one in northern France with no sleep in between. He wanted the possibility of shagging the wardrobe assistant.

'I'll sort him out.'

Matthew caught her expression and smiled wanly. 'Okay, I'll shut up. Recognize the talent of a superior smart-arse and trust that we'll all nurture him and keep him safe, get the best out of him for all our sakes.'

'That's about what I was thinking, yes.'

'You're such an angel. You know that, Ella? Clearly not an evil thought in your head. Come to Florent with us all tonight. Help me drown my sorrows. Tell me how you get on with Rory.'

'As soon as this day's finished I'm going back to my hotel room, and I'm going to sleep.'

'You're so wild.'

'No. Just been up since four.'

'So have I.'

The door of the trailer opened suddenly and Poppy Jones, their Second Assistant Director, leaned through and smiled at them both.

'Okay, Matthew? You ready to go? And Ella, Rory will be coming to you in a couple of hours. He's not due on set until . . .' Poppy consulted her call sheet, '. . . after lunch. Two thirty.' She smiled at Ella again. 'You're free until eleven thirty. Catch a snooze?'

She laughed. 'Exactly what I'm going to do.'

Meanwhile Matthew had got to his feet, and now Ella stood back to look at him one last time.

An eighteen-year-old soldier of the Great War looked back at her: pale, hollow-eyed, his uniform of the Shropshire Division of the Royal Horse Artillery battered and worn, the khaki trouser legs too short, the black boots full of holes.

'I'm scared, Ella.'

Matthew said this to her every morning.

'You'll be great.'

'But I'm *scared*, Ella,' he repeated and sighed again. 'Last day. This was meant to be my big break and I don't think it's happened.'

Poppy looked back at her call sheet. 'Anton Klubcic is on set today.'

Matthew leapt to attention. 'He is? How did I not know that? Is that meant to make me feel better?'

'Yes,' said Ella, 'because now you know he'll be watching you. Give it to him. Show him what you're made of.'

Matthew swallowed nervously. 'I don't know if it's better or worse that I know he's here.'

Ella caught Matthew's shoulders in her hands and leaned towards him.

'Don't be such a wimp. Get out there and make sure that if Anton Klubcic remembers anyone it's Lance Bombardier William Denman. You die today, you're never going to have a better chance. Do it, Matthew.' She stepped back, patting his moustache one last time. 'By the way, you do know you'll never get this off again, don't you? Now get out of the trailer and on to that set or you'll start to annoy Poppy.'

Matthew took a deep breath, then stood up. 'Okay, Ella. Thank you.' He hesitated. 'I wish you'd kiss me goodbye.'

'What, and spoil your make-up?' She leaned forward and kissed him very lightly on the cheek, handing him his khaki jacket, which he slipped on, then his greatcoat, which he carried over one arm. She did up his brass buttons one by one, then took one last considered walk around him, checking that everything was exactly as it should be. She straightened the brown leather Sam Browne belt that crossed his chest, rubbed her shoe over his boot, brushed at his shoulders, then checked his moustache a final time and held open the door to her trailer.

He paused on the top step and looked back at her.

'*Gladiator*,' he told her. 'I'd have been better in that, too, don't you think?'

She paused, pretending to consider. 'I see you more as a kind of Danger Mouse.'

'And you're a witch.'

Ella stepped back for him to descend the three steps and

watched Poppy lead him away, round the mass of parked trailers that made up the unit base and on through the early morning mist to the set, to where fifteen horses, six gun carriages, a hundred and fifty extras and sixty-six crew were waiting for him.

With Matthew gone, a beautiful peace descended upon her trailer. Two precious hours to enjoy it. Matthew's time with her was over; Rory's, on the other hand, hadn't yet begun. She curled up on the long sofa at the front of the trailer and fell fast asleep.

Two

Ella woke to rapping at the trailer door. She sat up in a rush and then, when she heard nothing more, pushed herself off the sofa and took two steps to the window. A girl was standing on the grass outside with her back to the trailer, bent over a cigarette. From the window Ella could see bony shoulders hunched inside a denim jacket and bare bluey-white legs.

A sixth sense must have told the girl that Ella was there, because instantly she spun around, flinging away the cigarette and waving at her at the same time. Then, even before Ella had had the chance to think *trouble*, she had leapt up the two steps of the trailer, opened the door and was leaning enthusiastically in.

'Hi,' she beamed. She looked behind Ella and around the trailer. 'Rory, he is not here?'

'No,' agreed Ella, stepping backwards and sideways to keep her in the doorway.

'Thank God!' The girl had a strong Russian accent. Now that they were face to face Ella could see she was beautiful, in a grungy, skinny kind of a way, her fingernails bitten down to the quick, yesterday's make-up ringing her dark eyes. She looked about sixteen.

'You don't want to see him?'

'Not yet. Vot vill he think?' She laughed, running her hand through her choppy black hair. 'I sleep on train. I don't look so good.'

'Okay,' Ella made a wild guess. 'That wouldn't be a train from Kiev, would it?'

'Ya!' The girl was delighted. 'How did you know?'

'Just a hunch.'

'My name is Olga. Rory is my boyfriend.' She held out her hand, and as she spoke her eyes flickered past Ella towards the five mirrors and chairs that ran the length of the trailer, then widened as she caught sight of all the trays and trolleys of eyebrow brushes, cream blushes, base foundations, lipsticks, hair tongs, tubs of pins, false eyelashes, Elnett hairspray, eyeshadows every colour under the sun. 'I stay here viff you,' she said with conviction. 'I vait for Rory here.'

'I don't think so,' said Ella.

'Ya, please. I see him here.' She looked confidently up at Ella. 'He vill be so excited to see me. I know this.'

'I don't know who let you in or told you to come to this trailer but you really can't stay. It's very strict, Olga, I'm sorry. Security would say it isn't possible.'

No they wouldn't, security wouldn't say a word. They would simply lift her up and carry her, legs kicking, far away from their irreplaceable, world-famous film star.

'Sit down there.' Ella stepped back and pointed to the sofa. She couldn't leave the girl free to wander off again. 'We'll give my friend Poppy a call. Perhaps she could send a car to come and pick you up. Do you know anyone here in France? Do you have anywhere you could stay?'

'I vill stay viz Rory.' She sat obediently down. 'He like me squeeze fish . . .'

'No!' Ella had to fight not to laugh. From what she knew about Rory, Olga probably had the translation perfectly correct. 'So, when did you meet him?'

Olga placed her hands on her knobbly knees and gave her a conspiratorial smile, but didn't elaborate.

'Did you know who he was?'

'Of course!' Now Olga looked at Ella as if she was demented. 'I vand know him every day. He is on film set in my home town!'

'And you met him somewhere, what, in a club?'

'Ya. I dance in Troishka. It was truly amazing night.'

'And he suggested you came out here?'

'Ya. He say hey baby, come to France and make love viff me. Boy, he is so fantastic. I rilly love him.'

Suddenly she bounced back to her feet and sprang towards the heart of the trailer. 'Is Laura Mercier, ya? Vis eez amazing make-up product. I cannot believe it.'

Ella couldn't stop laughing. If only she could let Olga stay, she thought, watching her pick up a soft, fat blending brush and touch it lightly to her cheek, just to see Rory's aghast face when he walked up the stairs into the trailer and found her there. At her laughter Olga turned back, still holding the brush.

'You must go and sit over there.' Ella said it very firmly and pointed back at the sofa. She waited while Olga did as she was told. 'And now I've got to make that call.'

Olga looked at her watch. 'Eez so enjoyable. Rory eez coming here now. I know this. Eez so unbelievable for me.'

Ella looked at the trailer clock in alarm and saw that Olga was right. How could she have slept so long? Rory was due in less than twenty minutes.

'How do you know?' Ella pleaded. 'Who helped you to find your way here? And while we're at it, Olga, how did you get in? Surely you met security somewhere?'

Olga shrugged. 'Why? Eez not a closed set.'

She was right, but what did Olga know of closed sets? Later the set would close – Liberty Boyd had requested that all her love scenes take place on a closed set with only the sound operator, director and one cameraman present – but, for all the scenes scheduled for the next few days, the set was open to anybody invited in. According to Ella's call sheet, today there was a journalist writing a piece for Armistice Day and a television presenter to interview Hayden for BBC. Not surprisingly there was no mention of a dancer from Kiev.

However she'd got in, Ella wanted to get rid of her fast. Ella didn't know Rory. She'd had no chance to talk to him prior to this first meeting. She'd learnt about Melinda's 'appendicitis' and sudden departure from the set only the previous morning when her boss, Rosalind, had asked her if she'd take over Rory's make-up (as if she might have said no – she might have denied it to Matthew but this was the biggest break of her career), and she wanted this, their first meeting together, to go seamlessly well.

She and Rosalind had snatched a few hours together to fine-tune Rory's look, all the prepping having been done

months before in conversations between Rosalind and
Hayden the director and developed by Rosalind and Ella
in the weeks leading up to the first day of filming. But this
was to be the first time she met him, and he was notoriously
short-tempered *and* he'd been up all night *and* he would,
no doubt, be appalled to discover she'd got a stalker sitting
waiting for him in her trailer. And people loved her trailer;
it was a refuge for everyone. People came in to talk, cry, get
away from the set, tell her their problems. She'd wanted the
trailer to be a refuge for Rory. She'd had a fanciful idea that
it might prove to be the oasis of calm in his turbulent life . . .
She had to get rid of Olga.

Ella had tried to meet Rory in advance of this day. The
previous evening she'd walked over to his trailer to introduce herself but had been held at the door by his PA, Liza
Nash. You must be joking! Absolutely no chance of meeting
him, Liza had snapped at her, so fast Ella could barely hear
the words. Rory wasn't available. Didn't Ella read the call
sheets? Why didn't Ella know that Rory was on the film
set in Kiev? Make an appointment next time. And please,
please, please . . . At this Liza had clutched her hair in her
weariness and exasperation . . . Ella *had* to appreciate how
necessary it was for Rory to keep his personal space free of
the *clutter* of the set . . .

Ella had kept her mouth shut and walked away, if anything feeling sorry for Liza, who, sat in Rory's lavish ivory
tower, hardly ever seemed to see him herself and had little contact with any of the rest of the crew. If *she'd* had to
look after Rory all day, constantly having to deal with all
the groupies, ex-girlfriends, hangers-on who trailed around

after him, she'd probably be tight-lipped and exasperated too . . .

She pulled out her mobile from a pocket on the front of her skirt, thinking she shouldn't really be surprised the first girl had turned up already. But however often it might have happened before, Poppy would not thank her for the disruption. At this time of day, just before lunch, she would be flat out, circulating any amendments to the script that had been made during the morning's filming, ensuring that all the crew had notes of last-minute changes, and that each actor was ready to return to set at precisely the right time. Ella took a deep breath and called her number. As she waited for a connection she couldn't bear to look out of the window in case she made Rory materialize just by looking, and then she did look despite herself, and even though Poppy immediately picked up, Ella cut her off again without saying a word because he was *there* – Rory Defoe, notoriously late for everyone, was walking towards her trailer at least fifteen minutes early.

She dropped her phone back into her pocket and watched him move into the shade of the tall cypress trees that separated the unit base – where all the trailers were parked – from the four film sets. A few more strides and he was clear of the trees and back in the sunlight, following the pine-needle path that wound towards her, long legs carrying him across the ground with easy strides. Now he was slipping alongside the first of the trailers, treading carefully over the snaking power cables that spread out across the ground. He was swinging a bottle of water from one hand and was wearing baggy shorts, a navy T-shirt and flip-flops, with a baseball cap pulled low over his face.

When he got to her trailer he didn't slow down but strode straight on by, passing her window with his head down, purposefully following the path, and at first Ella presumed that he was on his way somewhere else after all. But then about fifty yards later he met a fork in the path, stopped, turned uncertainly and stopped again. Then, as she watched, he opened his bottle of water, took off his baseball cap, tipped back his head and poured a long stream of water straight into his face. When he was done he rubbed his face with his hand and shook his head violently, then stepped off the path on to the barely there grass, sank to his knees, sat back on his haunches, then lay down, arms by his sides, long legs now stretched in front of him, baseball cap tipped down over his face. He stayed like that, so still she wondered if he'd passed out, but then, just as she was thinking about going over to see, he sat up, readjusted the baseball cap, screwed the lid of the bottle tight and stood up again, dusting the back of his shorts, and turned back the way he'd come, back towards her trailer. And this time as he got closer he looked up, caught her staring at him and grinned. It was a tired, unguarded, irresistible grin, just for her, and at that moment she finally understood what it was that all the millions of fans saw in him.

Ella couldn't seem to unfreeze her face enough to smile back. He looked exhausted, not the self-regarding egomaniac at all. He had a fresh smear of dust from the path across his cheek, and his T-shirt was soaking wet in places. And taking him in, she decided again that all that mattered was that she protected him from Olga.

'I'll be back in a moment,' she hissed to Olga. 'Wait there.'

She opened the door, stepped outside and closed it again quickly behind her. If she'd had the key she'd have locked it too.

He swayed as he looked back up at her with glassy, I've been up all night, blue eyes.

'I'd like to lie down.'

'I saw.' She smiled back at him.

'Please tell me you're Ella Buchan.'

She nodded, feeling surprisingly star-struck and shy. But instinctively, and despite the worry of Olga sitting five feet behind her, she found herself starting to assess his face: thick black hair cut very short, beautiful curving lips, great cheekbones, moustache perfect. Not only did it make him look uncannily like Ambrose, but it also gave a dangerous, rather rakish edge to the dramatic planes of his face. Wonderful straight black brows, but the week-old beard was much too long. She'd take down those red-rimmed eyes, add a few drops of Bedazzle – banned in the UK but still available in Europe and kept in the make-up bag of any self-respecting make-up artist – a magic formula that could turn the yellowest of corneas a clear bluey white. She'd use the shadows under his eyes and that bruised pale skin to her advantage, but, if anything, his skin tone would need to be darkened, not toned down – probably Jamie Carrier's matt foundation 06? Or possibly 07. Rory, after a night on the tiles, looked at least as bad as Ambrose March after eight months in the trenches.

He put out a hand to balance himself and for a moment looked as if he was about to slide down the side of the trailer.

'Sorry I'm early, but three hours with my eyes shut,

being stroked by soft brushes, I couldn't think of anything I wanted more.'

Without the trailer to support him she was pretty sure he'd collapse on to the ground, and yet his voice was clear, each word clearly enunciated. Probably not quite sober, exhausted, dehydrated, yet still she had never seen such a beautiful face as his. Her heart beat a little faster. She wanted to help him up the steps and lead him in. She wanted to sit him down in her make-up chair, turn him around to face her so that she could peer at him, prod him, stroke her fingertips across his high cheekbones and his full sensitive lips, test the spring in his thick dark hair . . .

And she could. And once he had stepped inside and sat down, she would. And what's more, she'd be paid for it too. And she thanked God for what surely was the best job in the world because there was no argument. This was what Rory would expect her to do. No one would dare to suggest that it was anything more than sheer professional curiosity that caused her to run her fingers lingeringly through his hair, or to take his hand in hers, to check the skin tone on the underside of his wrist, of course. And if anyone did wonder if perhaps she could work with quite the same level of enthusiasm and care on an eighty-year-old man with a face as wizened as a walnut, she would say of course she could, because she was a professional and every face interested her in exactly the same way, no more, no less.

Who was she kidding?

And for the next couple of hours he was all hers. She would have him completely to herself, none of her colleagues booked into the trailer, no one to get in the way.

She might have a few more girlfriends than usual knocking and coming in, borrowing make-up, or just breezing past his chair to have a good look, but that was only going to happen today, while everybody got used to him being made up there rather than in his own trailer. They'd be gone soon enough. And meanwhile she'd rejuvenate him – the trailer cupboards were stuffed with various rescue remedies and potions, she'd cover his poor tired eyes with cotton wool pads soaked in witch hazel, and then she'd get to work . . . But then the smile was wiped from her face as she remembered Olga. What could she do about Olga?

'Will you insist that I sit in the chair or can I lie on the sofa?' He laughed at the concern on her face. 'I'm joking. I'll sit wherever you want.'

'It's not that.'

She shifted from foot to foot, scrabbling around in her head for a solution, and saw the confusion on his face.

'I've come at a bad time?'

'I'd say you're a little early.'

'Does it matter?'

She took a deep breath and decided to go for it.

'Yes. I need a few more minutes, if you don't mind.'

'You're telling me to come back later?' Surprise made him push himself upright again. 'But what if I want to come in now?'

'You can't. Something I have to do first.'

He studied her with sleepy eyes and a half smile, tipping his head first to one side then the other as he tried to work her out.

'Something's wrong. What is it?' He took another swig of

water and wiped his mouth with his hand. 'Trust me. You know you can tell me.' He waited but she didn't say anything. 'Okay, it's our first day together and you're worried about messing up my face? Is that it? Yes? No?' He paused again. 'You're still not sure whether to go for the Peach Crème Blush or the Shout of Pink? Is that it?'

She shook her head, laughing despite herself. 'Interesting choices, but I'm not sure we'll be using either of them.'

'Thank God for that. Okay . . . So what? You've lost my mess kit? Is that it?' He liked her smiling, she could see him relaxing again. 'Tell me and I promise I'll lie to Hayden and say it was my fault.' He waited. 'It's not the mess kit? Of course, wardrobe keeps the mess kit. So what can it be?' Still she said nothing. 'You've spilled sticky blood all over my chair? Oh, no! You've sat on my *Aeroscope*? Oh my God! You haven't!' He suddenly cried out in what sounded like genuine horror. 'Tell me you haven't crushed my camera?'

She pulled her face straight. This had to stop.

'You know wardrobe looks after your mess kit and your Aeroscope.'

'And you know I'm joking.' He tipped back his head, closed his eyes and, without warning, sank down to his knees on the ground before her. 'Okay,' he groaned. 'Enough. Get me inside, I can't even stand up it's so fucking hot out here.'

He waited, but she still didn't respond and then in a flash of understanding he suddenly got it, thought like she'd wanted him to think, and with the knowledge his smile immediately vanished and his face turned flinty hard. He climbed back to his feet.

'Don't tell me you've got someone inside?'

She felt him reassess her swiftly, critically, her red vest top, her flimsy, turquoise silk skirt, her bare legs, and she felt her face burn again. Go on, she thought. Think I'm shagging a bloke in here if it makes you go away, but if anything he looked incredulous, as if he couldn't believe she was up to it.

'Five minutes,' she begged. 'That's all I need.' Five minutes to shoo Olga down the steps and away, anywhere but here. She looked down at him and tried the smile again, tried again to make it sound as if she was asking for nothing, but it didn't work.

'Oh, no,' he said, his voice now clipped and cold and perfectly sober. He took a couple of steps back from the trailer. 'I don't think that's nearly long enough. I'm sure the cast and crew would stop filming for a bit if you let me explain. Why don't I go and ask them, see what they say?'

'Don't bother. Hayden doesn't stop filming for anyone.' She laughed, working to keep her voice lighthearted but she could hear that she was sounding anything but.

'He's had me filming with a temperature of a hundred and one, just switched the scenes so I didn't have to speak, so yes, you're probably right. So, what can you do?'

What's the big deal, she thought. Surely you can't mind the thought of me having fun in the trailer? After all, I'd only be behaving like you.

'Do us a favour, Rory, push off for a bit,' he said softly. 'You're spoiling everything.'

'I'd never dream of saying that to you.'

'But you are. And why shouldn't you? Who's in there? Do I know him?' He shook his head. 'No. Of course you're not going to tell me that.' He swung the bottle of water between his fingers. 'Clearly I am in the way.'

Was that what it was? Being told that for once he wasn't the star of the show?

Rory closed his eyes and swayed sideways as if he was about to pass out. What am I thinking? Ella asked herself, appalled. He *is* the star. What was she doing keeping him out there, standing at the bottom of the steps, negotiating with her, squinting up at her in the heat of the midday sun. He should be sitting in a chair in the air-conditioned cool of her trailer, with Alka-Seltzer in one hand and a glass of freshly squeezed orange juice in the other.

'I'm going,' he decided, just as she was about to explain everything. 'I'm going over to those trees, over there, where it's cool. And I'm going to lie down for a moment.' He turned and waved the water bottle at the way he'd come, beyond the pine trees to a little wooded copse on the other side of the film set boundary. 'And then I'm going to get up again and walk slowly back. And I hope that will give you enough time to say goodbye and get him out of the trailer.'

'Thanks. That's very understanding.'

'No.' He rested his head against the wall of the trailer and looked up at her. 'I'll tell you something. I'm shocked. How is that? I met you two minutes ago. Surely you have to know someone to be surprised by them?'

'I've made an unexpected request, I guess.'

She didn't want him to be surprised or shocked. Still she hesitated, torn between opening the door to reveal Olga and letting him walk away . . . But he was offering her five minutes and that was all she needed, time to remove Olga from his life, and then she could bring him inside, and after Olga had gone she'd perhaps explain . . .

He started to turn away, and her heart lightened. It was working. She'd thought on her feet and made a good decision. Just a moment now, say nothing more, and he'd be gone . . . But then, unexpectedly, he spoke again.

'While I'm out of the way you should explain to whoever's inside that you've got a job to do and that it's completely unprofessional to keep me hanging around.'

What? In the heat of the day icy goose-bumps erupted all over her. She looked down at him, startled. No, he hadn't just said that. Had he?

'What would Rosalind say?' He held up a hand. 'See you later. Have fun.'

She was so dumbstruck she almost let him go.

'Wait. If you feel like that . . .' She ran down the steps. 'Why did you say it was all right if it wasn't?'

But he wasn't stopping to talk; if anything he picked up speed still more, long legs carrying him fast away, and before he'd gone ten paces more she knew she had to stop him. She had visions of him stomping down through the copse to the town of Florent, then hitching a lift with some passing stranger and disappearing, just to punish her because he'd just reminded her he was the movie star. He could do and say whatever he liked and, however unfair, she had to keep him sweet. She couldn't let him go.

'Wait,' she called again.

He still didn't stop, deliberately making her follow him, and she paced after him past the trailers and downhill towards the trees, feeling the sun burn against her hot face, sweat roll down her back. She'd not been outside the trailer since dawn and now the heat of the day took her breath away. She had to break into a trot to catch up with him.

'Please stop.' She jumped a web of exposed tree roots and slid on the dry dusty earth. Irritation rose inside her as he still insisted on walking on.

This was Rory Defoe, with an ego to rival Anton Klubcic's. But she mustn't let it show that that was what she thought. She must not challenge him. Nobody must ever challenge him. When she eventually got him to stop she had to be calm, conciliatory. And if that didn't work, she must be abject in her grovelling apology. That's what he was expecting.

'What's the matter? Got cold feet?' he called back at her, flinging the half empty water bottle into the undergrowth as he walked, still not turning back. 'Decided it's perhaps not such a good idea to hold up a two-hundred-million dollar production after all?'

'You know, you sound so ridiculous.' It came out of her mouth before she even knew what she was about to say, but at least it got him to stop. 'And by the way, I'll never ever keep you waiting. I'll never keep anyone on this production waiting, but you were early. *And*, I misunderstood. I thought you were finding our conversation funny.'

He turned back to face her.

'Tell me the funny part.'

Rosalind's appalled face swam into her head. Probably the whole crew had heard their raised voices. She wondered that Liza, with her ears alert to any whisper of Rory-Trouble, hadn't already dashed to his side.

'There wasn't one,' she said hastily. 'I'm sorry. None of it was funny.'

'You say I sound ridiculous but I'm only trying to help you keep your job.'

He had sounded ridiculous, he still did, and huffy and stuffy and self-important too.

'I can keep my own job.'

He folded his arms and stared back at her. 'I would say it's not looking good.'

'Why?' Was he threatening her now? 'I've done nothing wrong.'

'If you're so sure about that why are you running after me?'

'Because I'm supposed to run after you. It's my job.'

This had to stop. For all she knew Rory could be mean enough to walk straight over to the video-village to find Hayden and demand she was fired. And Hayden would do as he asked.

'You misunderstood,' she went on rapidly. 'There's a girl inside my trailer. She has come from Kiev to see you. Not me.'

His eyes widened but he didn't miss a beat. 'Is she pretty?'

'You'd probably think so.'

'Why didn't you say?'

She looked back at him stonily. 'I know, clearly a bad mistake. Might have got me fired.'

He smiled. 'I'm sure Rosalind would have fought hard to keep you.'

'Maybe. Depends what you were going to say.'

'Ella, I can be a grumpy bastard. You'd better get used to it.' He sighed. 'You sure there's no man in the trailer?'

She nodded.

'Good. So who is this girl?'

'She says she met you in a club in Kiev.'

'Ah, yes, Monika.'

'Actually Olga.'

He could smile at her now, but she knew she couldn't relax.

'And you were going to get rid of her before I arrived?'

'I was going to try. I thought you would prefer it. You must have this happen quite often.'

'But why pretend there was someone inside for you?'

'What else could I do? Why did it bother you?'

'Because I don't like being misled.'

'I'm sorry I misled you.'

'Why do you say it like that? You think I'm behaving like a jerk?'

Don't say it, she told herself, but it was as if some gremlin had got inside her mouth and was gleefully picking her words.

'Yes,' she agreed. 'You don't want anybody having fun if it doesn't involve you.'

'Too right I don't! Who does? But that doesn't make me a jerk.' He came forward. 'Ella, I said I was sorry.'

'No, you didn't.'

But she was starting to relax and smile back at him with grateful relief that he wasn't minding her talking back at him, and that they seemed to be moving back on track.

'Now your turn to apologize,' he insisted. 'Monika is none of your business.'

'You're right. I'm sorry.'

'She might be the love of my life.'

'I doubt it, seeing as you don't even remember her name.'

He grinned again.

'Let's go and meet her.'

'Please don't keep her long.'

'If she stays I'll make sure she doesn't get in your way.'

'No! Please, she has to go.'

He glanced across at her again and she thought she saw some warning in his look.

'As I said, Ella. None of your business.'

They turned together and began to walk back, and as they got closer to the trailer the door opened and Olga appeared on the top step, waiting for them. Even from a distance of a hundred yards or so, Ella could tell from the vampish way she lounged against the door frame that she'd used her time in the make-up trailer well.

At the sight of Olga Rory put his mouth close to Ella's ear.

'She looks interesting.'

'I thought you'd remember what she looked like.'

'What's her name again?'

She turned to him. 'You should leave her alone.'

'Why?'

'Because meeting you again is no joke to her.'

'Nor me.'

'And we need to get to work.'

'You'll get as much of me as you want.'

'She thinks she loves you.'

He looked at her scornfully. 'She's got a plan, just like every other woman I've ever met.'

'No!'

'Ella. Forgive me if I sound terribly unromantic but there is not a chance in hell that girl's here because she loves me. I'm rich and famous and she thinks I might make her a star. That's the way it is. She's a pro. She knows the form. And you're the only one who seems to have this wide-eyed idea that it's about anything else. She is not sweet but neither am I. So perhaps I'll send her on her way . . . or perhaps I won't. Either way, it's not your problem. Don't call Poppy. Don't try and get her frogmarched off set. And while we're talking . . .' Rory leaned towards her, '. . . if we're going to get along together, and I think we are, it can only work if you don't make any further decisions on my behalf that don't relate directly to my make-up. I don't want to know your opinions, not on my love life, my drinking habits, my sleep patterns, whatever. I don't want a nanny, I want a make-up artist who's good at her job. I want you to let me do exactly what I want as long as it doesn't interfere with you. Okay? I think it's best that we get that straight right from the start.'

She opened her mouth to speak but Rory interrupted her.

'Let it go.'

She looked at him, momentarily silenced.

'I'm entitled to an opinion about Olga.'

'Ella, you are not.'

'Because she's in my trailer. She's therefore my responsibility, not yours, and I don't want her there.'

'And I do. So, for now, she's going to stay.'

'But it'll be impossible to get you ready.'

'Find a way.'

'Rory,' Olga squealed in delight, unable to wait any

longer, and she danced down the three steep steps, leapt the last few strides and threw her arms around him.

'Olga!' He slid his hands around her narrow waist. 'Oh you angel, you came.'

'Ya.' She looked up at him, delighted with what she saw. 'I stay vis you always.'

'You can sit with me while Ella gets to work.' He kissed the tip of her nose. 'But listen. I have a very big headache so you will have to be very still and very quiet. And then I'm sure Ella will do as I say and forget that you're there.'

Three

Ella slowly climbed the steps to her trailer and opened the door, then turned back to Rory, who was still standing at the bottom with Olga protected by his arm.

'Whenever you're ready.'

'Don't even think of calling Poppy,' he called after her.

She stared stonily back at him. 'I'll give you five more minutes and then I'm calling everyone I can think of. You know we can't work like this.'

Rory looked down at Olga. 'Come on. Up the steps.' He took Olga's hand. 'Come and see a make-up artist at work.'

Inside the trailer there was nobody there. When Ella had first realized she was to have the trailer to herself that afternoon she'd rejoiced, but now, now she wished there was someone to share Rory's sheer bloody awfulness.

Ella and Rosalind always kept to their own working areas; they each had their own chair, their own section of the long fitted table that ran the length of the trailer, their own make-up and brushes and everyday equipment. Rosalind always took the first space, Ella the second. Their two assistants and a trainee took the other three spaces further down the line.

When the trailer was full, five actors could therefore have their hair and make-up done at the same time. But today Rosalind was making up Liberty Boyd in her own trailer and the other make-up assistants were all in the marquees working on the extras, so Ella was alone and the trailer felt desperately empty. Why wasn't there someone needing a quick retouch between scenes? Why was Rosalind not there when she needed her? But then . . . Ella thought about it and changed her mind. She would not want Rosalind witnessing this.

She beckoned Rory forward and he pulled back chair number two and sat down. 'Come here,' he told Olga. 'Up on my knee.'

Even Olga sensed that now was not the time to provoke Ella any more. She gave her a quick, uncertain glance – the first time she'd looked at her since she'd seen Rory – and slipped meekly on to his lap, then shrieked and flung herself backwards. 'Sorry,' she whispered to Ella. 'Bad boy!' she giggled, slapping under her bottom at Rory's hand.

'I said keep still,' he told her, firmly placing his hands on her shoulders and forcing her back down. Olga pulled one hand towards her mouth and kissed his fingers one by one, then lay back against his chest, her heavy-lidded eyes fluttering half closed.

'Vat eez good,' she whispered, reaching up for him, brushing her mouth against his neck. 'Ver good.'

'I've lots of friends,' Rory told Ella, catching her look of disgust in the mirror. 'Some of them might not be as well behaved as Olga. You'd better get used to it. And yes, an espresso please, black, one sugar.'

What could she say? What could she do?

He laughed. 'Don't look so glum.'

She went to the back of the trailer and made him a coffee, brought it back and placed it on the table in front of him. Then she stood directly behind his chair and concentrated on his reflection in the mirror in front of them, trying hard to put the man sitting there out of her mind, concentrating only on what he was to become.

She leaned in close, telling herself to focus on the shape of his face, his skin tone, the texture of his thick black hair. Silently she stared into his eyes and they stared back at her, up close so clear and sensitive, so full of warmth, that it seemed completely wrong that they were part of him. He wasn't to know how difficult this was for her, how scary and exciting the prospect of working with him had been. How, despite everything she'd said to Matthew, this was the biggest break of her career.

And now, at the moment of truth, her nerves had caught up with her, the certainty that she was about to get something wrong made worse by the sight of Olga there on his lap, smiling at Ella whenever she caught her eye. She was suddenly so distracted that she simply couldn't think how to start. *Cleanse, tone, moisturize.* It was the routine preached by a thousand beauty magazines, but Ella couldn't remember it, not today. She looked at the week-old stubble on Rory's cheek, and instead of a bottle of cleanser tentatively picked up a pair of scissors and weighed them in her hand.

'Your hands are shaking.'

'So keep still.'

She leaned in to him and carefully cut a few centimetres off the longer hairs of his moustache, and then when she had finished leaned in close and gently blew the cut hairs away from his mouth.

She saw the surprise in his face. And she'd never have done it if Olga hadn't been there sitting on his lap. But she was floundering now, and she'd wanted him to believe he hadn't affected her at all, when in fact she couldn't think straight. She put down the scissors on the table in front of her.

In the mirror, she saw Rory reach up and touch his face with his hand. She couldn't let him know that he'd got to her. Whatever else, he had to think she was in control.

Next she plugged in her electric razor, and when Rory saw it, he wrapped his arms around Olga and tilted her sideways so that Ella had the space to lift and push his head into the angles she wanted and very, very precisely finish what she'd done with the scissors, shaving centimetres off the stubble on his cheek and off each end of his moustache.

He caught her eye in the mirror. 'Careful you don't shave Olga.'

She ignored him. Silently she put down the razor on the table in front of the mirror and picked up her polaroids of the scenes already shot that had Melinda's notes attached.

Olga shifted position so that she was sitting sideways on Rory's lap. Ella saw that his hand was now resting on Olga's bare leg and she couldn't stop herself checking it again and again, waiting for the moment when it might move, creep under Olga's mini skirt or down her slim thigh. 'I lick you, Rory,' she thought she heard Olga mutter, but perhaps it was 'like'. She wondered dispiritedly just how much Rory expected her to watch.

She turned her back on both of them while she looked

through the polaroids. She'd seen enough genuine photographs of Ambrose, and had read Hayden and Rosalind's charts and notes so many times, she ought to know exactly what she should be aiming for. Beside her Olga gave a long trembling sigh. Ella had Melinda's notes too, detailing every base, every shade, every texture that had previously been used on Rory's face in the first days of filming. But Melinda's techniques were different to Ella's, and in any case the scenes that had been written up in the most detail were those covering Ambrose's time in England in preparation for the Front. Melinda had worked on the scenes where Ambrose was at home with his wife, then his interview at the War Office, the pivotal moment when he had first voiced his great idea – that he should ditch the usual shots of massed ranks of soldiers, whole battalions, marching, flags flying, and instead follow one regiment of the Shropshire Horse Artillery throughout its deployment on the Western Front. They'd filmed the scene where his idea had been coldly dismissed by the Generals at the War Office, who were still very wary of any permanent record of the war and had only recently agreed to allow filming of any kind. The Generals had been resolutely specific and detailed about what Ambrose should be allowed to film, and it certainly didn't involve dead British soldiers (only dead Germans or Turks), as the effect on the home public was supposed to be bad. Melinda had worked on the scenes that revealed Ambrose's anger, perfectly masked, as he'd listened to the Generals' plans, and his awkward agreement to do as he was asked.

Melinda had done Rory's hair and make-up for the next scenes too. Ella ran her eye over the notes covering a few weeks earlier, before the cast and crew had come to France, when the company had moved from London to Shrewsbury, where two hundred new army recruits from the Shropshire Light Infantry had boarded a train in 1916, as thousands more had done before and after them. This was a troop train that would take them to London, then on to Folkestone and from there to Boulogne and the Front. And faithful to the day, Hayden had filmed Ambrose March there among them, pumping up his Aerospace camera with air then running alongside the men as they boarded the train, filming as he ran, the air from his camera expelled in a slow controlled exhale. In a world of elaborate special effects and CGI, the clarity of his film and the youth and beauty of the soldiers as they waved goodbye to their friends and families were incredibly powerful. Now, nearly one hundred years later, Hayden was showing Ambrose's film to a new audience, dropping his original footage into *To End All War* in twenty-second sequences, and this time giving it the accompaniment of sound. Sometimes gunfire and bomb blasts, other times simply the sound of birdsong or the voices of men singing. There was one short section where Ambrose had filmed an officer and chaplain and three other soldiers standing together in no man's land, singing a hymn over the dead bodies that lay strewn all around them. Hayden had added the sound of the hymn. The combined impact of Ambrose's footage and the deep musical voices had been unbearably moving. The moment Ella saw it was also the moment she first recognized what a great film *To End All War* might turn out to be.

She turned back to her notes. Today and for every day forward Rory would need to look battle-worn. She would have to turn him into an entirely different Ambrose from the man who'd left London. Fastidious still, elegant always, his black hair continued to be neatly flattened with pomade, his moustache still to be perfectly clipped, but now she had to make him grey, filthy, lice-ridden despite his best efforts. With her make-up she had to suggest a haunted, exhausted weariness and she couldn't think how to begin.

Scene eighteen, the scene to be shot that afternoon, was simple enough, an exterior scene of a motorcycle despatch rider arriving at a stone barn where about a hundred new recruits were spending the night on their way to the Front. Ambrose had been on his way to a field hospital, had come upon the soldiers and had used the arrival of the despatch rider to practise filming and running at the same time. It was not a technically difficult scene, not a memorable scene, no battles, no crowds of soldiers. Rory would be on camera only at the end of the scene. He needed a bruise to one cheekbone, but that was simple enough to achieve; what concerned Ella was that it would be the first time that the crew, and specifically Hayden, would see her make-up rather than Melinda's and so it was critical that she got Rory perfectly right.

'Could you lift your head up, please.'

Rory did what she asked. His colour was heightened now, his eyes sparkling.

She looked back at his face. They were filming in high definition, which was very unforgiving. Every pore, every hair on his cheek would be on show, every brush of powder, every smudge of foundation or concealer had to be accounted for. She stared at his skin and tentatively ran her finger down his cheek, trying to decide on his tone, his texture: 05?

06? 07? 08? What should she use? She couldn't remember a time when she'd had to consciously work it out. She gently pinched the skin on his cheek, testing its elasticity. It was good clear skin. She reckoned 06 foundation. It must be 06. She put down the polaroids and swivelled his heavy chair around towards her, trying to lean in closer, but Olga, head pressed against Rory's chest, made it nearly impossible.

Ella was so close to telling him that she couldn't go on she felt as if she was trembling inside. This was the biggest moment in her career. She'd been so eager for this day, so confident she'd pull it off, and now everything was in danger of falling apart. She found herself glaring at Olga and noticed in a detached kind of way that she'd painted what looked like spirit gum on her cheeks. Another time perhaps she'd have found it funny.

'I think she's asleep,' Rory whispered.

'She could go and lie on the sofa?'

'I don't want her to wake up and start talking again.'

'Then why let her stay?'

Rory didn't reply.

She leaned forward, undid the three little buttons at the top of his T-shirt and clipped it back, exposing his brown throat, dark curls of chest hair, the pronounced ridges of his collarbones.

'It would help if you could sit further back in the chair.'

'It would help if you stopped fussing and got on with your job.'

He snapped the words at her so coldly that she had to turn away from him. Automatically she soaked cotton wool in cleanser and set to work on his face, wiping it clean.

She picked up the bottle of 06 crème foundation and was about to start applying it when she remembered that she hadn't primed his face. Any make-up artist would know to begin with primer. Even Rory probably knew you began with primer. Without it everything would slip within the first half hour of filming. She put the foundation back on the table, then picked up a bottle of primer and started to apply it to his face with a stipple sponge, stopping every few seconds to blend it in with her fingers, aware that Rory was watching her intently, but making sure she never caught his eye.

Silently she worked her way around his temples, blending in the colour towards his ears, trying to find something to break the tension between them.

'So, what did make up do about your moustache in Kiev?'

'Covered it up.'

'Must have taken ages.'

He yawned and didn't bother to reply.

She consulted her notes again, but she could only see the words *bastard*, *arrogant bastard*, dancing all over the page. It made her suddenly want to laugh. She turned away from him and Olga and read through the requirement of that afternoon's filming – a light bruise to his right cheek, showing through stubble, badly cracked bottom lip, further beads of sweat to be added minutes before the cameras rolled. She rummaged in her drawer and brought out a bottle of scar gel, and for a moment it was as if she'd never seen it before. There were instructions on the side of the bottle and she began to read: *allow layers to set between applications*. But she didn't want a scar, she wanted a bruise.

She laid her finger on his cheek.

'There's too much hair here.'

'Are you criticizing my stubble?'

'It's a beard, Rory.' She picked up the electric razor and touched it lightly against his jaw. 'You look like a polar explorer – on the way home.'

'But if you'd read your notes you'd have seen Hayden specifically asked for my own stubble, lots of it.'

Ella dropped the razor and grabbed her notes off the table.

Rory touched his finger to the patch of freshly shaved skin. 'Shame.'

She raised her chin defiantly, wondering how she could have done something so stupid and how long it would take to find all those shaved hairs and stick them back on.

She couldn't let him see her concern. 'I am sure Hayden will agree with me that this is not stubble. It's beard. He hasn't seen you for three days, he probably wouldn't even recognize you now. I am therefore going to thin it and shorten it and somehow hide the pink patch I have just created on your chin.'

'You're worried,' Rory said pleasantly. 'I want Rosalind.'

'You're not getting her,' she said sweetly back. 'You have to trust me. You can't check with someone every time I touch a hair on your head.'

'You look so uncertain.'

'I know what I'm doing.'

She turned and walked to the back of the trailer, opened a cupboard door that blocked her view from Rory and bent down behind it, searching through the cupboard inside, lifting out boxes of hairpieces, moustaches, packets of different lengths of facial hair, squirrel hair, rabbit and human. Eventually she picked out several packets of Ben Nye's crêpe wool hair and then, as she was standing up again, the phone in her pocket vibrated with a text. But she knew she shouldn't look at it now, she was running so late. She could picture Poppy bending around the door of the trailer arriving to take Rory to set, her face when she discovered him only a quarter made-up and with a shaved circle in the middle of his cheek. She could hear Hayden's anger and the whispers among the crew gossiping about how she'd cracked up, couldn't cope with him. And she could imagine Rosalind's mortification that the protégée she'd invested so much time in had proved to be such a hopeless flop.

She pulled out her phone from her pocket and read the text anyway. It was from Poppy.

Saw you thru the window. Keep cool!

Just a line, but it was enough to remind her that the world outside her trailer still existed and that she had a place in it and that she was good at her job. And of course she could ignore Olga sitting on Rory's lap. And of course she knew whether to use the 05 or 06 on Rory's smug face. She dropped the phone back into her pocket and picked up a bottle of 05.

'Who the fuck were you calling?'

She stood up and closed the cupboard door. Rory was on his feet, gripping hold of the back of his chair. 'I told you not to call anybody.'

She walked down the trailer towards him. 'Where's Olga?'

He looked momentarily taken aback but recovered quickly. 'Who was it?' he demanded again. 'Poppy? What did you say? *Help me Poppy, help me. Nasty Rory's got a girl on his lap and I don't know what to do.* Is that what you said?'

'Sit down, Rory.'

What she would have liked to say was that he was the most unprofessional and arrogant actor she'd ever met. And that she didn't want him to sit down, she wanted him to walk out of her trailer and never come back. And not only did she want to tell him so, she wanted to open the door of the trailer and shout it to the entire cast and crew.

He came to meet her. 'Why hide behind a cupboard to make a call?'

'I wasn't hiding, I was picking up this.' She showed him the bottle of 05. 'To cover up all those nasty spots on your chin.'

She saw a brief flicker of a smile. She carefully walked around him and went to the back of the chair and stood there, holding on to the back of it and looking out of the window, silently waiting for him to return, wondering again where Olga had gone.

He didn't come back to the chair. Instead he went through the narrow archway by the sink that opened again, at the front of the trailer, on to the sitting area with the sofa where Ella had first talked to Olga. There was a degree of privacy between the two parts of the trailer, but not enough to stop Ella taking a step closer so that she could see and hear what Olga and Rory might say.

She saw that Olga was lying the length of the sofa, her long legs side by side, a pair of grubby pumps neatly placed together on the floor beside her. As Rory approached, Olga opened her arms in welcome.

'You shouldn't have come here,' Ella heard Rory say.

'I am sorry but you ver so wunnerful,' Olga muttered back, her voice low. 'All I could think vas to see you again.' She pushed herself upright. 'Please, Rory. Let me be good vis you now. Ve have good fun, ya? You show me your big movie star trailer.'

'I want you to go.'

'No!'

Count yourself fortunate, thought Ella, sympathetic to her all the same because Olga clearly didn't understand what kind of a man she'd run after.

'Please Rory, I stay here. I come all this vay.'

Exactly, thought Ella. You poor girl.

'But I didn't ask you to, did I? Look at me and tell me. Did I ask you to come?'

Where was his compassion? Where was his remorse?

'Ya,' Olga said miserably. 'You did.'

'I don't think so.'

'You don remember. You ver so drunk.'

There was a long silence and then Rory spoke again.

'Olga, I'm going to call someone and I'm going to tell her to help you find your way to a train station and then you should catch a plane home.'

'Please. I come by train.'

'Train, get the train then. Poppy will get you a car to the station.'

Ella turned away. She didn't want to hear any more. All that chutzpah, all the misguided hope that had sent Olga rattling through the night from Kiev, all for nothing.

She went over to the table in front of her, picked up a collection of brushes that needed soaking in cleanser and dropped them into a bowl. And then she heard the trailer door suddenly open and Rory clatter down the steps, calling out Poppy's name.

And a little while later she heard the trailer door shut again and she looked out of the window to see Olga walking away with Poppy at her side.

Rory came back into the trailer and tossed a DVD in an envelope on the table in front of him.

'She's sharper than you think. Don't feel too sorry for her. She'll do fine.'

Whatever. Most importantly, she had gone. Ella was going to start again. She picked up a bottle of cleanser, squirted some on to a pad of cotton wool and started to smooth it across his arrogant, sexist, sanctimonious cheek.

'She's nakedly ambitious, or rather she'd like to be,' Rory went on. 'I told her she should go and sleep with Anton but she laughed and said she'd done that already. It made me wonder if that was why she came today, to see him, not me.'

Ella slapped more cleanser on his cheek and Rory shifted beneath her hand.

'Stop, I don't need any more of that in my eye.'

She stopped and waited.

'First,' Rory said, 'I don't have spots. Not one. Admit it.'

'I must have imagined them.'

'Second, I never, ever had sexual relations with that woman.'

'Where've I heard that before?'

'But,' Rory went on, 'I was in a club in Kiev last night, and I met people and perhaps at some point I did mention to someone the quaint little town of Florent, where I was making a film.'

'But not to Olga?'

'Not to Olga.'

'Come back to Florent and make love with me.'

He frowned at her in the mirror. 'Thank you, but I've had a very long day.'

'In your dreams, Rory.'

She started to wipe his face clean, pleased with the way she'd managed to sound just so bored with him. 'It's what you said to Olga.'

'But I didn't, did I? That's what I'm telling you. I've never seen her before in my life.'

Ella stopped. 'Now I am surprised.'

'Don't be. It happens all the time.'

'But why would she do that? And how could she come all this way if it was based on nothing? She'd have leapt straight into bed with you, straight into your movie star trailer, not knowing you at all. She must be out of her mind!'

Rory looked at her with amusement. 'I'm sorry you think it would have been so bad.'

'Absolutely it would!'

'She saw her chance and she took it, that's all.' He stretched forward for the DVD. 'She vands to be a movie star, ya. And here is her show reel to prove it. She asked me to give it to Hayden, see, she even knew his name. So, don't feel too sorry for her. She's got that show reel into the right hands, exactly where she wanted it. You should be impressed.' He glanced up at the clock. 'Anyway. Just thought you'd like to know. And now, Ella Buchan,' he touched his hand to his cheek, 'enough of the cleanser. Don't you think you'd better get some make-up on to my face?'

Ella followed his gaze and saw that three-quarters of an hour had already slipped away and immediately nerves prickled once more. She had to put away her shock about Olga, think about it later, when she could relax over a beer or a glass of wine and talk it through with Poppy, but now, now there was only time to think about Rory, who could not be late on set because of her.

But she wasn't uncertain, not any more. Somewhere between their stand-off and Olga leaving, the tension had freed inside her and fallen away and now she was clear-headed, confident, too, that, with the help of one of her contouring brushes and some packets of crêpe wool hair, she could repair his face, and nobody, apart from Rosalind, would even notice what she'd done.

Rory settled back in his chair and closed his eyes. 'Don't talk to me any more. I'm going to sleep.'

Even his rudeness didn't bother her now. She opened a packet of short black hair and some spirit gum, picked up one of the clips that had fallen off his shirt and re-pinned it.

What she'd said was true. Now that she'd properly begun, she felt clear-headed and professional, the old confidence returning. It was even a relief to find she didn't warm to him much; it stopped the mystique getting in the way, stopped

Kiss Like You Mean It

her caring what Rory thought of her. From now on, whatever else he said, whatever else he did, surely he wouldn't be able to throw her off course again.

She looked at his face again, that beautiful face, and her heart no longer stopped. She looked at the newly clean-cut curve of his jaw, the short straight nose and the perfect lips, and found no answering flutter in her stomach. Now she *could* stare at him as dispassionately and as professionally as if he was anybody else, his face fascinating and intriguing, but, after all, just a face like any other, an empty canvas waiting for her touch.

Four

A motorbike despatch rider with a wide blue and white band on his khaki arm chugged and bumped towards the cast and crew. As he passed the centre of the set the engine spluttered, coughed and died.

'Cut!' yelled Hayden, and the actor riding the bike straddled his legs out to balance himself. The boom operator and the two cameramen peeled back from the set, leaving Hayden to come striding between them, head thrust forward, long blond mane getting in his eyes. He stopped at the motorbike and at his nod the mechanic in charge of all picture vehicles – in this case a temperamental original 1915 army motorbike – ran in from the edge of the set and kneeled down to work on the bike's engine. To the left of the motorbike, actors playing infantry officers arguing over a couple of maps kept to their positions and didn't move a muscle.

'Ten minutes, please,' called the mechanic, and the two officers immediately started talking. Hayden sighed and kicked impatiently at the dusty brown earth, then went to speak to Sam Lucey, his first cameraman.

A prop hand ran forward and carefully lifted the maps out of the officers' arms, and a make-up girl ran on to re-powder their faces. And Ella, standing off set with Rory waiting beside her, watched Hayden's face and guessed that after two hours of unscripted spluttering and breaking down, this unreliable motorcycle was in danger of making them over-run again that afternoon.

Behind the motorbike was an abandoned stone barn set in a pretty orchard surrounded by fields and woods. Ivy, both real and artificial and supported by huge camouflage nets, hung down in great waves against its ancient walls. It was a billet occupied by men on their way to the Front, typical of hundreds of others – barns, abandoned cottages, cow byres – that were dotted around the countryside of northern France and had been requisitioned during the war as temporary shelter for battalions on the move. Stretched out, many of them asleep, khaki-clad soldiers lay everywhere. A few others sat upright, one standing smoking, leaning against the wall of the barn.

Ten minutes later the mechanic declared that this time he was sure he'd fixed the bike, and Hayden returned to his place behind his first cameraman, where he watched the scene on a little hand-held recorder.

'Roll sound,' called the First Assistant Director.

'Rolling! Rolling!' called the runners.

'Background action,' called the First AD.

Two soldiers opened a gate to the right of the barn and tracked into the orchard below, while most of the extras in front of the barn stayed still, though one or two began shifting, stretching. One who had been lying down got to his feet and started to cough, and, with a grin, the one standing smoking against the barn wall offered him a cigarette from a tin.

'Action Freddie!' called the First AD.

Again the motorcycle made its wobbly path through the set, and this time when the despatch rider reached the two infantrymen the noise of the engine did not cut out.

'Have you heard anything from Stevenson?' asked the first officer to the despatch rider.

'Cut,' yelled Hayden and leapt out again, running on to set, blond hair flying behind him. 'I couldn't hear a word. Cut the bike before he speaks. Okay?' He ran back to his chair. 'Reset.'

The despatch rider re-started his bike, the extra who'd stood up lay down once more, the soldiers returned from the orchard and the overhead cameras on cranes swung back into position as the motorcycle turned a wide circle and prepared to enter for the second time.

'Action,' called the First AD.

The motorcycle made it across the set and met the infantrymen. The engine cut at the right time. Again the extra stretched and rose to his feet.

'Have you heard anything from Stevenson?' the first officer asked the despatch rider for the second time.

The despatch rider violently shook his head.

'Cut,' yelled Hayden, marching over to the despatch rider. 'Do it like that and you look as if you've got a frigging wasp in your ear.'

'And he sounds as if he's got a frigging wasp up his arse,' said Rory. He turned to Ella. 'You know that man on the bike is not an actor? He was riding in a display team at the Shrewsbury flower show and Kate Janner saw him and signed him up. She never warned him he was going to have to speak.'

'Oh, the poor guy,' said Ella, watching Sam Lucey slowly unfold from his camera and stretch his back.

Hayden ran back to his assistants. 'Can I have playback,' he called and then he leaned in to see the action that had just been shot, placing his huge hands on his big muscled thighs and glaring at his monitor. With his paunch and his stack-heeled cowboy boots and his long blond hair, he looked as if he would have been more at home with a bass guitar in his hands, on stage with a German rock band.

He nodded to his First AD.

'Roll sound.'

'Rolling, rolling,'

'Background action.'

'Action Freddie.'

And again the motorcycle set out from its corner off set. It reached the infantry officers. The first officer said his lines and the despatch rider successfully shook his head.

'I sent out a couple of patrols last night and Corporal Daltry was killed – damn nuisance, one of our best NCOs – and I haven't heard a squeak from Hawkins since yesterday afternoon,' said the first officer.

'Hawkins is in Field Hospital 29, sir,' said the despatch rider. 'He was with Corporal Daltry.'

The cameras continued to roll. This was unheard of: ten, fifteen seconds of action without Hayden shouting 'Cut'. Beside Ella, Rory shifted restlessly and the prop hand beside him lifted the Aeroscope carefully off the ground and cradled it in his arms.

73

'Cut,' called Hayden.

The First AD turned.

'Ready, Rory?'

As soon as he said it, Ella felt the shiver of expectation all around her. What was it about him that made everybody stop what they were doing and turn towards the set? She didn't know. She wondered if he noticed and thought that he probably didn't. He was preoccupied, fidgety, checking his belt, shifting inside his heavy army uniform, only half still with her.

She picked up the tripod Ambrose carried on his back and helped Rory to sling it across his shoulders and hold it steady with a frayed piece of rope and an old iron hook. As a cameraman Ambrose would not have been expected to carry as much equipment as a regular soldier into battle, although during fighting it would have been recommended that he kept his gun – if only for the use of the bayonet – close to hand, as well as the first aid kit and rations in sandbags. But even without spare ammunition and grenades the complete kit was very heavy, and with the tripod and Aeroscope too it became almost impossible to stand for long in the heat of the day without breaking a sweat.

He turned to her silently and she reached down into the roomy cotton pouch tied around her waist, bringing out some loose powder and a brush and quickly stroking it across his reddening face and neck, toning down his cheeks and carefully avoiding the khaki cotton of his shirt. The heat of the day meant that as fast as she applied the powder, beads of sweat appeared somewhere else on his face.

'Water,' he whispered, sounding like a dying man.

She remembered how hungover he'd seemed when he'd first arrived at the trailer and looked at him with a flash of concern, then silently fished in another pocket, unscrewed a bottle of Evian and held it for him to drink without touching the bottle with his lips, so as not to disturb the web of cracks she had created across them.

He nodded when he'd had enough and she re-screwed the bottle.

'Tell me when you want some more, and now look at me again.'

She reached up for a thick strand of hair that had dropped down on to his forehead and lifted it back into place. She could feel the pomade melting in the palm of her hand.

Behind her Sam Lucey rolled his camera forward into position, stood up to re-tie the bandana that was keeping his hair out of his eyes, then bent back to the camera, ready for Rory.

Hayden swung round in his chair, took out a handkerchief of his own and wiped his sweating brow. 'Ready?' he asked Rory.

Rory nodded and moved to the edge of the set.

'Come here,' Hayden told Ella. 'Come and watch with me. See what a good face you've put on your man.'

She smiled at Hayden in surprise. It was a kind gesture. He'd never troubled to take notice of her before. She moved quickly to his side and stood beside him, watching through the little hand-held camera that was wirelessly connected to the main cameras and meant he could get instant playback on the scene.

This time the crew would film a reverse-angled shot, taking into account Rory, who was to walk in from the left as the despatch rider kick-started his bike. Almost as an after-thought, Rory was then to run to the stone barn, quickly set up his camera and film the despatch rider's departure with his Aeroscope before venturing inside. And, for the first time in shooting, he was using a genuine Aeroscope camera, on loan from a museum in Los Angeles, so precious that it had been given its own prop hand to guard it when-ever it went on set. For the battle scenes and for the scenes that did not demand such close-ups, the props department had made two further Aeroscopes, so beautifully and care-fully copied that visually they were indistinguishable from the real thing, the only difference being that they did not work, whereas this real Aeroscope did, and Rory worked it, pumping up the camera and filming exactly as Ambrose March would have done nearly a century before. Later, when Ambrose came to film men on the move, running into battle beside them, he would make do without a tripod. But here, with time and opportunity to set up as he wanted, he would pump up the camera, unfold the tripod, mount the Aeroscope upon it and begin to film.

'Action, Rory,' called the First AD.

Through Hayden's hand-held camera Ella watched Rory start to walk across the set. The despatch rider kick-started his bike and came towards the cameras and Rory, seeing him, ran closer.

'Cut,' called Hayden.

Rory waited for his instructions and didn't move. Even then, in those few seconds when he'd done nothing more than walk and briefly run, he had become Ambrose March to the point that every eye remained glued on him still.

'Rory, it's beautiful, exactly right.' Hayden flicked back his hair, then wiped the sweat off his forehead with a sleeve. 'And pleased to see you know how to work that thing. But stay back. You're crowding the shot. I don't want you so close to the bike. Sam . . .' Hayden turned to the first cameraman. 'Cut in to him really fast. And Freddie, I want you to stop ten feet sooner, about here.' He ran forward once more to the centre of the set and kicked at the ground, stirring a cloud of dust. 'Here. Otherwise you're obstructing Rory. Okay?' He looked around, nodded at his crew. 'Let's try again.'

'Hayden, wait,' said Rory.

Ella sighed. It had all been going so well. Everybody stayed in place.

'I must get close to that bike,' Rory went on. 'If I stay back, where you say, I won't get anything. It's either close up or it's not worth shooting.'

Hayden dismissed him without a pause. 'Rory, I hear you but I want you ten feet back. Trust me, it looks better that way.'

Ella listened in surprise. Something was up. It wasn't like Hayden to be so clumsily dismissive of him.

'That's ridiculous.' Rory, clearly rattled, pointed to the Aeroscope cradled in his arms. 'You know this lens is three inches long. The camera has to be close enough to get a good shot.'

'Four inches,' said Hayden.

Rory looked at him scornfully.

'Anyhow,' Hayden added briskly, turning away, 'it doesn't matter.'

'Say that again.'

'We're not going to see your shots.'

'So?'

'So stay back.'

Hayden turned his back on Rory, bent down to a holdall and picked out a pen, then carefully wrote something on the script.

'I'm not wanting to be difficult here,' said Rory. 'But let's face it, this is just a despatch rider arriving at a resting station. From Ambrose's point of view, it's probably not the most exciting moment of the war so far.'

Answer him, Hayden, Ella wanted to shout to him, as Hayden continued to bend over the script, writing, saying nothing. What was his problem? What was he doing, playing with Rory's temper? Couldn't he hear it beginning to fray?

'What I'm saying is, if Ambrose can't get close enough to see this guy's face, I don't think he'd bother with the shot at all.'

Hayden continued writing. Without thinking, Ella glanced over his shoulder.

At the top of the page he'd crossed out the film's title, *To End All War*, and had replaced it with *The Carey Sloan Disaster Movie*, and he had gone over it again and again, so hard that the short, angry little capitals were embedded on the page.

'It matters, Hayden!' Rory raised his voice. 'You know Ambrose would never cover a shot like that. And you shouldn't either. You just care more about getting your own fucking angles right.'

Abruptly Hayden stopped writing and dropped the pen and the script back in the holdall.

'I won't shoot from the barn, the pictures would be crap,' said Rory. 'I must come in. Ambrose risked his life to get close to his subjects. I find it offensive that you're even arguing about this.'

'Don't talk to me about offensive.'

'What the hell's that supposed to mean?'

Tension crackled in the air, as it did most days, but this spat was decidedly worse than normal. She glanced again at Sam Lucey. She thought she'd seen a little nod of agreement when Rory spoke, and on balance she had to agree with Rory too. Would anyone watching the film ever notice that Ambrose was filming too far away from his subject to get a good reel of film? Probably not, but it felt right to hear Rory defend his man, who had surely been at least as much of a perfectionist as Rory was. Good front line shots had depended on the cameramen being prepared to stay close to the action and run exactly the same risks as the soldiers they were filming; they'd not been gained with a long lens set up hundreds of feet away, nicely out of danger. Ambrose had filmed inches away from his men, men who had sometimes dropped to the ground beside him, taking bullets that could just as easily have been for him. Rory knew it and of course Hayden knew it too, and the truth was that any other day Hayden would probably have agreed with Rory, which was why this stand-off was clearly about something else, little to do with authenticity and, Ella suspected, more serious than the usual daily tussles that occurred between them, more than simply the sound of two large egos squaring up to each other. For some reason Hayden was furious with Rory.

'What do you think, Sam?' Rory asked, swinging around to him without warning. 'You're the cameraman.'

Sam shook his head, fiddling with his view-finder. 'Don't ask me.'

'But I want to know what you think. Christ, are we not allowed to discuss anything here?'

'I just shoot what I'm told.'

'What? Even if you think what you're being told is crap? I won't work like that.'

'You should. He's the director,' Sam told him softly, suddenly looking up from what he was doing and staring at Rory with calm brown eyes. 'And he's not talking crap.'

Ella, like everybody else on set, stared at Sam with un-ashamed surprise and more than a little respect. Even Rory seemed momentarily thrown off stride.

'But you're a cameraman. You're the closest thing to Ambrose that we have,' he retorted. 'How can you not defend him?'

Sam fished in the back pocket of his jeans and brought out a cap which he clipped on to his view-finder, then bent to his camera bag and brought out another lens.

'Sam?'

He looked up at him. 'Hayden has the whole of the film in his head. You know that. I wouldn't argue about a scene I know far less about than him. You can, if you want to, but don't involve me.'

Sam was so cool, so unfazed by Rory's noise and bluster, holding the lens in his hands and calmly polishing it, that Ella felt an involuntary swoop in her stomach and for the first time found herself clocking him properly and liking what she saw.

For a few moments more Rory continued to face him, but it was as if he knew he'd lost the round. And that the longer he remained there in the ring the worse he would look.

'I'm going to get a drink.' He strode off set, searching out Ella and waving at her to join him.

'A drink,' muttered Ella, feeling for the bottle of water in her pocket.

'Here,' said Sam, walking over to her with the bottle. He handed it to her. 'You left it by my camera.'

'What a prick,' Rory said furiously, as Ella unscrewed the water bottle and held it out once more for him to drink.

Hayden? Sam? Himself? Who did Rory mean?

Hayden came over to him. He stood, arms folded, looking at Rory with a certain degree of resignation.

'You should come in. You're probably right.'

What! Hayden was conceding. Ella couldn't believe it, and from the look on his face neither could Rory.

'You'd better leave the tripod,' Hayden added. 'We'll film without it.'

Ella bent and unclipped the tripod and felt the collective exhale of relief from the crew as Hayden returned to his post beside the main camera.

Unsuccessfully suppressing a little smile of satisfaction, Rory waited for the prop hand to come forward and collect the tripod.

'I didn't do it only to be difficult,' he insisted as she powdered his face once more. 'I did it because I'm right.'

He walked back on set, slowly over to the barn.

Sam bent back over his camera.

'Action,' called the First AD.

Rory walked then ran once more. The motorbike halted at the right place and he ran towards it and began to film.

To a man the cast and crew watched intently. Standing small and alone on a scrap of dusty earth, black hair dropping over his eyepiece, it was no longer Rory, but Ambrose. Even the seasoned pros who would never usually think in character were doing so this time. Rory cradled his little camera that measured just twelve inches by six by seven, a small oak box weighing less than twenty pounds, while rearing up on each side of him, so close they were almost touching him, were the two high-tech cameras of the twenty-first century, each costing half a million dollars, both taller than the men who operated them, all matt black and shiny chrome. And as Ambrose filmed his footage of the despatch rider, so they filmed him, rolling silently forwards and back on their gliding bars like predators, with vast vacant eyes, moving in for the kill.

And finally the despatch rider kick-started his bike and drove off in a cloud of dust and Ambrose stopped, brought the camera down, and with an arm raised over his eyes to shield out the sun, watched him go.

'Cut,' yelled Hayden.

There was a collective pause.

He looked around the crew and said, with quiet satisfaction, 'It's looking good.'

The crew burst into spontaneous clapping, then quickly fell silent for the second time, turning to him, and waiting expectantly.

Everyone knew it was early enough to start another scene, that they were behind on the day's work and the light hadn't yet started to fade. Hayden didn't have to let them go, and no one would begrudge him asking them to film some more. But in the past six days there'd been six 4 a.m. calls and perhaps, just perhaps, he was remembering that. He paused, stared back at his script, then at his watch, scratched his head, then looked around at everyone once more.

'You guys,' he sighed, then gave them a grin. 'Okay, check the gate. And if you buy me a beer I'll say it's a wrap.'

There was a whoop of delight. Checking the gate, when the camera was checked for dust, a hair, anything that might have interfered with the day's filming, was a sure sign that work was over for the day, and without waiting any longer, several of the crew – those with nothing more to do now filming was finished – broke into a sprint, tearing off through the orchard and into the fields beyond, barging past each other on the steep downhill slopes that led to the valley and road and the little town of Florent.

As Ella watched the cameramen closing down their cameras she felt somebody touch her shoulder as they passed.

'Don't even think of going back to the hotel.'

Ella saw her clothes before she saw her. A clash of shocking pink and yellow, dungarees, cut off mid-thigh, a bright yellow long-sleeved T-shirt, a spotted blue and white polka-dot hankerchief knotted around her neck.

Watch out! Flamboyant, crazy wardrobe girl approaching. That was what Sacha wanted her clothes to shout, but somehow, they never quite did.

They'd worked closely for months, first before shooting while they prepped for the film, and now, with their trailers parked up side by side, sorting out the actors who moved endlessly backwards and forwards between them and the set. Put some work in front of Sacha and she was always confident, knowledgeable, interesting, fantastically creative. Take it away and she was one of the few people on set who could get under Ella's skin.

Sacha let the others run on ahead of her and looked back at Ella, pink and breathless with expectation and curiosity.

'Good day? Bad day?'

She waited, all nervy and giggly and gossipy, for what Ella might say. She was, of course, referring to Rory, and she was the last person Ella wanted to talk to about him. And yet she knew that if she didn't, Sacha would be deeply hurt.

'He was nothing like I expected.'

She tried to sound vague, but Sacha looked as electrified as if she'd just been plugged into the mains. She came closer and dropped her voice to a theatrical whisper.

'Please don't tell me you *liked* him?'

When Ella didn't immediately reply she ran with the question, convincing herself of the answer as she went. 'So, what happened? What did you do? No! I knew it. All those hours on your own. I said to Poppy that it was a bad idea, leaving you together for so long, but she said she couldn't avoid it, it was the way the scheduling fell. And, of course, Rosalind had to make up Liberty in her own trailer, and all the extras were in the marquee, and anyway, Poppy said I was being ridiculous, that of course nothing would happen, that you'd got a brain and oh, Ella, Ella! We had faith in you.'

'So you should have.'

'But for God's sake, woman!' Sacha put her hand to her mouth, her eyes gleaming with laughter, black curls dancing around her face. 'You were meant to put up resistance. Don't you remember? He's a ruthless womanizer, remember that? On this one production he's already given poor Hattie, my assistant, a nervous breakdown, and we've spent the last few weeks discussing how none of us would ever fall for him. You were meant to hold out *at least for one day*.'

Ella so wasn't in the mood for Sacha tonight. Irritation curled her toes. She tried not to let it show. 'Of course I would have done. But I didn't need to hold out. He didn't try to seduce me. Not even once.'

Why did she tell Sacha that? Why tell her anything? Now she was going to have to talk to her some more.

At that Sacha's face fell and she stepped back in amazement. 'No! I don't believe it.'

Ella laughed. 'You look really upset.'

'I am. You mean nothing? Not even a subtle flicker of a move for you to grind into the dust with your stiletto heel?'

'Flip-flops.' Ella shook her head. 'They're useless.'

'I don't believe it. You mean he didn't do anything?'

'I think I'd have noticed.'

'But that's all wrong. How could that be? He's a total shagabout. He goes for everyone.'

Everyone but you, thought Ella unkindly. Oh, and me.

'He was meant to flirt and, on behalf of all the women on this film set, you were meant to spurn him.'

'I didn't get the chance. Really sorry, Sacha. I can see I've let you down.' As she talked she turned away, aiming for where she'd left an extra satchel of make-up on the grass.

She picked it up and slung it over her shoulder. 'Do you suppose anybody will speak to me in the bar?'

'I doubt it. People will be extremely disappointed.'

'Perhaps if I'd made more effort, put on some make-up . . . Look, don't worry about waiting for me, Sacha. I could be ages yet. I'll see you in Florent.'

Sacha looked at her in sudden doubt. 'Are you OK?'

'Of course.'

'You've had a bad day, haven't you? I saw you through the window. You did not look pleased.'

Ella agreed with a smile and a nod, not about to explain about that.

'You know I was only joking about Rory.'

'Of course. I'm fine. Please don't wait.'

Then, thankfully, Ella saw Poppy appearing from inside the stone barn, deep in conversation with Luca, the set designer. When Poppy saw Ella and Sacha she waved at them.

'Don't go,' she called.

'She won't,' Sacha called back before Ella could answer. 'She has to wait in case Rory wants her.' She winked at Ella, then added. 'But not in the way you're thinking.'

Ella gritted her teeth, but it seemed Poppy and Luca hadn't heard. Together they moved to examine the wall that ran out from the left-hand side of the barn to enclose a little yard. The wall looked identical to the barn, as if it too had been built many centuries before, from the same ancient stone. But now, as Ella watched, Luca reached up and rocked it gently with his hands, then bent down to examine its base and Poppy bent down beside him to look too.

Come on, come on, thought Ella as she and Sacha stood

silently side by side watching them. Poppy's golden curls seemed to sparkle in the slanting rays of the early evening sun. Moments later, the two of them stood up again and Poppy broke from Luca's side and came jogging over to Ella and Sacha.

'Are Health and Safety out to get you?' asked Ella. 'That wall is clearly about to come tumbling down to crush us all.'

Poppy rolled her eyes. 'Of course it is. And it wobbles at an angle of more than forty-five degrees, which Health and Safety have noticed too, so Luca is going to have to strengthen it, tonight, in time for shooting tomorrow, even though it's made of polyurethane and couldn't crush a raspberry. Luca was so pleased when I told him. He said he hadn't been looking forward to a beer at all. So, I don't feel bad,' she smiled. 'That's his job, isn't it?' She looked from Ella to Sacha. 'Ready to go?'

'Back to the trailers?' asked Ella.

'Yes. Got some final amendments to pass around. How was Rory?'

'Let's say your text came just in time to stop me punching him.'

'Please don't tell me that. Hayden wouldn't like a black eye.'

Of course Poppy knew Ella was joking, but still, professional second assistant director to her core, she couldn't quite hide her concern for her major star.

'Don't worry,' Ella reassured her. 'He's fine. But why did you never warn me that he was such a big misogynist pig?'

'I did warn you over and over. And who the hell was that girl?'

Ella turned to include Sacha. 'She was a nice girl called Olga who wanted to meet Rory.'

'Who somehow got on set,' added Poppy. 'I'd like to know what she did to those security guards to persuade them to let her in.'

'Can't you guess?' laughed Ella. Now, with Poppy beside her, she felt her mood lifting.

'Put it like that,' said Poppy, 'and I suppose I can.'

'You know, I think she squeezed fish,' said Ella. 'It's a difficult manoeuvre, very delicate, takes a lot of practice. But pull it off and I've heard it's incredible, works every time.'

'I don't understand,' said Sacha.

'But pretend that you do,' said Poppy, 'otherwise she might show us how it's done.'

'God no,' said Sacha, wrinkling her nose.

They reached the fork in the path that led either back to the unit base or down to Florent.

'We'll find you down at the bar,' Poppy told Sacha.

Sacha blew kisses to each of them. 'Don't be long.'

They continued along the path back towards the trailers.

'My guess is she wanted to know all about Rory?' said Poppy.

'How do you do that?'

'It's easy. She's transfixed by him.'

'Not another one.'

'They don't know him like we do.'

'I don't know if I can face the bar tonight. I'm going to be bombarded.'

Poppy slowly shook her head. 'Oh, no, you don't. Don't you even try to get out of it. You're coming to L'Oignon and it's going to be fun. What else would you do? Go back to your hotel room? Take your knitting down to the bar there and sit in a corner, all on your own?'

'Don't be rude about my knitting.'

Poppy smiled at her sympathetically. 'I'm not. I love your knitting. I'm hoping that cushion cover is going to be my birthday present.'

'You must be joking. I want my cushion cover.'

'Of course. It's far too nice for me.'

'I might do some now, while I wait for Rory. Why did I forget to ask him if he was coming back to the trailer to take off his make-up?'

'Because he was deep in a row with Hayden and he wouldn't have answered you anyway? But he will come back, of course he will. He's so vain, won't want to risk a spot.'

'I saw arrogant, argumentative, definitely irritable . . . But I didn't particularly see vain.'

'Oh, was he all those things? Poor Ella. I knew you were having a hard day. I saw you through the window of the trailer and you stared straight through me.'

'You're the second person who says they saw me through the window. I'm sorry, but why did neither of you come in? It would have been nice to see you.'

'I sent you a text.'

'So you did. And I suppose it did get better after Olga left. And once I could remember how to make a bruise I was fine again.'

'So, it didn't work out like we expected. No invitations to Rory's trailer for a private screening of your favourite film?'

'Hang on a minute, have you turned into Sacha?'

'I'm just asking about your day . . . and checking whether you fancied Rory. All that talk of punching him made me wonder.'

Ella paused, sighed. 'I think I should tell you how he behaved with Olga.'

Briefly she explained what had happened.

'She was shameless. But don't you think Rory comes out of it surprisingly well?' asked Poppy. 'When I met them, he was rather patient with her and kind. He even told me to organize her a flight home.'

'Wow! How generous of him.'

'He wasn't offering to pay,' Poppy quickly put her right. 'Production has to pay for it.'

'Not so generous. He wanted her out of his life as quickly as possible, that's why he asked you to put her on a flight. It wasn't anything to do with helping her. And why did he have to get her to sit on his lap? That's what I want to know. What was that all about?'

'He wanted to wind you up.'

'But why?'

'I don't know. Must have been very awkward.'

They walked on for a few paces more, then Ella spoke again.

'But Poppy . . . speaking of fancying.'

Poppy glanced at her. 'Yes?'

'Why am I saying this?'

'I don't know. Say it anyway.'

'On set today. Not Rory, somebody else. Who, I have to tell you, is absolutely gorgeous and I can't believe we've never noticed him before.'

'Sam Lucey?'

'Damn you!' Ella laughed. 'How?'

'I simply followed your stare. Ella, I think the whole of the crew followed your stare. You weren't the only person to notice Sam Lucey today.'

'Wasn't I?'

'All the girls love Sam. Don't you know that?'

'I only looked at him once, and that was just a little peep. All I thought was *he's nice*, and then I looked away again. How did you notice?'

'Sorry. It's my job. I see everything.' Poppy was clearly not sorry at all. 'And I agree he is gorgeous. I, and most of the rest of the crew, on the other hand, noticed that weeks ago. And now you've noticed, and you've even told me you've noticed – such a big step forward – you must definitely come to the bar because I know he'll be there tonight.'

By now they'd reached the unit base and they stopped together outside Ella's trailer.

'I said I think he's nice,' said Ella. 'I haven't even spoken to him.'

'Then tonight's your night to get talking.'

Ella looked up at her trailer. 'I'd better put on some make-up, brush my hair.'

'You had,' Poppy agreed. 'And quickly. God knows what he must have thought looking at you on set just now.'

'Yes, thank you, Poppy. If you didn't have a boyfriend, I'd think perhaps you were jealous of me liking Sam Lucey.'

'I am really jealous,' Poppy agreed. 'I'm thinking, Bitch! Leave him alone.'

'Good,' Ella laughed. 'So, I'll wait here for Rory and if he doesn't show up, I'll come and find you. How long will you need?'

'Half an hour?'

'Perfect.'

'Don't be late. I can't face Sacha on my own all night.'

'I won't be. And please shut up to everyone about Sam Lucey.'

'Don't even say it. Of course I will. And don't wait too long for Rory. He and Hayden could be arguing for hours. Why don't you leave him a note on the door telling him to take off his own make-up?'

'Signed Poppy?'

'Yes, if you want. I'm not afraid of Rory.'

'Nor am I!'

'Good.' Poppy started to walk away. 'Because you've got him twenty-four-seven for the next ten days, right to the end of the shoot. I just got a call this evening. Melinda is not coming back.'

Five

When filming finished for the day Ella usually headed straight over to the marquee that housed the extras – invariably soldiers making up numbers for the battle scenes – and helped remove moustaches and wigs and sometimes, if there'd been a bloody battle scene, no end of prosthetics, blood-caked stumps of limbs and gory facial wounds that were generally too difficult for the extras to remove themselves. It was often an hour or more before she could join the others at the bar, and too often, by the time she had finished, she was so tired that all she could do was creep back to her hotel room and yes, her knitting, or perhaps a book. But not tonight.

Letting herself into the trailer and switching on the lights, she wished again that she'd thought to go and find Rory and ask if he was planning on returning to her trailer. But then, the last thing she'd wanted was to get caught between him and Hayden in the middle of a row. And as Rory had no prosthetics and only spirit gum and make-up to remove, she knew he'd manage on his own, even if he was the star of the show, used to everybody doing everything for him. But she knew too that if she didn't wait and went straight to the bar in Florent, he'd be bound to show up outside the locked trailer and would, no doubt, make a monumental deal of the fact that she'd not been there to meet him when he came back to her for a six-thirty call the next morning.

Soon the unit cleaners would be along, but still she tidied everything she could see, wiped clean the workspaces and threw away the empty Coke cans that had, as usual, multiplied tenfold across every surface in the course of the day. Then she cleaned her brushes and finally dropped into her make-up chair and stared at herself in the mirror. An exhausted, bare face stared back at her. She shook her head, ruffling her hair – which could do with a wash – then pulled at her fringe, leaned forwards and rubbed at a patch of sunburn between her eyes that had started to peel. For a make-up artist, she was looking very rough. If Rosalind had been around that day Ella would never have got away with it.

She got back to her feet and fetched a bottle of wine from the fridge and a pot of Face It from its own designated shelf. Face It was her own concoction that she blended in a liquidizer at the back of the trailer on every set she ever worked on. It contained extracts of rose, liquorice, mint and aloe blended with spring water and was halfway between a spritzer and a lotion. It was soothing and moisturizing, smelled like heaven and was loved by everybody who knew about it; mixed by Ella then decanted into individual 25ml glass pots, each pot containing just enough for one application, kept on its shelf out of the sunlight, to be nicked continuously by anyone who knew what it was and that it was there. Ella found that flattering. When she'd come for her first interview, for her first job with Rosalind, she'd brought a pot for her. Whether or not it had got her the job she didn't know. Rosalind always insisted it hadn't, told Ella she'd nearly turned her away for being such a crawler. But still, ever since, she'd used nothing else and because of Rosalind's support it had become a trade secret, big stars loving the exclusivity and also insisting on walking off with pots of their own.

She clipped back her hair, tipped some Face It out of the jar and on to some cotton wool pads, then poured herself a glass of cold white wine and sat down in front of her mirror, the glass of wine within easy reach. Half an hour more, she thought. Then, if Rory still hadn't arrived, she'd join the others at the bar. She knew they'd be waiting for her, all her friends on the crew, dying to hear how her first day with Rory had gone, nobody doubting that she would have been next in his sights. She hoped Sacha would have explained by the time she got there. Not funny the first time, she really didn't want to have to have the whole conversation all over again.

She tipped back the chair, rested the cotton wool pads on her eyes and lay back, trying to relax. She managed it for just a few seconds before she found that her eyes were wide open again and she was lying there, not relaxed at all, her brain whirring as she wondered whether she should admire Olga or disapprove of her and how it was probably a combination of the two. She dashed off the pads and sat upright again, then took a welcome slurp of wine and stared at her face. She'd been about to pick up her usual brown mascara, which, together with a dash of lip conditioner, probably MAC's Gentle Coral, would usually have been enough to see her out of the door. But tonight she put it down again, unopened. Tonight she wanted more than the usual bare minimum. Something to do with Sam Lucey being in the bar, perhaps? But more likely it was simply the prospect of walking in late, knowing that the others would be at least an hour ahead of her, that made her want to make an effort. It was her war-paint, she thought as she smoothed more Face It across her cheeks and chin, but it would of course be so subtle and discreet that nobody but another make-up artist would know she was wearing anything at all.

She studied herself again. She'd caught some sun. Working on location in France in the middle of a heatwave, it would have been difficult not to, even though she had spent most of her days in the trailer. Her usually pale skin had finally turned a golden brown and she had freckles on the bridge of her nose. She wiped her face clean, then added moisturizer, dabbed concealer under her eyes to take care of the shadows of tiredness, and drew around the insides of her eyelids with a tan pencil to hide any traces of red. She added a little mineral powder and then a highlighter to her eyelids and temples, blending it into the sockets with her fingertips and brush, then dotted and rubbed a trace of pink into her cheeks that brought out the tan. She used brow finisher on her eyebrows, outlined and coloured in her lips with a dark raspberry red, then shook and ruffled her hair and looked at herself again. An immaculate face, with dark auburn hair, even golden skin tone, subtly highlighted cheekbones and wholesome lips – yes, she loved the lips, loved the colour and the plumping effect: she'd definitely use that again – and large, dark blue eyes stared coolly back at her. And then, as she looked, she saw in her own face the moment when the blank look turned into one of alert attention, as there came the sound of feet stomping up the steps outside.

She quickly turned up the lights, dropped the cleansing pads into the bin beside her, and leapt up, out of her chair. Then, carrying her glass of wine, she went to let him in.

It was not Rory on the other side of the door, but Hayden.

He gave her the briefest of nods as he moved past her and into the trailer. 'Where is he?'

'Rory?' She shook her head. 'Not here.'

At that Hayden literally tore at his hair. 'Oh, bloody hell, then where's he gone? Oh, what the fuck am I going to do?'

'Hayden!' She touched his arm. 'What's wrong?'

He didn't reply, walking past her and on into the trailer, up the length of it, striding past the chairs one by one then swinging around at the far end and staring back at her.

'I can't tell you.'

'Okay.' She nodded. 'I think he will be here. Poppy said he would. I thought you were him.'

Hayden closed his eyes and gripped the back of the furthest chair.

'Do you know, that sex-starved mother-fucker might ruin my film?'

'No. No, I didn't know that.' Shocked, she said it very politely.

'I don't know what the hell to do about it.'

She thought she saw tears fill his eyes.

'Oh, I shouldn't even have told you that. I'm crazy to have said a word.'

She walked towards him and held out her hand, but he stayed back and didn't immediately move. 'Come back here.' His agitation was so deep that she found herself reaching out again for his hand. 'Come and sit down.'

He gave her his hand, and as she took it he walked forward, stopped and turned towards her, then dramatically fell against her and buried his head in her shoulder, groaning aloud.

Ella slid her other arm around his back to support him. If he hadn't called Rory a sex-starved mother-fucker she'd have thought someone must have died, he was so upset. But surely he couldn't be referring to his little spat with Rory about the camera angles? Something else must have happened, something awful.

She continued to pat his back, thinking how he was volatile and extremely sensitive, how he shouted and cried all the time, how perhaps she didn't know him well enough to judge, but that this felt different. And she didn't know whether to press him to explain or keep quiet, stand there indefinitely, supporting and patting and waiting for him to say something more. And then he decided it for her by lifting himself off her shoulder and stepping back from her.

'I'm so sorry.' He managed the ghost of a smile. 'Bad day.' He glanced at her glass of wine. 'Do you have some more?'

'Of course.'

She rushed to get another glass and poured him one and then let him lead the way back to the sofa at the front of the trailer.

'Do you want to sit down?'

'No. I'm too full of nerves and rage. You think he'll be here soon?'

'I don't know. Would you like me to call him?'

'There's no point. I think he's turned off his phone. Jesus!' he exploded, suddenly. He went to the door of the trailer and pulled it open, looking out across the unit base, and she knew from the way he hung there, looking, that there was nothing to see.

'Have you tried his trailer?'

'Not there either.' He turned back to Ella, his voice back under control. 'I'm sorry. I'm probably sounding quite deranged. And I can't tell you a thing because if I did and anybody else found out about this, it is no exaggeration to say it could be the end of this film. And it can't be, Ella, it can't be.'

'Of course it can't. But you know, if you did tell me, that it wouldn't go any further than this trailer?'

'I know that, of course I do, and I know that you are a soul of discretion, and that your little trailer here is a haven of all kinds of secrets. And indeed, I'd like to tell you mine, share the burden, share the agony . . .' He screwed up his eyes at the pain. 'Oh, it's too good, my film is just too good. Oh, isn't he such a monumental arsehole to even think of jeopardizing my beautiful film? Why did I ever hire him? Why the fuck did we ever put his fucking name on the fucking line that said star of my fucking film? I knew it would be like this. Everybody told me it would be like this but I didn't believe it, or I chose not to see it because he's so good I could kill him. I knew he'd be the best Ambrose we'd ever find.'

Hayden bit his lip, his eyes far away, staring out of the window of the trailer, but she knew he was struggling with whether to tell her, knowing he shouldn't but unable to keep it to himself.

He turned back to her and took the plunge.

'He's screwing Carey Sloan.'

She looked at him cautiously. 'I know who she is.'

'But you haven't come across her?'

Ella shook her head. 'Not to talk to. She's with Anton Klubcic, isn't she? Is that difficult? A conflict of interest?'

He collapsed into the sofa.

'You could say that.'

Ella was concerned for Hayden, of course she was, but she couldn't help but feel a sense of anti-climax, because surely Rory shagging someone inappropriate was hardly front-page news? Clearly, Carey Sloan was an unfortunate choice. Clearly Rory had misbehaved again, like he'd done so many times before, and no doubt his personal publicist was about to have another sleepless night as she tried to spin it straight. But surely this misdemeanour would be forgotten? The crisis would blow over? The story ultimately just one more to add to the stack of others, providing a few more headlines, to be embellished where necessary?

'Anton's obsessed with Carey,' said Hayden. 'People say that it's only because he's got wind of the fact that Rory fancies her – which is transparently true because he's knocking her off. How fucking mad could he be? But the point is that nobody, *nobody* goes *near* one of Anton Klubcic's girlfriends, least of all Rory.'

'Rory does what he likes.'

'You've noticed? So now you see why this could jeopardize my film?'

'Would Anton cut our finance?'

'He'd chop Rory's balls off if he got the chance! And yes, our finance too. Oh, and he'd probably throw Rory off the film – as we're halfway through shooting, he'd be somewhat hard to replace. Or, even if he couldn't do that, say Rory's contract's so watertight even Anton can't break it, then he would bribe and blackmail and blacklist and make sure *To End All War* never sees the light of day. I'm not exaggerating this, Ella. Either way our film would be finished.'

She was completely stunned. 'But he's financing us through his own studio. He'd lose millions if the film didn't get shown, and he loves us. *To End All War* is his great project, his big hope for the Oscars next year. Surely he couldn't bring himself to destroy it?'

'You don't know him very well, do you? Anton is a bully with a dangerous mix of fragile ego and massive self-love. What's more, he would like to be an actor. Wrong – I think he even *was* an actor, in Russia, about ten or fifteen years ago, not in anything anybody's ever going to see. The fact that he failed gives him another reason to hate a success story like Rory, but then he managed to turn his life around, made his millions – I dread to think how – and became the man we know today. And right now, he's very proud of *To End All War*, because *To End All War* gives him credibility and he cares about that a great deal. Right now, he loathes Rory, loves the film. But believe me, if he finds out about Carey and Rory, he won't think about anything more than revenge because Rory will have made him look stupid. And

Anton cares about that more than anything else. Yes, it was his idea to make a film about Ambrose March. And yes, his studio, Studio X, is financing and producing us. Yes, he's personally putting up most of the cash. And yes, of course, he'd like it to be a smash hit. But when *To End All War* wins its wonderful reviews and its Oscars, we all know that nobody will think of it as Anton's film. They probably won't even think of it as my film. It will be Rory's film and Anton knows that. And right now he can just about stomach the thought, but let the Oscar winner be that guy who stole his girlfriend, on the film set, right under his nose . . .' He shook his head at the thought. 'Anton would rather die.'

'Okay, but . . .' she nodded. Clearly this was serious, much more than just a scurrilous indiscretion. 'Right now, he knows nothing?'

'As he has Carey followed twenty-four-seven I don't know how not. But it seems he doesn't. Not yet.'

'When did you find out?'

'I didn't find out. Rory told me. He hinted about it last week, but at first I didn't react, thought he was just talking. I suppose some part of me was trying not to make it into an issue, hoping it would go away, thinking of course, of course Rory wouldn't do something so insanely stupid as go after Carey . . . But then, this afternoon, he told me again. They're definitely together.'

'And was he telling you that to bait you?'

'No. He was telling me because he thought it was funny.'

'He's crazy.'

'Because, as you say, he thinks he can do what he likes. And right now, he's enjoying himself. Oh, Ella. I can't bear it. They'll be all loved up, hands all over each other, probably thinking nobody will notice, and not caring if they do.'

'Nobody has noticed yet. I've heard nothing about this.'

'That's my only hope. And that's what I was trying to explain to Rory – that if he could just leave her alone now we might still be okay. That's if we can persuade Carey not to breathe a word, but she's almost more of a liability than him. She's in seventh heaven, can't get enough of Rory, and it's making her silly and careless. I have a feeling she's as naive as Rory is about this; neither of them understand. And Rory, Rory does not take kindly to being told what to do. In fact he positively enjoys being told so he can then do the opposite. But I have to get him to see sense on this. I have to get him to leave her alone. Tell me how, Ella. What do I do?'

He downed the glass of wine in one and held out the glass for another. Ella filled it up.

'Say Anton does find out. What about the other co-producers? Couldn't they overrule him, save the film? Or what about Liberty Boyd? Surely she's got enough clout to make sure the film survives?'

'She's a star, and in other circumstances she might have been powerful enough to have some impact. But she's paid her dues on his casting couch too. She owes Anton her whole career. So she might protest a little if he sinks this film but she's not going to make a fuss, she'll want to keep him sweet. But look, say I'm wrong, say Anton wants to keep her sweet too. So instead he decides to act discreetly and stay under the radar of the press – and there's no history of him ever doing that before. But say he does. Then he leaves the finance in place, lets the film get finished and still ensures that it never sees a cinema. He could kill *To End All War* with the lightest of touches. He controls the schedule. All he would need to do is move it, and then move it again, stall it indefinitely or perhaps, if he had to, release it in a few art house cinemas for such a short run that nobody ever goes to see it. He's done it before; he loves the power to break a movie, break a career, just as much as he loves to make one. Sometimes he does it just for fun, it's what makes everyone so afraid of him. But give him a good reason, and then, despite our American co-producers, despite our stars and all the buzz, all the hype already building about this jewel of a film, despite everything we poor souls have put into it, we're finished.'

'So, somehow, you have to get Rory to start listening to you.'

She saw the defeat in his face.

'I started to explain and I tried to be calm, but I know I wasn't. I said it all wrong, and in any case I'd hardly begun before he walked off. I suppose I talked Anton up, tried to make him understand the importance of keeping Anton happy, and it was the worst thing I could do. Think about it, Ella. Rory's known only wonderful reviews, million-dollar pay-cheques and the adoration of a thousand beautiful women. In all his career he's never had a failure and it shows. So show him a bully like Anton and you know what he does, he laughs at him. And when I tell him laughing's bad, laughing makes Anton see red, he laughs at me too, laughs at my fears. And then when I still don't stop, and I start to shout, he walks away, says he's disgusted with me for being such a coward. And I know just what he's going to do now and I can hardly bear it. Tonight he'll take Carey under his arm and out on the town and he'll make sure all the paparazzi are there to see them.'

She'd known Rory for all of one day, plenty long enough to believe that what Hayden said was true. She looked back at him, at the desperation in his face, and saw he was waiting, with a wild hope that somehow she was about to speak aloud and tell him what to do.

She tried again. 'Is there another way to get Rory to drop Carey? How about you lift her off the film? You could re-shoot her scenes, find her a better part on another movie on another continent, one that she simply can't turn down?'

'And how would I square that with Anton? She's here because of him.'

'No. Of course.' Even as she started she'd known it wasn't a solution at all. She swallowed the last of her wine and poured them both another glass.

'I tried to keep them apart. When Rory hinted to me about Carey, I'd just had a call from Sydney, his director on *Life As You Know It* in Kiev. He wanted him back for a day's re-shooting. Have him, I told Sydney. Keep him as long as you wish. Sydney couldn't believe his good luck. I've never been so kind before. But I took the opportunity to separate them, even though it buggered up our schedule here. I thought if I could get through most of Carey's scenes before he got back perhaps they wouldn't have time to get into any more trouble ... Wasn't that naive? Rory's come back and straight away he's picking up from where he left off. And, by the way, you know something else? You know what makes this even worse? She can't even act. She's not even good. She's awful, can't do the French accent and giggles at the sight of a camera. There's absolutely no way she'd have got the part if she hadn't worked on Anton first.' He rolled the stem of the glass between his fingers. 'I think he gave it to her because he knew it would involve her kissing Rory. It gave him some strange thrill, but that was when he thought he was controlling them. Day after tomorrow we have the scenes in the hay barn. Rory's requested a closed set. I can't think why.'

'You must talk to Rory again, talk to both of them.'

'How? What can I say?'

'You have to apologize to him.'

'I want to tear off his head.'

'I'm sure, but you can't. It's such a fine and handsome head.'

At least she made him smile.

'It might help to remember one thing, and that is that Rory truly cares about Ambrose. That's his weak spot and it might be your way through.' She pushed herself back on the sofa, thinking about it. 'Nobody who has been on set these past few weeks can have missed the fact that he is incredible in this film – Rory least of all. See today, how defensive he was of Ambrose? He loves him and he wants to tell his story. That's probably his only vulnerability. So that's where you must hit him. Appeal to that, remind him how, without this film, what Ambrose did will never be recognized. No one will know of him. Give him the evidence. If he argues, show him other films that Anton has destroyed. Remind him that right now no one's heard of Ambrose March and that is how it will stay if this film doesn't get made. And make him see that there will be other opportunities, better chances to stand up to Anton. But that he shouldn't do it now, not with this film. Jesus, I don't believe him!' Abruptly Ella ran out of steam. 'How can he be such an idiot?'

But this time, while she'd been speaking, Hayden had begun to sit straighter, and he'd been listening and nodding, encouraging her on, and now he downed the last of the third glass of wine.

'You could be right. I've got to go and find him and tell him what you said.'

'I hope it might work.'

'It could. If I put it like that, there is a chance he'll listen. As you say, he cares about Ambrose. I must appeal to him. What else can I do?'

'I'm sorry. I can't think of anything else.'

He stood up. 'You've been calm and rather wise. Nothing like me.'

'You're going?'

'Of course. This can't wait.'

'Where will you go?'

'I don't know, but he's not coming here now. Look outside.'

He moved to the window and she came and stood at his side and they stared out together at the fading light, the yellow sunset already spreading across the empty, silent trailer base.

'Most of the crew will be in L'Oignon,' said Ella.

'You too? Is that where you are going?'

'That was the plan.'

'Do call me if you see him. Would you mind? For God's sake don't say anything. Just tell me where he is.'

'Of course.'

She wouldn't dream of confronting Rory. Let Hayden do that.

'And thank you for the wine. And thank you for listening to me.'

At the trailer door he paused again.

'And Ella?'

'I know.' She went to the door to see him out. 'Of course. I won't breathe a word to anyone.'

'No one. And certainly not Poppy. If she knew, she'd have to try and sort it out, and this needs to be contained.' He glanced around the trailer once more. 'Did I tell you Rory looked great today?'

'Thank you.'

'Something different about his face.'

She winced.

'Don't worry about it. I liked it. That's what counts.'

'Why did I ever think you wouldn't notice?'

'I don't know, but I'm deeply insulted.'

She hung her head. 'Sorry.'

She opened the door for him to go and then reached out to stop him as he started to make his way down the steps.

'Rory's not the only one who cares about Ambrose March. If you think of anything I might do to help, please let me know.'

He looked back up at her.

'You're going to regret telling me that.'

Six

By the time she had locked up the trailer, called Poppy to arrange to meet in Florent, and walked through the orchard that took her down to the town, it was late enough for the sky to have turned from mellow yellow to streaky pink and red. By the time she made it through the trees and out on to the lane below, it was almost dark.

The lane wound for about half a mile before it arrived at the little town of Florent. As she walked along, silently and alone, she thought how, nearly a century before, it had borne the noisy footsteps of thousands of British soldiers marching to the Front and how it was more than likely that the little stone barn that was now providing shelter for soldiers in the film had once done so for real.

She crossed the narrow humpbacked stone bridge, then walked up the cobbled Rue de Valour and into the pedestrianized main square and stopped to look about.

Florent was a small pretty town. Its architecture was Flemish, on a smaller scale but very similar to Arras, which was just ten miles away. But, unlike Arras, Florent had survived the First World War relatively intact. Now, in high summer, the town square was full of noise and people, children chasing each other around the fountain, families – at this early hour, it was always the British ones – eating supper at the restaurants, gaggles of pretty teenage French girls slowly promenading and eyeing up gangs of handsome boys.

Florent had countless pensions and guest-houses and two major hotels, both of which had been taken over by the crew for their ten weeks of filming. Up a narrow cobbled street, in the oldest, most beautiful part of town, was the gorgeous boutique hotel La Sauterelle – the Grasshopper – which had just ten rooms and one suite. The rooms had been taken over for the producers, for Liberty Boyd and a couple of other actors and for Hayden. Rumour had it that Liberty Boyd was not best pleased that the suite had been given to Rory.

At the opposite and definitely the unfashionable end of town was Le Sport, a modern, three-star hotel with sixty-six cheap rooms that had been block-booked for the rest of the crew. It was an unappealing place, and the crew used it to sleep in and not much else, preferring to do any after-hours partying at L'Oignon instead.

L'Oignon was in the old part of town, halfway up the cobbled street that led to La Sauterelle. It was a bar and restaurant, pretty and perfectly French, with pots of geraniums, pale blue shutters and square painted tables and rickety wicker chairs that spread out, up and down its wide pavement outside. Early on it had been picked as a discreet, unofficial watering-hole for a select few of the crew and some of the less starry members of the cast. Then, as the weeks had passed, and word had got around, inevitably more and more of the crew had arrived and L'Oignon had been wholeheartedly taken over. Those who had discovered it first now sat at their tables muttering grumpily, hardly aware of the few locals – mostly old men – who sat stubbornly beside them, among the heaving throng of noisy crew, refusing to be turfed out of the restaurant that had been their favourite for years.

But although L'Oignon was a smash hit with most of the cast and crew, as far as Ella knew, neither of the film's two stars had ever been seen there. In all the time they'd been filming in France, Ella had never once heard of Rory or Liberty Boyd joining any of the crew in any social gathering whatsoever. She knew she wasn't going to find Rory here.

As she climbed the steep cobbled street towards it now, she could see Matthew, sitting with his back to her, with a couple of other actors, but she didn't want to get caught by him. She walked forwards, slowly, bending away from his table through the crush of people, looking around for Poppy or Sacha but not seeing either of them.

Inside there were fewer people, but it was so stiflingly hot that she was about to turn and go outside again when she saw Sacha and then Poppy sitting at a table beside the bar. They were in the corner of the room, beneath a window that was wide open to the street outside.

'Ella,' Poppy called, seeing her at just the same time. 'Over here! Come and sit down.'

'Ella, darling. Just a moment before I leave,' said another voice at her shoulder, Rosalind's voice, deep, insistent, no messing.

Ella turned to her, and Rosalind leaned forward and

theatrically kissed both her cheeks then held her back as if to look at her better, as if she hadn't seen her for weeks rather than just one day.

As always, Rosalind looked spectacular, exactly as a make-up artist should look, Ella always thought. She was tall and thin and had long dark grey hair that fell to just below her shoulders and was tonight held back off her face by a wide red silk scarf. She was a make-up artist who never wore make-up, and didn't need to either, as she had the most startlingly beautiful face, with bony high cheekbones, a small neat nose and wide navy eyes that missed nothing. At sixty she could still wear anything she liked. While filming *Skin Tight* in a Russian winter, she'd once arrived on set in a black, full-length, fitted velvet coat-dress, trimmed with sable, and had looked so stunning the director had insisted that he put her in the film. Tonight she wore a floating, hippy-chic dress in dark violet silk which clashed beautifully with the red silk scarf. As usual, she made Ella feel boringly underdressed.

Delighted to see her but still expecting a bollocking, Ella waited for what she might say next.

'Darling, I am bristling with expectation,' declared Rosalind pointedly, over the din of the crowd. She continued to grip Ella's shoulders with fierce, sinewy hands.

'Bristling?' Ella was relieved to see a twinkle in her eye. 'Are you referring to Rory's beard?'

'Or rather lack of beard. Do you have an excuse?'

'No.'

'Good. Excuses are preposterous. What happened? Did you not look at your notes?'

Ella grinned back at her. 'No.'

'Everybody needs to look at their notes. Apart from me.'

'I agree. Never again.'

'But, I suppose you did do a good job patching him up. What did you use?'

'I tried cutting the top off one of my contouring brushes but the hair was too shiny. So I used Ben Nye's crêpe wool hair instead.'

Rosalind nodded. 'Brunette?'

'How did you know that? It took me at least five tries to get the colour right.'

'Years of practice.'

'Don't tell me you've ever accidentally shaved off a bit of beard?'

Rosalind pulled Ella closer. 'This afternoon I accidentally stuck a few of Liberty's false eyelashes to her upper lip.'

Ella snorted with laughter. 'Accidentally on purpose?'

'Perhaps.' Rosalind cast a quick glance around the room, not that there was any chance Liberty was there to overhear. 'She was being so poisonous to Heidi.'

Heidi was sixteen and was on a month's work experience. She was very sweet and very shy and also happened to be the daughter of one of Rosalind's oldest friends.

'After about half an hour I took them off again and of course Liberty never even noticed. She was under a couple of eye pads, enjoying that cream of yours. Blah, blah, blah . . .' Rosalind opened and closed her hand like a beak. 'Blab, blab, blab. When she talked she made the eyelashes open and shut like a couple of Venus fly traps. Very Liberty.'

Ella laughed delightedly. 'I'm afraid Rory did notice what I'd done.'

'Darling, don't worry about it. The important thing is you put it *right*. If anything you did him a favour. I told him he looks far more handsome now.'

'Oh, he really needed that.'

She laughed. 'But he does look better, doesn't he? I don't know why I didn't insist on getting rid of that beard myself. I suppose I let it go because Hayden was so adamant and I didn't feel that strongly. But, looking at him today, I realize I should have done. You did a good job on him today, Ella. And I liked the plains dust too. That worked very well.'

'Thank you.'

'Right.' Rosalind nodded, patted her shoulder. 'Good girl. Glad I caught you.'

'You're leaving?'

'Yes, I certainly am. Can't stand around here. It's far too hot. I'm out for dinner with Hayden. I told him, after a day on my own with Liberty I needed some good wine and a delicious dinner so he's taking me to Le Grand Surprise.' She leaned forwards and kissed Ella's cheek. 'Christ, she was a monster today,' she whispered. 'And what stinky breath! Truly the worst. She's joining us in the trailer tomorrow.'

'Oh, good,' said Ella. 'That sounds like fun.'

'We'll burn lots of candles. Must be because she wants to get close to Rory but also I have a feeling she's realized she's missing out, spending her whole time cocooned in her own trailer, she's not getting any of the gossip.'

'Is there any?'

'Don't ask me. I'm always the last one to know anything.'

Which wasn't the slightest bit true.

'It'll be great to have you back,' said Ella, wondering if Rosalind knew about Carey Sloan and, if she didn't, whether Hayden would tell her anything over dinner. From what he'd said to Ella, he wasn't about to, but Rosalind and Hayden were close and even if he wasn't planning on telling her anything, Rosalind was not the sort to miss that something was wrong.

'No. It was much the best thing that you got to know Rory on your own. If I'd been there I wouldn't have been able to resist hanging over your shoulder, telling you what to do.'

'You can do that tomorrow instead.'

'You've got him cracked. You don't need me.'

She said it with such confidence that Ella was touched. 'Thank you.'

'And we'll have Minnie and Jemima back from the marquee. We'll be a full house.'

Ella was glad. She loved the chat and bustle of a full trailer.

Rosalind finally dropped Ella's shoulders and stepped back from her. 'I must go or Hayden will be waiting for me.'

'Of course,' Ella nodded, thinking Rosalind might find herself waiting for Hayden.

Over at the bar she saw Sam Lucey standing with his back to Poppy and Sacha's table, a trio of pretty girls crowding in on him.

'See you in the morning.' Rosalind squeezed her shoulder. 'Have a good night.'

Ella let her go, then turned and walked over to the table where Poppy and Sacha were sitting, facing the room, waiting for her.

'Why were you so late?' asked Poppy, as Ella dropped down into the chair, and she could see from her face that what she meant was, how could you leave me with Sacha so long? Sacha, who was lying back against her chair, with her eyes closed, arms loose at her sides, a drunken smile upon her face.

Poppy followed Ella's stare. 'At least it means I don't have to talk to her.' She poured Ella a glass of wine. 'Did Rory give you a hard time?'

'No. He didn't show.'

'So what kept you?'

Ella looked back at her, momentarily lost for an excuse. 'Nothing. I waited for him, that's all. Then I came here.'

'Took your time.' Poppy's eyes narrowed. She took a handful of chips from a bowl in the middle of the table and ate them one by one, but she said nothing more.

Ella held her stare. She wished she could tell her, or at least give some meaningful look that would say she would tell her later when Sacha wasn't in earshot, but she couldn't, and so instead she laughed it off. 'Don't look at me like that. I sat in the trailer and then I put on some make-up and I drank a glass of wine and then I came here.'

'Of course you did,' said Poppy.

Sacha, missing the undercurrent completely, rocked back in her chair and opened her eyes.

'Look at us,' she told Ella, looking around the room, her eyes shiny with wine. 'It's so much fun. Look at us, sitting here in sweet little onion. I love it.'

Poppy passed her the bowl of chips. 'Eat some. You've had too much wine and not enough food.'

'Yes, but it doesn't stop me being happy. Gen-u-ine-ly,' she enunciated carefully, 'happy to be here.' Then she frowned at Poppy. 'You don't know how lucky you are to be here, Miss Jones.'

'How lucky would that be?' said Poppy, looking bored.

'*You* didn't spend the whole of last summer under an umbrella in Wales.'

'No, I didn't,' Poppy agreed. 'And you did. And you've told me that before.'

'You don't know how hard making a film can be.'

Poppy let out a long sigh. 'Sacha, I've heard it all before.'

'But I haven't,' said Ella jumping in. 'What was the film?'

'*The Italian Stallion.*' She stared at Ella. 'No, don't laugh. It could have been great.'

'But it wasn't,' said Poppy.

'So, why Wales?' said Ella, trying to keep a straight face.

'It was meant to be set in Tuscany,' Poppy said, 'but Wales was cheaper.'

'Low budget then?'

'Low budget, I wish. Non-existent budget more like.'

'Soft or hard?' asked Poppy.

'It was not porn!' Sacha looked crushed. 'He was a racehorse. He ran in the Palio.'

'In Wales?'

'Leave her alone,' mouthed Ella to Poppy.

'Yes, leave me alone!' insisted Sacha. 'I had to dress eleven jockeys and I didn't even get paid. It wasn't funny then and it's not funny now. And the only reason I'm bringing it up is because I think you should appreciate what we have here, on this film.'

'Why shouldn't Ella appreciate it too?'

'She does.' After such a long speech Sacha abruptly ran out of steam. 'And that's why I am so happy to be here, working with her, here in L'Oignon.'

'But you don't like being here with me?'

'Stop it, Poppy,' said Ella.

Sacha didn't mind. 'And with you,' she conceded.

She reached, affectionately, across the table for Poppy's hand, then changed her mind, stretched for the wine bottle instead and refilled her glass, then drank two-thirds of it straight down.

'You should slow down,' Poppy told her, taking the bottle out of her hand.

'Don't bug me,' said Sacha, looking cross-eyed. 'You'll spoil my evening.'

Yes, don't bug her, thought Ella, aware that Poppy was needling Sacha because she was irritated with Ella, because she felt Ella was keeping something from her, which, of course, she was.

Sacha was too drunk to care. She put down her glass of wine and stretched happily in her chair, swinging back both her arms, and promptly caught Sam Lucey smack in the groin with the back of her hand.

Ella, facing the two of them, with her back to the rest of the room, had been the only one to see Sam leave the bar and move into Sacha's range. She closed her eyes.

'That's one way to get his attention,' muttered Poppy.

'Oh, no! Oh no!' Sacha leapt off her chair and turned to Sam's bent figure then dropped to her knees, trying to see his face. 'Sam, I am so sorry!'

In answer he whistled through his teeth then slowly straightened up again.

'Did you want something?'

Sacha laughed, hot and pink with embarrassment. 'No. Of course not. I mean I didn't realize you were there.'

She stood up with him, then swayed violently and clutched at his arm. 'Are you okay? Water? Do you need some water? Or a chair?'

Sam didn't look so bad. Clearly it had been only a glancing blow.

'I think I'll survive.' He held her steady. 'Are you okay?'

Poppy pulled back her chair. 'Sit down, Sacha.'

Sacha fell heavily back into her chair and put her head in her hands. 'I can't believe I did that.'

Sam looked from Sacha down to Ella sitting beside him. 'Hello, Ella.' He turned to Poppy. 'Hello, Poppy.'

'Good to see you, Sam,' said Poppy.

Sacha kept her head on the table and looked up at him with love in her eyes. 'Are you sure you're okay, Sam?'

'Absolutely.'

He stayed standing at Ella's side. She sat with her cheek in line with his hip and looked down at his feet in a pair of navy Converse trainers, then up his long legs, in navy linen trousers, then up again to a crisp, pale blue shirt. She couldn't see any more without tipping back her chair. She tipped back her chair.

'Hi Sam,' she smiled up at him. He looked lovely, tanned, freshly shaven, damp dark hair just starting to curl.

'Wine?' Poppy offered, holding up the bottle. 'Take away the pain? Promise we won't hit you too.'

He laughed and shook his head, still looking at Ella. 'Thank you, but I can't. I'm off, out for dinner.'

'Where?' asked Poppy.

'Le Grand Surprise.'

'Oh!' said Ella. 'With Hayden and Rosalind?'

'Yes. Are you coming too?'

She shook her head.

'Sure you can't?' He was still staring at her.

'Sure,' she laughed, as if he'd said nothing at all, which, perhaps, he hadn't. She looked back at Sacha, eyes closed, resting her cheek on the table in front of her. 'I have a feeling she needs to go to bed.'

He laughed. 'I know that feeling.' He paused. It was as if he wasn't quite ready to go, hoping she might say something else.

'You think Rory was happy with his scene?'

'Yes. In the end.'

'Good. Okay.' He nodded almost to himself then lifted a hand in farewell. 'I'll see you tomorrow.' And he was gone.

'Damn,' said Poppy, turning back to Ella. 'What a shame.'

'Whasha shame?' said Sacha, sitting up again, taking the bottle and pouring herself another glass. 'God, I love him.'

Poppy swapped her glass of wine for a tumbler full of water. 'Drink this.' She looked restlessly around the room.

'Why's it a shame?' Sacha asked again.

'Because the night is still young.'

Ella knew what Poppy meant. She meant that she didn't want to spend her whole evening sitting at the back of the room, trapped at their little table for three, listening to a rambling drunken Sacha. And neither did she. She looked around the bar and then the wider room but she knew no-body else in there.

'You should have gone with him,' Poppy said to Ella.

'Of course I couldn't have done.'

'He asked you.'

'He was being polite.'

'I suppose there'll be other nights.'

'And you'd never have forgiven me.'

'No.' Poppy downed the last of her own glass. 'I wouldn't.' She laughed. 'You couldn't have done that to me.'

And there was no way Ella could have walked into Le Grand Surprise with him either, and Sam must have known it too. She'd been once before and Le Grand Surprise was Grand, with a hushed and formal dining room, thick white tablecloths, amuse-bouches between each course. The thought of turning up uninvited, breaking into that little dinner *à trois*, Rosalind's look of uncomfortable surprise . . . Much as she might have enjoyed walking across town with Sam, walking into the restaurant at the end of it would have been a price too high.

So instead, here she was, left behind with the weight of Sacha and a secret she couldn't tell Poppy.

Sacha shoved back her chair and stood up. 'I need *La Toilette*,' she mumbled at the floor.

Ella looked at her, calculating whether she'd make it there and back on her own and deciding she probably wouldn't.

'No, don't,' said Poppy, as Ella stood up to help her. 'She'll be fine, won't you Sacha?'

Sacha stared back at her. 'Watch you trynimply?'

'Nothing. Off you go.'

They watched her unsteady progress towards the bar, watched her stumble against a girl carrying two full wine glasses, then totter down the shallow step towards the washrooms.

'We're going to have to take her home,' sighed Ella.

Poppy closed her eyes. 'I know, stupid drunken idiot. I was looking forward to this evening.'

'I'll go and help her.'

'Wait. In a moment.' Poppy hesitated. 'While we've got a chance, I wondered if you wanted to tell me what's up?'

Ella froze. She hadn't thought about it like this, how listening to Hayden would mean she would have to lie to her closest, dearest friend.

'Something happened between when I left you at your trailer and now,' Poppy went on. 'And don't tell me it didn't because I know you and there's something you're not telling me.'

'There's nothing.'

'Then what's the matter?'

'Irritated that our evening's spoiled, that's all.'

A flicker of hurt crossed Poppy's face. She leaned closer to Ella. 'If that's so, then great, because of course I don't *want* anything to be wrong. But, my sense is something happened after I left you and it's upset you and all I want is to help. I don't understand why you can't tell me what it is.'

So uncomfortable that she couldn't think of a word to say, Ella could only shake her head.

'Rory did turn up, didn't he?'

'No.'

'Yes, he did. He came to the trailer after I'd left you and

maybe he said something or did something that you feel you can't tell me about?'

'No!' Ella cried. 'What do you mean? Of course not. You mustn't think so badly of him.'

'Ella, I wouldn't tell a soul, you know that.'

Ella took her hand. 'Of course, but Rory's not mean. He's full of himself, not dangerous. And if he had upset me, you'd be the first person I'd turn to. So please, trust me when I say he didn't come and that I'm only late because I took my time in the trailer.'

Poppy continued to grip her hand and then, after a few seconds, her face cleared and broke into a wide smile of relief. 'Thank God for that.'

'Thank you for caring about me.'

'Any time. So, go and collect Sacha from the *toilettes* and let's get out of here.'

'You go.'

'I think, after worrying me like you did, that you owe me. You go.'

'Okay, I'll go.' Ella rose to her feet. 'We'll take her back to Le Sport? Yes? Put her to bed and start again.'

'She'll have to go to bed. There is no way she'd stand the pace of our evening out.'

'Are we going to party?'

'Absolutely. Our partying will be legendary. People will talk about us for years. Do you know I lasted until ten thirty last week?'

'Ten thirty p.m.!' Ella shrieked. 'Are you crazy?'

'I knew I could do it if I just kept focused.'

'Wow. You have such staying power.'

'I wondered if, tonight, we might try eleven?'

'No way!'

'I think we could do it. I really do.'

'No way. You're on your own, girl. I did ten p.m. once last week and I still haven't got over it.'

'Yeah, you're right.' Poppy finished the last of the chips and ran her finger around the salty bowl. 'It was a crazy thought.' Then she looked at her watch. 'Okay, you go and find Sacha or we'll run out of time and then we may as well go back to Le Sport and you can get on with your knitting . . .' She stopped. 'Actually, you don't need to go and get her, because here she is.'

Sacha, looking pale and a little more sober, made her way carefully between the tables and sat quietly down. 'I need to go back to the hotel.'

'I know,' said Poppy gently, happy now. 'We'll take you there.'

'I'm sorry if I've spoiled your evening.'

'You haven't,' Ella reassured her. Sacha seemed so subdued.

'I feel absolutely terrible.'

Ella rubbed her arm. 'It's okay.'

'I mean I'm terrified I didn't lock my trailer.'

'You must have done. Don't worry about it. It's the wine, making you paranoid.'

'But what if I didn't lock it?' Sacha stared at Ella with teary, troubled eyes.

'Forget about it,' said Poppy dismissively. 'Security will keep an eye on it.'

Sacha bit her lip. 'I could get fired.'

'We can walk over and check if you want to,' said Ella.

'Would you?' Sacha looked at her gratefully. 'Would you really come with me? I don't want to go on my own.'

'No way,' said Poppy. 'I'm not walking all the way back through those woods in the dark.'

'I will,' Ella told her. 'I don't mind. Sacha won't be able to sleep otherwise.'

'Oh, I think she'll sleep just fine.'

Ella stood up and helped Sacha to her feet.

'Then I'll come straight back here.'

'I feel so bad,' Sacha moaned.

'Good,' said Poppy. 'You should.'

'It's okay,' Ella insisted to both of them. 'Ten minutes to the trailer and back. Ten more to Le Sport, tuck Sacha up in bed. Ten minutes and I'll be back here. What time will that be?'

'If you do it exactly as you say, I calculate . . .' Poppy thought about it carefully. 'If you don't decide to stay in Le Sport – and you had better not because I'll be waiting here for you – then you will be back here at exactly ten past eleven.'

'I have to do it because it would be a new record,' said Ella. 'And by a whole ten minutes.'

Seven

EXT: *A MILE FROM THE FRONT LINE, NEAR ARRAS (SHIMMERING HOT): 1916.*

To the east, fields of wheat, trampled, with trenches cut through. Away to the west a vast expanse of blasted battlefields.

Out of the heat haze materializes a group of figures, waist-high in the corn. We soon see that it is a group of young Frenchwomen dressed in brightly coloured peasant clothes. Each one carries a basket.

We hear their voices, laughter.

Close-up of Pascale, one of the girls. We see that her basket is full of oranges. She turns to Beatrice, giggles nervously.

PASCALE: I told you they wouldn't shoot us.

BEATRICE: They will when they hear the price.

PASCALE: I won't make them pay. I will give them my oranges.

BEATRICE: No. You will sell them.

PASCALE: *They are heroes.*

BEATRICE: *Who steal our eggs from the henhouse and our*
cherries from the orchard.

PASCALE: *Why did you come with me if you are so angry?*

BEATRICE: *Because I know what you would do if I was not*
here.

PASCALE: *Yes. I would have fun.*

INT: REMAINS OF A BRICK-BUILT COTTAGE.
SOLDIERS SITTING ON UPTURNED PETROL TINS IN
FULL BATTLEDRESS.
   It is much darker inside. The room is moderately crowded.
   We see AMBROSE MARCH sitting among the men, but
separate from them. He is looking straight ahead at the doorway,
which is covered by an oilskin cloth.
   Through the cloth pokes the head of a young soldier. He is very
appealing. This is WILLIAM DENMAN. His smile falls away at
the sight of Ambrose.

WILLIAM: *We've got company, lads.*

   AMBROSE jumps first to his feet and lifts his Aeroscope and
his tripod from the corner of the room. Without a word he strides
out of the cottage.
   Several of the soldiers follow him out.

EXT: BRIGHT SUNLIGHT. CORNFIELD.
The girls are waiting for the soldiers.
Behind them AMBROSE is impatiently fiddling with buttons and knobs on the Aeroscope.

Ella stopped reading and returned to the head of the page. On the table in front of her she had the original script, which she was reading from, and beside it another annotated script that had been marked up and rearranged in the order of filming. She checked from one to the other. Scene 62, the scene where Pascale and Beatrice first appear in the cornfield, had been shot two days before on the third set. Scene 63, the scene with Ambrose in the cottage with the soldiers, had been shot on the first set and had been completed three weeks earlier.

She skipped forward a few pages and began reading the scene scheduled for the next two days of shooting.

INT: HAY BARN.
There are coils of rope on the floor beside some cotton sacks of flour. A wooden ladder climbs to an open trap door. PASCALE is halfway up the ladder. At the base is AMBROSE.

PASCALE: *Let me show you what I mean.*

Ambrose follows her up the ladder to the loft above. He carries the Aeroscope on his back.

INT: HAY BARN LOFT.
Wooden floor. Piles of loose hay. Pale soft light, sunbeams streaming through dusty glass window.

AMBROSE: *What are you doing?*

PASCALE is sitting on a bale of hay unbuttoning her blouse.

PASCALE: *Film me.*

PASCALE continues to undress. AMBROSE is still, watching her.

PASCALE: *Film me.*

He walks unsteadily towards her and she falls against him, unbuckling his Sam Browne belt, ripping at his clothes. Briefly AMBROSE kisses her back, then, horrified, jerks away from her grasp.

The scene was scheduled to take two days to shoot and would ultimately provide no more than fifteen seconds of finished film, but it would form a pivotal moment in the plot. This was the first time that Ambrose had shown the potential to lose control. Until this point nothing had seemed to affect him. He'd kissed his wife goodbye in Doncaster but had revealed no sadness in leaving her. Throughout his time at the Front, he'd displayed a calmness that at times had bordered on coldness, never hesitating, never showing any signs of doubt or fear. He had run headlong into the chaos of smoke, the rattle of gunfire, and had stood tall as men had dropped, dying, beside him. He'd filmed close-ups of limbless bodies, of faces contorted with pain, and had not flinched. Even when those faces had called out his name, he had not stopped filming. Until this unexpected moment in the hay barn he'd been so single-minded in his purpose that he'd hardly seemed alive, which was why it was all the more startling and satisfying when, for just those few seconds, he'd responded to Pascale's touch and had kissed her back.

But Pascale is nothing to Ambrose and he does not seek her out again. In the scenes that follow there is no apparent sign that the kiss has affected him in any way. But it has. It has made him responsive again, forced open a tiny part of his mind to the memory of women. So when, the following week, he travels to the outskirts of Arras, and to Field Hospital 29, and for the first time he meets Nurse Helen Dove, perhaps he has been made vulnerable to the possibility of falling in love?

Ella dropped the script back on the table and sat back in her chair. She didn't think so. Something about this did not ring true at all. It wasn't that Ambrose and Pascale shouldn't kiss in the barn – if anything that scene came as welcome light relief – but she didn't buy the change it brought over Ambrose, and, in her opinion, it lessened the impact of Helen Dove when Ambrose met her for the first time the following week. Far more effective to have Ambrose steely, heartless, ruthless, then struck by Helen Dove like a thunderbolt. Far better not to warn the audience that he had a heart. She was sure she was right. She felt so strongly about it that she wondered about talking to Hayden. She certainly wouldn't approach one of the prickly, protective script editors, but Hayden might listen, particularly as it was the scene concerning Rory and Carey. They'd shoot anyway, it would be in post-production that the scene would be cut.

A new set had been built for the scene in the hay barn. Ella had visited it the day before, as the set designers were adding the final touches to the exterior, and had loved it enough to want to move in. It was, of course, historically accurate, beautifully built from reclaimed wood, with perfect dovetailed joints and original mangers for the cattle or horses that might have sheltered there through the winter, and there was something so peaceful and wholesome and sturdy about the barn that it seemed appalling that it would be used for just a few scenes before being broken up, when it was so beautifully made that it could have lasted a generation – indeed, it had been built to look as if it had already lasted at least that long.

Lighting had managed to persuade Hayden only to film the scene in the early mornings and early evenings, to take full advantage of the quality of light that would stream through the old glass window-panes and into the loft. In fact they had originally requested that Hayden film only between 5 a.m. and 8 a.m., but the tight schedule had made that impossible. Hayden had conceded to a point, scheduling Liberty Boyd on the second set in the morning so that he could then move across to the barn for rehearsals in the early afternoon before filming Carey and Rory for real towards the end of the day. Simple to look at, it was a complicated scene to stage, with special-effects technicians on hand to spray clouds of treated 'dust' seconds before the cameras rolled, dust that would hang in the air and sparkle as the sunlight streamed through the window.

A few days later the same special-effects team would move to Field Hospital 29, another set built from scratch.

Following the trajectory of the film, summer would quickly slip towards autumn, and special effects would switch from providing shimmering heat to autumnal mists and early morning fogs. Inside the set of Hospital 29, they would create steaming uniforms and clouds of frosty breath rising above the long lines of hospital beds, while carefully placed air-conditioning units blasted out freezing air, trying to help the actors remember how it felt to be cold when in reality it was still blisteringly hot.

Over the past two days it had been so hot that, even with the air-conditioning running almost twenty-four-seven, tubes of make-up were turning to liquid in the make-up trailer, moustaches were sliding across grease-painted faces as soldiers ran into battle, dark patches were appearing on Liberty Boyd's heavy cotton uniforms and Rory frequently had to stop to wipe away the rivulets of sweat from the eyepiece of his Aeroscope. Hayden tried half-heartedly to hide his pleasure at their discomfort, knowing that Liberty especially was not enjoying the temperature, but there was no doubt that the sweat and the heat was only adding authenticity to his film.

Despite Rory's request, the hay barn scene was not to be filmed on a closed set. Word had it that, among the large crew, Anton also planned to be there, behind the cameras, no doubt watching with gritted teeth as his girlfriend pounced on Rory. But, two days after Hayden had come to Ella's trailer and told her about Rory and Carey, Ella had heard nothing more, nothing from Hayden, and no whisper of Rory and Carey's relationship on set, leaving her to hope either that Hayden had exaggerated the relationship in the first place, or that he had succeeded in persuading Rory to leave Carey alone. Much as she'd have liked to know for sure, Hayden had not sought her out to tell her, and she had not asked. And if it wasn't for one small niggle of doubt, she'd probably have been able to let the whole episode slip from her mind.

But instead she couldn't help remembering what had happened as she'd returned to L'Oignon to find Poppy.

Having found Sacha's trailer safely locked, she and Sacha had turned back towards the town. They had made their way slowly through Florent. Ella had manhandled Sacha up the stairs of Le Sport, had helped her undress, fetched her water and put her to bed, and then she had made her way back to L'Oignon. And it was then, as she'd climbed the street towards Poppy, that she had seen Carey walking into La Sauterelle, with Rory a couple of steps ahead. In itself there'd been nothing compromising about the sight of them together. It wasn't late. It was Rory's hotel. No doubt Carey was on her way in to see Anton. But something in the way they walked through the door told Ella that they had been out together and that they had no intention of separating now. Something about the way that Carey moved towards him as Rory held the door open for her made Ella think she was about to kiss him.

They hadn't seen her, and she'd quickly turned her back on them and walked away a few paces before stopping in a shop doorway to call Hayden, as she had promised him she would. Hayden had been just a few streets behind her, making his way back to La Sauterelle, and from the short, rather dismissive way that he'd spoken to her, without mentioning her name, it had been clear that he hadn't been alone. When she'd finished the call she had put away her phone feeling very uncomfortable, wishing that he hadn't confided in her.

Eight

Liberty Boyd leaned forward and touched her reflection in the mirror in front of her.

'Christ, I look appalling.'

As Rosalind hadn't yet begun work on her, it couldn't be deemed an insult. Rather it was clearly an invitation to the trailer at large, to protest that, of course, she didn't.

Behind her, Liberty's personal assistant shifted uneasily in her chair, waiting for someone, anyone, to respond.

Rory reached across and patted Liberty's hand. 'Rosalind will see you right.'

'What do you mean? Bastard,' she flicked at his shoulder beside her, jolting Ella's arm as she did so but not noticing. 'You're not meant to say that.'

'Sorry, what am I meant to say again?'

'That I look beautiful?'

She pouted at him, waiting.

She was, undeniably, beautiful. She was also undeniably flirting with Rory and undeniably poisonous, thought Ella, stepping around her and wiping off the smear of plains dust from under Rory's eye, in order to start all over again.

'Mmm,' Rory considered her carefully. 'Almost Angelina Jolie.'

Liberty didn't know what to make of that. She gave a humph, and tossed back her dark glossy hair.

She was twenty-two, smaller and more delicate than Ella had expected. When she had first entered the trailer she had slipped off her pumps, lifted her bare feet beneath her and curled into her chair like a little cat, before carefully clocking the room with wide, pale green eyes. She'd looked the make-up girls, Jemima and Minnie, up and down, had smiled at Jemima (size sixteen) and ignored Minnie (size eight), then nodded dismissively at Carey who was sitting two chairs away. When Rosalind had introduced Liberty to Ella she had languidly taken Ella's hand and shaken it briefly, and had hardly seemed to see her at all.

Then, with a bang and a crash of the trailer door, Rory had arrived and all in an instant Liberty had come alive, trying to jump out of her chair to greet him, before finding herself pulled back by her hair, which was still attached to her stylist's comb.

Rory had bent his head to kiss her smooth cheek.

'Ow!' he commented, smiling at her sympathetically.

'Ow indeed.' She'd spun around to her stylist. 'Stupid bastard.'

'No, Liberty,' said Rory quietly, moving to his chair, to where Ella was waiting. 'We don't speak like that in here.' Then he leaned across to Ella and unexpectedly kissed her cheek too. 'Good morning.'

At that Liberty gave Ella a frosty stare. Behind her, her personal assistant opened a notebook and wrote something down.

'What was that?' Rory asked, sitting down in front of Ella.

'Nothing.' The assistant coloured, snapping shut her book. 'A memo, that's all.'

'She's probably making notes about you,' Liberty answered for her. 'For Janine, my PR.'

'You're kidding!' Rory snorted. 'What kind of notes?'

'Nothing compromising.' Liberty had a precise, upper-class English-girl way of speaking. 'Nothing you wouldn't like. I keep notes on everyone I work with.' She paused. 'Tell me your name again.'

Bent over her trays of make-up, Ella didn't realize that Liberty was now addressing her.

'She's called Ella,' said Rory.

'Ella what?'

'Ella Buchan,' said Ella, standing up to look at her.

'B-U-C-H-A-N,' Rory spelled it out. 'Now, what would you like to know about Ella?'

'Nothing more, thanks,' said Liberty, then gave him a flashing smile. 'I'm only interested in the actors.' Then she looked down the length of the trailer, at the other artists all busily working. 'Excuse me. Is anybody free to give me a hand massage?'

Laughing, Rory slipped his hand over hers. 'No. They're not.'

'But where's that girl of Rosalind's gone? She could do it.'

'Stop it,' he insisted.

She looked at him wide-eyed. 'Honey, my hands are very dry.'

'Then ask Rosalind if she has any hand cream.'

Dutifully, Liberty's PA got to her feet.

'It's okay,' Rory told her. 'I'll ask Rosalind.'

'Tell Rosalind only Crème de la Mer.'

He got up again and moved two chairs down the trailer to where Carey Sloan was sitting, head back and very still as her make-up artist carefully applied individual lashes to her eyes. Carey was scheduled to leave first for the set and was already dressed, a protective gown covering her ankle-length burnt orange dress and white cotton blouse, and a gauzy veil tied over her dark red, ringleted hair. While Ella watched, Rory bent his head to Carey's ear and whispered something that made her smile.

Rosalind, meanwhile, had made her way from the back of the trailer to meet him. Without a word she glanced down at the table in front of Carey and picked up a pot of hand cream, which she handed over to Rory with pursed lips.

'Is that the right one?'

'Do I care?'

Rosalind and Rory then made their way back to the front of the trailer and Rory handed the pot to Liberty's PA, who hurriedly unscrewed it and silently began to massage cream into Liberty's pale white hands.

'Heidi is working in the marquee today,' Rosalind told Liberty with a polite smile. She turned to the hair stylist, who had finished dividing Liberty's hair into neat and identical sections and was now deftly rolling it up on to fat curlers.

'How long, Ben?'

'Five minutes?'

'Perfect.' Rosalind looked around at them all. 'Anybody like a coffee? Ella?'

Ella nodded towards the can of Coke open on the table in

front of Rory, her hands full of crêpe wool and spirit gum, her mouth full of pins. Still early morning and already she felt as if she'd been there all day.

Rosalind shook her head in wonder. 'Ella, it's ten past six in the morning!'

Ella took the pins out of her mouth. 'And if my hands start shaking, I'll jog around the base a few times to burn it off.'

Liberty looked at her incredulously and now she finally addressed Ella directly for the first time.

'But it's not even diet!'

'Apparently it's much better for you than diet,' Ella told her cheerfully, reaching forwards and taking a swig before bending to examine Rory's cheek. 'Pure sugar rather than chemicals.'

'Gross,' said Liberty. 'Think what it's doing to your internal digestive system.'

'As opposed to your external one,' Rory said, quietly enough for only Ella to hear, loud enough for Liberty to know he'd said something.

Ella smiled but didn't answer. With Rory in front of her and less than an hour left to get him ready for set, she was already focused, mentally dividing her time between the various tasks ahead of her, and, because she was still smarting slightly from day one and the incident with the razor, determined not to make another mistake. Before Rory had arrived she had prepared the table in front of her, and among all the usual tubes and pots of make-up and powders was everything else that she would need for him that morning, including a bottle of spirit gum and a packet of prosthetic wax, and one pot of purple rain powder and another of chimney smoke, which she would add to her other colours to make the bruise on his cheekbone, almost the same colours, but now a darker blue than the bruise she'd made for him the day before.

This was their third day of working together. After the dramas of day one and then the revelations from Hayden, she'd been full of misgivings about day two, but, as she had reported at the end of it to Poppy – and to Rosalind, who had had her own misgivings about Rory – Rory had been the model subject to work on, at times almost subdued. A couple of times they'd been left alone together in the trailer and he had made little attempt at conversation, and when Ella had talked to him, it had felt as if she was jolting him out of some heavy preoccupation that he returned to as soon as he politely could. There'd been no mention of Carey Sloan or any other girls, no annoying telephone calls coming in on his mobile at exactly the wrong moment; he had sipped only bottled water and had made no starry demands. But now, as she and Rosalind settled down to work on their respective faces, Ella realized that the gleam in Rory's eye had returned. Was it having Liberty beside him, to talk to and laugh at? Or was it the presence of Carey, two chairs away, that had brought back his good humour?

When she had finished preparing his face she painted a circle of spirit gum on his cheekbone then warmed the little piece of wax in her hand before moulding it into place with her fingers. It would create a swelling on his cheekbone and would slightly close his eye. Automatically she glanced up at the trailer clock to check that she was still on time.

Standing beside her, Ben had meanwhile finished taking out the rollers from Liberty's hair. Silently – Ella didn't think she'd heard him speak to Liberty once – he brushed her hair out again, then parted it in the middle and, with deft fingers, twisted it up and rolled it into a fat shiny bun, which he secured with several pins.

Rosalind, watching behind him, nodded supportively. 'That's absolutely perfect, Ben.'

Pleased, he rubbed at his unshaven cheek. 'I won't put on her cap until she's been to wardrobe and then we'll loosen her hair a little.'

'Please may I see?' said Liberty.

Rosalind passed her a hand mirror and Liberty held it up so that she could see the bun.

'It's darling, Ben. Thank you so much.' She laid the mirror down in front of her and folded her hands demurely.

Ben gave a little nod. 'No problem,' he said, and then got away from her as fast as he could, squeezing past Rosalind and down the trailer to join Minnie and Jemima and make a last check on Carey's hair before she left for the set.

'See,' said Liberty playfully, turning to Rory. 'I can be nice.'

'Shhh, I'm busy,' said Rory dreamily, head back, eyes closed, as Ella bent over him and delicately painted his cheek with the finest eyeliner brush she had.

'You're boring. You know that?'

When Rory didn't answer Liberty turned away with a little laugh and looked critically around the trailer, her fingers drumming against her thigh.

'Are you okay?' Ella asked her.

'Shhh,' said Rory.

Liberty turned to Ella and stared at her with her extraordinary eyes. 'I guess I'm kind of missing my home comforts.'

'Is there something that you need?'

'Vivaldi?'

'Fuck off,' said Rory, shaking with laughter under Ella's hands.

Carey edged her way past them on her way out to set.

'See you later.' Rory caught her hand as she passed.

'Go for it, girl,' said Liberty, giving her a critical up and down.

'She's pretty,' she told Rory, Carey undoubtedly still in earshot. 'But boy, she is way too tall for that part.'

He didn't reply.

'Rory?' She was back, buzzing around him again, and this time there was an insistence to her voice that made Ella stop what she was doing and sit back in her chair.

'What?' Rory opened a lazy eye.

Ella stretched deeply, then rubbed her back.

'Has your PR said anything about a piece for *Hollywood Whisper*?'

Ella stiffened.

'Forget it,' said Rory.

'Oh, darling, come on! They want us for the front cover.'

How could she think he'd be pleased? Even forgetting the fact that Rory had vowed never to speak to *Hollywood Whisper*, a day hardly passed without his face on a front cover somewhere. When he didn't answer, she ploughed straight on. 'You're going to have to forgive them some time.'

'No, I'm not.'

'Yes, you are, and you know you are.'

'You do some pictures with them if you want to . . .' He settled back in his chair. 'Ella. Come back.'

Ella returned to his face, and beneath her Rory's eyes dropped again to the sensation of her fingertips and brushes against his skin, but she could tell from the grim set of his jaw and from his hand, fiercely gripping the side of his chair, that he was far from relaxed.

Liberty hadn't given up. 'Didn't you break that guy's nose *and* his camera?'

'Neither. I knocked his teeth out.'

Dressed in a long white linen tunic, and giving every impression of serenity, ignoring the conversation running on either side of her, Rosalind bent over her trays and continued to select and lay out everything that she would need for Liberty that morning, choosing things for the bag she would take with her. She would prep Liberty in the trailer, and then go with her to the set, where she would continue to maintain her face and oversee the hair and make-up of the rest of the cast at the same time.

Liberty's character, Helen Dove, was a nurse who had first come out to France as a hospital letter-writer, there to take dictation from the soldiers who could not write letters themselves. But she had stayed for only a short time, quickly seeing enough to decide she would be far more valuable to the war effort if she had some sort of medical training, and she had returned to England to train with the VAD, the Voluntary Aid Detachment, which had instructed so many girls in basic nursing and hospital care before sending them out to hospitals to work alongside professional nurses. Many of the VAD girls had remained in England throughout the war, but, having trained in a London hospital, Helen Dove had left for France on the same ship and at the same time as Ambrose March. Upon arrival she had been sent to Field Hospital 29, and it was there, two months after her arrival, that she had first met Ambrose.

Ella stole a glance at Liberty, who was waiting, wide-eyed, clearly hoping that Rory would say something more. Not yet in costume, but with her hair pulled back and her face ostensibly bare of make-up, she looked fresh-faced and innocent.

'Wasn't that enough?' she asked him. 'Come on. Speak to me.'

'I don't want to talk about *Hollywood Whisper*.'

'You have to.' She was playing to the trailer at large, smiling at him, coaxing him, still acting as if all they were indulging in was playful banter. 'You owe it to me. If I have to turn them down, it's the least you can do.'

Ella stopped her delicate brushstrokes because she had the distinct sense Rory was about to swat her irritably away. He sat up again in his chair.

'I thought we were going to do joint PR,' Liberty wheedled. 'And I don't want to do *Hollywood Whisper* on my own. I want to do it with you.'

Of course you do, thought Ella. Liberty was 'A' List with him, 'B' list without. But why did she have to bang on about *Hollywood Whisper*? How come she didn't know never even to mention the name? Or perhaps she did know. Perhaps that was the problem, that she did know and didn't care.

'I Will Not Work With Them.' Rory turned to Liberty's

nervous PR girl. 'Got that? I want you to put a line through them in your pad.' Then his face broke into a smile. 'Now, come on. Tell me what you wrote about me.'

The girl blushed but didn't answer.

'"*In the flesh Rory Defoe has that magnetic quality that makes it hard not to touch him.*" Do you ever find that?' He stretched out his hand to her. 'Hello. I'm sorry. We were never introduced.'

'Kate,' said the PR, shaking his hand. She cast a worried look towards Liberty's back but there was a guilty smile on her face that she couldn't quite suppress.

'You don't need to know her,' Liberty snapped without turning around. 'I was going to say that the *Hollywood Whisper* photographs were stunning.'

'I never saw them,' said Rory.

'Let's just say they did you no harm.'

'No. Let's not say that.'

Please someone stuff Liberty's mouth with a roll of cotton wool, thought Ella. She looked around for Rosalind, but it was as if Liberty's words had cast some spell over her and had her rooted to the spot.

Liberty was so persistent. It was as if, in her mind, Rory was being deliberately difficult, a bit starry, a bit precious. It was as if the *Hollywood Whisper* pictures had been no more invasive than snaps of Rory, perhaps leaving a restaurant, or climbing out of a cab.

'They were monochrome, very brooding and atmospheric,' Liberty went on. 'You looked like Heathcliff, there among the gravestones.' She reached across and covered Rory's hand with hers and, amazingly, he didn't pull away.

'What I mean is, I'd never seen you look so beautiful. Perhaps I shouldn't admit this, but when I saw those shots I just knew I had to be in this film with you.'

Ella stepped back as Rory swung his chair to face Liberty. 'Where's your boundary?'

Liberty smiled at him uncertainly. He'd come so close. 'What do you mean?'

He didn't back off. 'What I mean is where's your limit? Where do you say *stop*? You seem to be implying that as long as you're looking good, it doesn't matter where you are or what you're doing? Is that right?'

'It's our job, Rory.' She rolled her chair backwards, away from him, and for the first time she looked a little uncertain. 'I don't know. I suppose I've never thought about it like that.' Then she rallied again. 'Okay. Of course I wouldn't have wanted to be in your shoes that day, but hey, sad day, great pictures. I was envious of them. I'll admit it. Is that so bad?'

'Sad day? You're suggesting it was simply a *sad day*?' He didn't shout at her, but his voice was so full of passion and anger the trailer seemed to shake. '*I* have boundaries, Liberty, and one of them, definitely the most important one I'll ever know, was drawn around that churchyard in Narrow, in Yorkshire, on the day I buried my mother. But still, *Hollywood Whisper* walked straight in.'

'No, they didn't.'

'Jesus, you know what I mean.'

'They stayed back.'

'Why are you defending them?'

'Because I think you're over-reacting.'

At that, suddenly, spectacularly, Rory lost his temper.

'Then you are a crazy bitch.'

Angrily he shoved his chair backwards, crushing Ella's foot beneath it, and before she could react he'd leapt to his feet and stormed out of the door.

A few seconds later, Ella had recovered enough to hobble and dive after him. As she got to the front of the trailer he had opened the door, jumped down the three steps and was striding away, half made-up, ripping off his gown as he walked, in the direction of the wood and Florent.

She seemed always to be running after him. She caught him up and he stopped, eyes wide, breathing hard.

'I'm sorry for what she said.'

'I can't sit next to her any more. All she sees is an opportunity. She's a poisonous, shallow publicity machine.'

'So try not to care what she says. Don't let her get to you, not Liberty.'

'She was talking about my mother.'

'I know, I know. I'm sorry.' She went to touch his arm but he flinched away. 'Look, would you like me to make you up in your trailer? It wouldn't be a problem. I could just run back and get my things?'

He shook his head. 'I'm taking a break.'

Ella's heart sank. 'Please, Rory. You know we haven't got time for that.'

'For just a moment could you try not to think about the fucking film schedule?'

She looked down at the ground. 'I'm sorry. Of course. How long do you need?'

'I don't know. I'm going to go and find Carey.'

'No!' she said in horror. 'She's on set! Please don't do that.'

'Ella. Let go of my arm.'

She hadn't realized she'd taken it. She had to let him go. And, with dread for what was going to happen next, she watched him set off again, towards where Carey was filming. Hesitantly, heart in her mouth, she started to follow after him.

Whether he cared she was following or not, Rory didn't turn back. Now that he'd decided where he was going, he turned rapidly along the path away from the base and through the trees down towards the orchard that led to the hay barn, to where Carey, as Pascale, was filming an outdoor sequence with another actress called Sophie Simms who was playing Beatrice.

Ella hung back as Rory approached the set, then stood silently in the shade of the trees and watched as he zig-zagged through and around sound recordists, runners, boom operators, costume assistants, grips, sparks and all the other crew and came to a halt right on the edge of the set. And then, even though the cameras were rolling, he walked, straight out, into the arc of bright white light.

'Cut!' came Hayden's angry shout. 'What the hell are you doing? What's wrong?'

Rory stopped at Carey, and took in the stunned, wide-eyed crowd. He nodded to them briefly, took Carey's arm, and without a word of explanation or apology started to walk her away.

But blocking his exit was Hayden. With legs like jelly, Ella walked close to the edge of the set, where she stopped beside Sam.

'I've come to see Carey,' Rory told Hayden.

'That's it?'

'That's right.'

'Could you, please, wait?'

'But I would like to talk to her.'

Rory went to move on but Hayden stepped to block his way.

'She's busy. You don't just walk in here and fuck up my scene.'

'I'm sorry about your scene.'

'No, you are not.' Hayden leaned angrily in to him. 'You don't care about my scene or my film.'

Ella turned and searched the crowd of people who had been watching the filming, dreading that she would find Anton Klubcic there among them.

Rory looked decidedly unbothered at Hayden's anger. 'Shoot the scene again. Can't have been that much of a fluke.'

'Why should I have to? What's the matter with you?'

Hayden raised his hands and for a moment looked as if he was about to punch him, then let them fall again, hopelessly, to his sides.

Full of sympathy, Ella ran towards him. 'Five minutes, Hayden. That's all he needs. Isn't it, Rory?' She gave Rory a desperate stare. 'Yes? And then you're coming back with me.'

Rory shrugged. 'I might need five minutes. I might need ten. You'll know when I'm ready.'

'It's better if you let him go,' Ella told Hayden.

Hayden couldn't look at Rory. 'Stop him taking her back to his trailer.'

'Is that what you want to do?' Ella asked Rory.

'Of course not. Don't be ridiculous.'

'You think *she's* being ridiculous?' Hayden spluttered.

Rory laughed into his face. 'See you soon.'

Then he took Carey's arm and led her away.

Ella turned back to Hayden, who was staring after the two of them with despair all over his face.

'What do I do?' he asked her.

'Don't start crying,' she offered. And don't ask me, she wanted to add. You're the director. You carry this film. Don't keep asking *me* what to do.

'Ten minutes,' called the First AD, and with a sigh Hayden slowly unclenched his fingers.

'Couldn't you have stopped him?'

'Better to let him go.'

'Carey.' He shuddered. 'Why does it have to be Carey?' He gave a furtive look around the set. 'If nobody knew about them before they're certainly going to now.'

'Yes,' Ella agreed, 'especially if you give them a whopping clue like that.' She dropped her voice. 'Act like nothing's going on and they'll believe it! You have to. Let them think it's just Rory, behaving like a spoiled movie star, doing what he wants, just like he always has. They're used to it. Sloping off with Carey doesn't mean he's having an affair with her.' As she spoke she looked away from the set and happened to see the pair of them sit down, beneath a white canvas awning, one of many put up around the set to provide shelter from the sun. They were sitting, very circumspectly, side by side, in two white cotton director's chairs, not touching, Rory speaking, Carey listening.

'I thought I'd made him understand,' said Hayden. 'I pitched it like you said and I thought I was rather convincing. I reminded him about Ambrose and how much he matters to us all and I thought it had worked.'

'It might have done. He was upset. Liberty has been driving him mad.'

He looked at her. 'I'm sorry if you think I'm going to pieces. Truly I'm not. It's just a relief to be able to tell someone what's going on.'

'I'm not sure I like it. I think I'd prefer to be kept in the dark.'

'Tough. I need you now. You're going to tell me what to do.'

'But I don't want to. You're meant to tell us what to do.'

He laughed quietly. 'What I mean is you're off the radar. You're not some studio head. I don't have to pretend with you. I don't have to continuously reassure you that everything is perfect and that you did the right thing, giving me all your millions of dollars to make this film. I can tell you how screwed up Rory makes me feel, and I know it's not going to make the film collapse around my ears.'

'Did he ruin much just then?'

'Yes. We'd just about bagged the scene. But what will I do about it? Nothing. That's what I mean. I am completely in his hands. Jesus! I try to do angry. I try to do don't mess with me. I try to look as if I'm directing him, not the other way around, but surely everyone can see it's not true, that he's the one in control.' He chuckled miserably. 'Yes, look at your face. They know.'

'Of course they don't. The thought never crossed my

mind until you said it. And you mustn't let on, not to me or anybody else, because it's not true.'

'I'm not so sure.' He kicked the ground with his shoe.

'Hayden, you want me to tell you what I think you should do?'

He looked back at her.

'Get back to your crew.'

'Yes, I know. Act like nothing's wrong.'

'Absolutely.' She stopped him. 'Because nothing is wrong . . . Is it? I looked around for Anton, but he's not here, is he? Tell me I didn't miss him.'

'He's not here. Thank heaven for small mercies. He's more interested in the filming we have scheduled for this afternoon in the hay barn. Christ, Rory had better behave himself then.'

'He promised you that he would?'

'Yes. I told you. He didn't explicitly agree to giving Carey up. He was never going to make life that easy for me. But when I left him, he said he would talk to her, and I was sure that he'd understood. I'd got him on side, which is why this is so distressing. What the hell is he doing? Oh God, tell me how to handle this man.'

She glanced across to the two of them. 'All they're doing is talking. They're not even touching each other.'

'Everyone can see what's going on.'

He gave another tension-filled stare around his crew.

'You must not do that!' Ella insisted.

'Sorry?'

'They need you to look as if nothing's wrong. And then it won't be.'

'Okay.' He nodded weakly. 'Okay.'

He left her, walked uncertainly back to his director's chair, sat heavily down and dropped his head in his hands.

Ella let out a long exhale, then turned and saw Sam and immediately he came over.

'What the hell was that about?'

'It's just Rory being Rory, throwing his weight around.'

He gave her a look, as if to say he didn't quite buy it, and she smiled easily back at him. Hayden might not be able to act but she could. Change the subject, she thought, change the subject.

'How was dinner?'

'Ah, well.' He stood up straighter, and looked at her consideringly. 'Not quite as good as it would have been if you'd been there too.'

'Oh.' Wrong-footed, she felt herself blush. 'I'm sorry I couldn't come.'

'That's easily put right.'

She laughed. 'Sam, are you asking me out on a date?'

'Could be.'

'This is very exciting. I haven't been asked out on a date for . . .'

Months, she'd been going to say. Years, would probably have been closer to the truth, but she wasn't about to admit that. Her last relationship, two years with a London barrister who'd loved himself a lot more than he'd ever loved her, had ended a few weeks before she'd left for France. Dates, weekends away, romantic surprises, they hadn't featured much, unless she'd organized them.

'Ages,' she said instead, and then she couldn't help herself glancing away again, towards Carey and Rory, because Carey was now standing up from her chair.

Sam followed her stare and sighed heavily. 'So, it looks as if we're going back to work. I'll have to catch you another time.'

'No, wait,' she said, throwing caution to the wind. 'Catch me now.'

He grinned, and took a step closer towards her. 'I like the sound of that.'

'Tell me when. Quick! Rory's coming and I don't want him to hear.' She was laughing but desperately meaning it at the same time.

He watched Rory walking towards them and frowned. 'But I do want him to hear.'

'Shh! I'm only coming if you stop talking before he gets here.'

'Why? Why does it matter?' He lowered his voice. 'So what if he hears?'

'It sounds ridiculous, doesn't it? Because,' she winced. 'Because it's private. I don't want him to know about the rest of my life.'

'So what if he does? You work with him, that's all. He doesn't remote-control you.'

'No,' she agreed, laughing. 'You're right.'

Left alone on the edge of the set, Rory bent his head under the crane that was lifting the overhead camera and walked up to the two of them, looking at her coolly, taking in her fluster, the laughter still there in her eyes.

'Let's go,' he told her shortly.

Ella turned back to Sam.

'Had you somewhere in mind?'

Sam blinked in surprise. 'Hmm,' he paused, deliberately taking his time. 'Not Le Grand Surprise, the chairs are too hard. Not L'Oignon, much too noisy. . .'

'Ella, I said let's go,' said Rory.

'Have you been to La Mas d'Antigne?' asked Sam.

'No, but I want to, that would be perfect.' She turned back to Rory, who was now staring at her stony-faced.

'Shall I come and pick you up from your trailer?' said Sam. 'Or would you rather meet me there?'

'Come to the trailer.'

Sam was clearly now enjoying himself. He reached to take her hand. 'I've been meaning to ask you for ages.'

That was too much for Ella.

'Come and pick me up at about eight.'

She turned to Rory. 'I'm ready. Let's go.'

'No, hang on a minute.' Rory turned to Sam. 'There's something I've been meaning to ask you, too.'

'Oh?' Sam turned to him in friendly surprise. 'What would that be?'

Ella held her breath, sure it was going to be something sarcastic and horrible.

'It's the Aeroscope. I wondered if you would mind taking a look at it with me.'

'Sure,' said Sam, his interest immediately caught. 'Is there something wrong?'

'No. Not at all. It's me, not the camera. I've been filming with it all day. I know how it works but it's annoying me that I'm not using it better. I need a cameraman, someone like you, to help me, someone who knows what they're doing.'

For Sam the surprise was quickly over-shadowed by his enthusiasm.

'I'd love to take a look. When were you thinking?'

Rory hesitated.

Oh, I wonder when you have in mind, Ella thought, watching him bitterly. Might you, possibly, be thinking about this evening, perhaps about eight o'clock?

'I've got these big scenes with Carey this afternoon and tomorrow. Is there any chance . . . Any chance you might be able to take a look this evening, once filming has finished? I don't want to get in the way of your evening with Ella, but perhaps, could we find half an hour before you go?'

Or an hour, thought Ella, glaring at him. That would no doubt stretch to two hours, or three. Because getting in the way is exactly what you want to do. Because you don't like people having fun if it doesn't involve you.

'It depends when filming finishes,' Sam frowned, thinking about it. 'We've had the delay, we're certainly going to run over this afternoon. If I know Hayden we'll be out until it's dark.' He looked across at Ella, caught her eye again and smiled reassuringly. 'I'm sorry, Rory, but not tonight,' he said, still looking straight at Ella. 'This evening could be difficult.'

He was turning Rory down. Ella couldn't believe it. She had to look down at the ground so Rory wouldn't see her smile.

'Of course,' said Rory easily. 'I understand. No problem. I doubt anyone watching the film is going to know how to film with an Aeroscope any better than I do. I can't be doing it so wrong.'

Sam nodded. 'From what I've seen, you're doing a fine job.'

Oh, Sam! she thought. Kind Sam, to risk a chance of filming with the Aeroscope, all for a date with her. She was damned if she was going to be the reason he had to say no.

'Wait,' she insisted. 'Sam. You must take a look at the camera. Stay with Rory after filming tonight. It's fine by me. If it gets late, I'll go straight to the restaurant and you can meet me there.'

'Would that work?' Sam looked at her, delighted. 'You think there's time?'

'Why not? What's the problem? You think I'd never make it there on my own? Say eight thirty, and call me on my mobile if it's going to be later. Here,' she felt around in her pockets and brought out a pen. 'What can I write on?'

'Try his hand,' suggested Rory. 'Isn't that what people arranging first dates usually do?'

'My hand,' said Sam, offering it to her. 'Good idea.'

She took the weight of it in hers. It was a big hand, a brown hand. She bent over it and wrote down her number.

'There,' she said, looking up at him again.

'I'll look forward to it.'

'Me too.'

'He's probably exactly right for you,' said Rory, as they walked back to the trailer. 'Kind, helpful and just that little bit boring.'

'I like him.'

'So do I. I mean boring in a good way.'

'I don't care what you think of him.' She looked at him frostily. 'And I don't think he's boring at all. I think he's cute and funny. Truly, I really fancy him.'

'Truly? Christ, lucky Sam! I'd better make sure he's not late.'

'Thank you,' she said sweetly. 'I'd appreciate it.'

They walked on.

'Now, Ella, how well do you know Sam?'

'Why?'

'No reason at all.'

'Why?' she insisted. 'What are you trying to say?'

'If I said anything you'd think I was interfering.'

'Too right, because you would be.'

'Just keep an eye on him. That's my advice.'

'I thought you just said he was boring?'

'He is. But I've heard it hasn't stopped him having loads of fun on set.'

'Rory. Shut up.'

'Sorry.' He nodded. 'None of my business.'

And they walked on together, without speaking again, until they arrived back at her trailer.

He hesitated at the bottom of the steps. 'I did apologize to Hayden, by the way.'

'What did he say?'

'That I'd behaved like an unprofessional arse, which was accurate, I suppose. I can't believe I walked on to his set.' He winced and looked up at the trailer door. 'I was just so bloody angry. I thought I'd go down there and watch them for a bit, cool down and come back again. And then I saw Carey, and there was something I wanted to ask her and I didn't think, just walked straight on in.'

'You knew she'd be there. It was hardly a surprise.'

'Okay! So what if I did?'

'So don't pretend you didn't know what you were doing.'

'Ella!'

'What?'

'Stop bullying me.'

She shrugged. 'So tell me what you wanted to ask Carey. What was it that couldn't wait until she'd finished her scene?'

'That's nothing to do with you.'

She hesitated, then went for it. 'Hayden told me what's going on.'

'What would that be?' he asked easily.

'I know about you and her.'

'You do? Then surely you'll understand why I wanted to see her.'

'Oh, God, Rory, stop this, please. Please, please, leave her alone.'

'After tonight I will.'

'Why? What's happening tonight?'

He started to walk up the steps. 'You'll know soon enough. Hayden and I had a little disagreement about the script. It's why I need Sam, to show me how to film, and don't ask me why because I can't tell you or you'll try and stop me.'

'Then that's because you shouldn't do it! Whatever you do, please don't involve Sam.'

'Christ, no! I wouldn't want Sam there. It would be like being watched over by a boy scout. Sam is the last person to get involved. Not Sam's kind of thing at all.'

'Now this sounds really bad.'

'Stop sounding so scared. Trust me. You'll love it. Hayden will love it.'

Louise Harwood

The more he tried to reassure her, the more worried she was.

'Rory, can I trust that you are not about to do something that will upset our psychopathic Russian gangster, Anton Klubcic?'

'Absolutely not.'

She looked up at him. 'Please, Rory.'

'But you can trust that he'll never find out it was me.'

'That's a terrible answer. Be serious.'

He took her hands and looked down into her eyes. 'I wish I could.' He sounded full of regret. 'And I promise I won't have anything more to do with Carey after tonight. And know this, too, that I have always had this film's best interests at heart and that you can, absolutely, trust me when I say that.'

'Actions speak louder than words.'

He put his finger to his lips. 'Now you're sounding like a nanny again. Do you remember what we said about how you mustn't sound like a nanny?'

'You only need a make-up artist who's good at her job.'

'Exactly. Leave me alone, and trust me.'

She would, about as far as she could throw him.

Because he was up to something. He was impatient, excited, full of anticipation, and just looking at him made her full of foreboding. And, as there was no chance that he was going to tell her what it was, and as she had to find out, she wondered if the only way to do it was through Sam.

160

Nine

Later in the afternoon, rehearsals in the loft of the hay barn began and the whispered consensus quickly grew among the crew that Hayden hadn't exaggerated when he'd said Carey couldn't act.

Not that she could have told them so, but Ella had to disagree. In her opinion, Carey was acting out of her skin. It was just that she was doing it all off camera. Between takes, she was brilliant. Nothing in the way she acted around Rory suggested anything other than an easy affection between them, and there was none of the studied indifference that so often signals a secret relationship. She imagined that they must have planned how to behave during the filming of their love scene, particularly as Anton Klubcic was expected to arrive at some stage to watch, and it was clear to Ella that what they'd decided was to take full advantage of it, because no one could ever argue that they were doing anything other than acting out their parts.

The set was so tiny that with all the cameras and crew it was terribly cramped. Ella forced herself into a little space behind the cameras and worked with her back flat against the wall, with so little room she could barely move her arms to re-powder Rory's nose.

Late in the afternoon, Carey and Rory finally moved on to rehearsing the kiss. Out of earshot of the rest of the crew, Hayden first talked through what he wanted them to do, then returned to his position behind the cameras to watch their first attempt.

He was nervous, Ella realized, understandably so, his eye often returning to the doorway to the set, to where Anton Klubcic would surely soon make his entrance. And Ella was nervous on Hayden's behalf, unable to believe that Rory wouldn't take advantage of having his girl in his arms and take their kiss just that one step too far.

'Carey,' called Hayden, almost whispering. 'Remember, keep it subtle.' He clenched his fist against his heart. 'Feel it here, and we will too. Trust yourself.' He nodded. 'Okay.'

'Action!' called the First AD.

With trembling, fumbling fingers Pascale undid her buttons.

'Film me,' she told Ambrose, her voice coming out in a throaty whisper.

'Cut,' called Hayden immediately, letting out a sigh. 'Carey, that was much too frantic, much too nervous. Slow down. Be confident. Remember, Pascale knows exactly what she's doing.'

They rehearsed the scene again, over and over, for an hour, delivering their lines, but never quite making it to the moment where Pascale ran into Ambrose's arms. And then, just as Hayden was finally pronouncing himself happy, and the filming was scheduled to begin for real, and the golden hour began, when the yellow evening sun cast its soft light through the window of the barn, there came a sudden shuffling among the crew, a flurry of excitement. Ella saw Hayden glance again to the doorway, and turn a shade paler under his tan, and, without immediately turning to look, she knew that Anton Klubcic must have arrived. She'd never met him, never even seen him before, and curiosity meant that she couldn't help but turn, with the rest of the crew, towards him.

For a few minutes he stayed back, behind the cameras, a short, heavy-set middle-aged man, with pale smooth skin and thick white hair tied back in a stubby pony-tail. He was wearing shiny black trousers, a white shirt and a pair of white trainers. To Ella, he looked scary and, strangely, rather cool. Ignoring everyone around him – he happened to be standing next to Sacha, who was wearing a hot-pink tutu, but he didn't even flinch – he waved to Hayden to continue with his rehearsal and immediately closed in on the nearest video monitor, watching with interest as Carey tried and failed once more to undo her buttons in the way that Hayden wanted.

Then there came a little more shifting and shuffling, and suddenly Ella found he'd moved again and she was now squashed against the hard sweaty bulk of his body. She didn't move away, she couldn't, and although she tried to catch his eye in order to say hello, he didn't acknowledge her, all his attention on the filming ahead of him.

'We'll take a break before we begin shooting,' called Hayden. 'Five minutes.'

Immediately he came over to greet Anton.

'Anton,' he said pleasantly. 'Good to see you. Have you met our make-up artist, Ella Buchan? Ella is in charge of Rory.'

Anton ignored Ella and studied Hayden's face with pale, impassive eyes. 'We should see the girl's breasts.'

Hayden swallowed in surprise.

'All this fiddling with the buttons. We should see a breast.'

'You think so?' Hayden tried manfully to recover himself. 'I must say, I was thinking, probably not, leave it under-stated.' He laughed uneasily. 'But it's certainly an idea.'

Anton looked at him with disdain.

'I was giving you my opinion. It does not mean I am right. I am not the director.'

'Thank you. Yes.' Hayden nodded again. 'As I said, it's a thought.'

Anton turned to Ella, gave her a strip search with his eyes, then held out his hand. 'Hello. Redhead.'

'Ella,' she answered, shaking his hand.

'I know what your name is. Hayden has just told me.'

She let her hand fall back to her side.

'A pretty colour. Is it natural?'

'More or less.'

'It suits you.' He nodded. 'Keep it like that.'

Then he turned back to Hayden, dismissing her. 'I have one hour. When will you begin the filming?'

'Now. Of course,' said Hayden.

Stop grovelling, Ella thought. Can't you see how much he dislikes you for it?

Hayden found his First AD, gave him a brief nod and seamlessly the crew moved back into position.

'Roll sound,' called the First AD.

Sitting on the bale of hay, her back against the wall, Carey gave a frightened look towards where she knew Anton was standing, then stared down at her hands. Ella saw her take a deep trembling breath. Her heart went out to her. For all that she was taking a chance with Rory, she imagined Carey had had little choice where Anton was concerned. And she hoped, so badly, that Rory with all his wild stunts, and ridiculous plans, was not about to embroil Carey in anything that might hurt her.

'Action Carey,' called the First AD.

Pascale again unbuttoned her blouse, this time keeping it slow, doing as Hayden had instructed, and keeping her eyes on Ambrose as she did so; and this time, to the surprise of everyone, the scene was allowed to progress, to the moment where Pascale, her blouse falling open, rose to her feet.

She flew across the room, towards Ambrose, and when she reached him, Ella felt Anton's sharp intake of breath, could smell the heat of his body beside her. From what Hayden had said, Anton had cast his girlfriend, all for this moment. But why? Was it purely for the sexual kick of watching her kiss another man? Or was it more for the pleasure of thwarting Rory, giving Carey to him, but not for real?

Standing in the middle of the hay barn, Carey clung to Rory – Pascale clung to Ambrose.

'Film me,' she said again, and as she did so, time seemed to slow down. 'Kiss me.'

Ambrose touched her face and then bent and kissed her, first her neck, then her closed eyes, her trembling mouth, and Pascale immediately responded by pressing closer and passionately kissing her back. At that, Ambrose sank to the wooden floor with her tight against him and continued to kiss her, while one hand deftly undid the last few buttons of her blouse.

'Cut,' shouted Hayden.

Rory continued to kiss her for a few more seconds before Carey managed to twist out of his arms and leap to her feet.

'Sorry,' he grinned mischievously, wiping his mouth and looking around at the crew, taking in Anton Klubcic without missing a beat. 'Let no one ever say that filming a love scene isn't fun.'

Half the crew, the ones who hadn't noticed Anton watching from the wings, burst into spontaneous applause. Ella jumped up and made her way over to Rory with her powder brush.

'Why did you make us stop?' Rory asked Hayden quietly, as Ella joined them. 'It was great.'

Hayden laughed with relief. 'It was perfect. I can't believe it. In the can after only one take. There'd be no point doing it again. Those shots couldn't possibly be improved upon.'

'Coward,' said Rory. 'Carey shouldn't have gasped like that. You know we need to shoot it again.'

'Hold still,' said Ella, lightly brushing across his face with her powder brush.

'No, Rory. I'm serious,' said Hayden, his eyes flickering over to Anton Klubcic, then hastily looking away again. 'She sounded fine. We don't need to do the kiss again. We'll pick it up from where you push her away.'

'Oh, no,' Rory insisted. 'However perfect it was, we have to do it again. Another take, just for Mr Klubcic.'

'For Mr Klubcic, or for you?' asked Hayden.

'I can't say I'd mind trying that kiss again.'

'She's not yours. That's the only reason you want her.'

'No, seriously, I'm not sure we got it right. It was too quick and I'd like to try some teeth-clashing, don't you think? And at the beginning, she's looking down at the floor and really, it should be up into my eyes.'

'Don't push your luck, Rory,' said Hayden.

'I'm not, I'm not. I'm just giving you my professional opinion. I can't believe you're risking an important scene because you-know-who is watching!'

'Of course I'm not.' Hayden looked at him, irritated. 'Don't be insulting.'

'Watch it.' Rory dropped his voice. 'Calm and confident, because he is coming up behind you now . . . ' He smiled at Hayden, warning him. 'Right behind you.'

'What were you saying to Hayden?' Anton demanded.

Rory stepped aside to bring him into the circle and Ella went with Rory, feeling in her pockets for the right brushes and more chimney smoke for the bruise on his cheek.

'I was saying that I thought Carey's teeth and mine should bash together when we kiss,' he told him, taking him on. 'I like that sound it makes, but perhaps only we can hear it. What do you think?'

Anton stared back at Rory. 'Very unpleasant thoughts. Particularly about you.'

Rory laughed. 'I'm not surprised, given the circumstances.'

Ella dropped the powder and brush back into her pouch and brought out a comb, for all the world looking as if the only thing on her mind was her job, when the truth was she was only aware of the conversation going on on each side of her, and was not concentrating on what she was doing at all.

'You think we should see her tits?' asked Anton.

'No,' said Rory, looking at him with sudden disgust. 'Don't even think it.'

Ella combed down a lock of Rory's hair that was refusing to lie flat, caught his eye and frowned at him.

'Why not?' Anton insisted. 'Believe me, they are great tits.'

'I'm sure they are,' said Hayden, uncomfortably stepping in. 'But at this point, it wouldn't be appropriate. I know Carey wants Rory,' he paused, correcting himself awkwardly and making it worse. 'I mean, I know that *Pascale* wants him. But she's nervous too, she's not as brazen as that.'

Anton nodded. 'She is shy.' For the first time he searched Carey out, beckoned to her and immediately she came over to meet him. Even in low shoes, she was several inches taller than him. When she arrived at his side, Anton reached up and wiped across her lips with the pad of his thumb, then reached up and kissed her mouth lingeringly, reclaiming his territory.

'You were rather good.'

'Baby, I was thinking of you.' She snuggled up to him. 'I told you not to come and watch.' She kissed his cheek. 'Or did it turn you on?'

'I enjoyed watching you. But Rory says he would like to see more passion. He would like your teeth to gnash.'

'Would he just?' She raised her eyebrows, laughing easily, keeping her eyes on Anton. 'Jesus! Isn't he so demanding?'

'I'm interested to hear this sound. What do you think, Rory?' said Anton.

'Forget it. Hayden's happy with what we have.'

'But I think you are right and I would like you to show me.'

Rory shrugged. 'If you really want me to. You don't mind, do you?' he asked Carey.

'No,' said Carey firmly.

Ella didn't know what she meant. Yes, she did mind? Or no, she didn't? She found she could hardly look as Rory took Carey by her shoulders and manoeuvred her so that she was protected from the rest of the crew by Ella in front of her and Hayden behind.

'Stand like this.' He brought her a few inches closer to him before setting her free again.

'Okay,' he said quietly and smiled down at her. 'I'll kiss you again. Don't worry about it. Nobody's watching you now. So, we'll try again. Yes?' He nodded. 'Take it from when you first come to me.'

He looked up to Hayden and Anton. 'Now, what I was thinking . . . was if she relaxed against me.'

He turned back to Carey. 'First I'll hold you, yes. Like this.' He put his arms protectively around her shoulders, waiting for her to relax. 'Okay?'

Carey nodded against his chest.

Now Rory seemed aware of nobody but her. Not Anton, standing only a foot away from him, breathing hard; not Hayden, looking as if he was about to pass out with nerves.

'My feeling was that first I should kiss you more like this.'

He held her face in his hands and kissed her gently on her mouth.

Beside her, Ella heard Anton gasp. She looked down at the floor.

'And then, more like this,'

Again Rory kept her steady with his hands, but this time he kissed her harder, more passionately, bending her backwards and then after only a few seconds more he stopped.

'Enough.'

Now Ella looked up again. Rory had gently pulled Carey upright and, with his arm still around her, was looking back at Anton, eyes gleaming but otherwise seemingly completely unruffled.

'How was that? Any better than the first attempt?' He looked back at Hayden.

'What do you think? Did you like that way more?'

'The first way was better,' Hayden managed to mumble.

'That was horrid,' said Carey. She slipped away from Rory's side, threaded her arm through Anton's and looked up at him with a playful frown. 'And don't ask me to do it again. It was weird.'

Anton laughed and kissed her cheek. 'I loved it.'

You are such a strange man, thought Ella, unable to stop herself staring at him in uneasy fascination. But Carey's words had been perfectly judged, letting Anton know she hadn't enjoyed the kiss and flattering him at the same time.

Hayden had had enough. He turned to his crew. 'Guys.' He clapped his hands. 'We're moving on to the next scene. Back to work.' He turned to Rory.

'Now. Be careful when you push Pascale away, not too hard. You're a gentleman, still. Carey. He is going to catch you here.'

He put his hands on her shoulders.

'He'll do it like this.' He pushed gently. 'You take two

steps back, and then you wait for him to come back to you again.'

Ella quickly added a smudge of shadow to the corner of each of Rory's eyes then let him go.

'Behave,' she told him, under her breath.

'It's acting,' he told her. 'I'm feeling the part.'

'And Carey.'

'Stop being a nanny.'

'Stop underestimating Anton Klubcic.'

She stepped back, over the cables and ropes, and waited off camera for them to begin filming the next scene. And as she watched the first take, and then the second, she felt the tension slowly start to leave her. None of the crew was looking as if they'd seen anything untoward, and, having got the kissing over and done with, it seemed that Carey was relaxing now, and was finally beginning to act; and although Anton Klubcic was still there, motionless at her side, but for the heavy rise and fall of his chest, it seemed that they had all survived and surely whatever came next would be straightforward by comparison? Her visions of Anton storming into the middle of the set and dragging Carey away from Rory had proved groundless, and now, with luck, they would make it to the end of the day. And then Carey's part would soon be over and she and Anton would leave the set, leave France, and the rest of the crew could move on.

They continued filming for the next hour, and then, even though the sunlight had still not left the barn, Hayden called it a wrap, making no attempt to disguise his relief that he had survived the day, and full of exuberance at what they had captured on film.

Anton stayed until the final take and then immediately made his exit, not even waiting for Carey to say goodbye, and as soon as he had been seen to leave the set Carey turned to Rory and jumped up into his arms and wound her legs around his waist.

'Steady, darling, steady,' he said, holding her still for a few moments and smiling up at her.

'But he's gone,' she shrieked loudly. 'Can't I be happy?'

Everyone in earshot started to laugh. Rory dropped her gently back to her feet.

'I've got two hours,' she went on, telling Rory, Ella, anyone who was listening. 'Then he's taking me out for dinner. Jesus, have I had enough of this man?'

'Not so loud,' Rory cautioned. 'He's probably bugged the set.'

'Sod it,' Carey retorted, tossing back her long ringlets. 'I'm sick of him.'

She looked towards the doorway that led out of the set and outside and finally dropped her voice, turning to Ella, who was standing, with Rory, beside her.

'He promised me a part in this thriller he's making,' she told her. 'What was it called, Rory? *The Broken Wing*? Something like that. So I figured I should stick around. Two months, I think I've been with him now. Urghh! Yuck! Disgusting!' She pretended to stuff her fingers down the back of her throat. 'What a creep.' She dropped her voice to a whisper so that only Rory and Ella could hear. 'He's got me wearing a blindfold in bed now, thank God. It's the only way I can face fucking him.' She glanced quickly at Rory and whispered, 'Makes it easier to pretend it's you, darling.'

'Carey! Please!' cried Rory. 'I don't want to think about it.'

All around them the crew were packing up, coiling up cables, pulling covers over the cameras. Thankfully none of them seemed to have heard. Ella caught sight of Sacha, standing in the doorway that led out of the barn, and when Sacha saw her, she ran lightly over to join them.

'Carey,' she said, standing there in her ridiculous little pink skirt, ballet pumps on her feet, looking up at her. 'I should get you back to wardrobe. Is Ella going to take off your make-up?'

Carey frowned and Rory immediately stepped in.

'She's not. Not straight away,' he explained to Sacha. 'Carey needs to leave the make-up on for a little longer. She wants to go over her lines a few more times before to-morrow. Isn't that right, Carey? We were going to work on your lines?'

'Absolutely,' Carey agreed brightly.

'What?' said Ella, surprised. 'You mean you two want to practise your lines *in here*?'

'Where else?' said Rory. 'And no one must tell Hayden because Carey doesn't want him to know. He puts her off, makes her nervous. We're going to practise our lines and then Carey won't need so many rehearsals tomorrow. Tomorrow, she's going to surprise Hayden – and everyone else – by getting her lines right on take two rather than on take two hundred and two.'

'You bastard!' said Carey, laughing and pushing him backwards. 'I'm not that bad.'

'Yes, my darling, you are,' said Rory.

'Okay,' said Ella, trying to work out how much, if anything, of what he'd said was true. 'So, you're helping Carey learn her lines, in here. What about Sam? I thought he was going to look at the Aeroscope with you?'

'He is. And *then* Carey and I go over our lines.'

If Ella hadn't been in a hurry to go, she'd have thought about it a little more.

'So, would you like me to take off *your* make-up now? I presume you're not coming back to the trailer?'

'Christ no. Do it here,' said Rory. 'If I come back to the trailer I might have to sit next to Liberty.'

'But I'm Carey's dresser for these scenes,' Sacha told Rory, looking very uncomfortable. 'I need to take back her dress to wardrobe. I need to check it back in, so that they can clean it and press it for tomorrow.'

'No, you don't. It's perfectly clean,' Rory said firmly. 'And Carey will bring it back safely. Tell them she'll have it back by eight o'clock. Sweetheart,' he gave Sacha his most persuasive smile. 'Please. Do us a favour. Turn a blind eye, just this once, and help Carey. You're not going to get into trouble for it.'

Sacha looked to Ella for reassurance. 'What do you think?'

'Don't worry,' Ella told her. 'I'll make sure the dress gets back to wardrobe.' Whatever Rory was planning – and Ella had a bad feeling about what it might be – it was better if Sacha was not involved.

'Thank you.' Sacha still looked doubtful. 'You'll be here with them?'

'Sacha!' Rory said. 'Of course she won't, she'll be getting

ready for her date. Didn't you know? Ella has a date tonight with Sam Lucey.'

'Thank you for remembering, Rory,' said Ella, wishing that he hadn't told Sacha. 'Make sure you let him go on time.'

'What! Why didn't you say?' Sacha said to Ella accusingly, suddenly rather white-faced and so thrown she didn't care that Carey and Rory were listening.

'Because he only asked me this afternoon and it's not a big deal.'

At that Carey looked at Ella with amusement. 'Yes, it damn well is! Sam Lucey's *hot*. Go for it, girl.'

Rory looked at Carey, with narrowed eyes and a tight little frown. 'What is it about Sam Lucey? I'm sorry but I don't see it at all.'

Ella ignored him and walked forwards to take Sacha's arm.

'Listen,' she told her, walking her away, towards the door. 'I'm sorry I didn't tell you. And trust me to look after the dress. I promise I'll get it back to wardrobe. You go now and then Rory and Carey can get started, and the sooner they start, the sooner they will finish. Sam's having to wait too, because Rory needs him to go over something with the Aeroscope.'

Sacha sighed. 'I might have guessed Sam would notice you eventually. You're really going out with him?'

'Only as in tonight.'

'You are so bloody lucky.'

'Sacha?'

She looked back at Ella with huge wide eyes, ruined by

too much peacock blue eyeshadow.

'Why not me?'

'Don't say that. Would it help to say that it's just supper? That I've hardly talked to him, and it's not a big deal?'

'No, it wouldn't. It wouldn't help at all.' She turned away. 'Don't listen to me. I always set my sights too high. Try and get Carey's dress back by eight o'clock, before lock-up, and then no one will notice it's not there now.' She stopped, sighed, ran her hands down the frills of her short little skirt. 'I don't mean to make you feel bad.' She gave Ella a half-hearted smile. 'You're lovely. He's lovely. Just don't go and fall in love with him. You do know that's not a good idea, don't you? Have fun and promise you'll tell me about it tomorrow.' She turned away then gave Ella a little woebegone wave goodbye, and as Ella watched her slip through the doorway – clearly dying to escape – her first thought was that she wished she'd known how Sacha had felt. But then, her second thought was why? when knowing wouldn't have made her turn Sam down. If anything, it was easier that she hadn't known.

Ella turned back to Rory. She poured cleanser into a ball of cotton wool and reached up for his face.

'If you don't mind me asking, why do you need Sam tonight? Do it tomorrow. He's not going to help Carey learn her lines.'

'Don't you worry your pretty little head. I'll make sure you get your dinner on time. I need ten minutes with your boyfriend and then I will release him to you.'

'Boyfriend?' Carey was still listening in. 'This gets even better. Sam is your boyfriend?'

'No, he is not,' said Ella firmly. She turned back to Rory. 'Sit down somewhere. I can't reach your face if you keep walking around.' She looked around the room and saw the hay bale and pointed to it. 'That will do.'

Rory followed her over to it and sat down and Carey immediately joined him. She put her hands in her lap and shuffled a little bit closer until they were touching, hip to hip.

'You sure you don't want me to take your make-up off too?'

'Should she?' Carey looked questioningly at Rory.

'Leave it on.'

'Why?' Ella insisted. 'Don't leave me out. Tell me what you two are up to.'

Carey shook her head. 'We would if we could but we can't. You go and have supper with Sam. Better watch out for him, Ella, from what I've heard.'

'Stop trying to distract me. I want you to tell me what you're doing tonight. I know you're not learning any lines.'

Carey giggled, then grabbed Rory's hand. 'You'll see soon enough.'

The more Ella got to know her, the more Ella liked Carey and the more dangerous she thought she was. When Hayden had so casually dismissed Carey as just another wannabee actress, with too few scruples and plenty too much ambition, he surely hadn't noticed how exuberant she was, how much fun, how likely it was that Rory might be genuinely falling for her. Hayden had conveniently presumed that Rory's interest in her was all about beating Anton, and perhaps, at first, that had been true. But now? Now Ella would say that Rory genuinely liked her and would hold on to her if he could. And Carey? Carey was covering it up well, but Carey, she feared, was falling in love.

So, when Carey was rude about Anton, when she loudly dismissed him, despaired of having to sleep with him, it wasn't because she didn't take Anton seriously and it wasn't because she underestimated the risk of saying such things aloud. Ella thought she said those things because she didn't want to lose Rory and, from all that Ella had seen that afternoon, she hadn't. It made Hayden's confidence that the relationship was over seem ridiculous.

Just as she finished taking off Rory's make-up, Sam came over to join them.

'Aeroscope,' he said to Rory, folding his arms and watching Ella pick wax from Rory's cheek.

'A man of few words,' Rory said, looking up at Ella. 'Might that be a problem?'

Ella ignored him.

'It's being guarded by that prop-hand over there,' Rory told Sam. 'Could you take it off him, on my behalf? Don't let him make a fuss. You can tell him we'll deliver it straight back to the props department when we're finished.'

'What do you want to film?' asked Sam.

Rory flashed a glance at Carey. 'Any ideas?'

'You pick a subject,' Carey told Sam, smiling at him innocently.

'All I need to know is how Ambrose would cope once the light starts to fade,' said Rory. 'Want to watch?' he asked Ella.

'No, thank you,' said Ella.

She'd finished his face and was ready to go, ready to get

back to Le Sport to turn her cupboards inside out and find something to wear. She wanted to soak in a bath, wash her hair and put on a dress for the first time in weeks.

'If you don't need me, I'm going right now.'

'Fine by me,' said Rory. 'Because if we don't hurry up we'll find ourselves sitting here in the dark.' He looked over to the window. 'What do you think, Sam? How much longer have we got?'

'Probably about an hour.'

Ella caught his cheek in her hand and pulled him back to face her.

'Be off with you, Ella, there's a darling,' Rory told her. 'And then Sam won't be late. We wouldn't want to delay you.'

Everything Rory said seemed to have a hidden meaning, but whatever was going on, he wasn't going to tell her and right then, she didn't care. She finished cleaning the make-up off his face, pushed herself back to her feet and carried her cleanser and the dirty cotton wool pads and emptied them into a bin. Then, at the doorway, she turned back.

'Bye, Sam.'

She hoped that she sounded relaxed, casual, when the reality was that just looking at him, there on his knees in front of the Aeroscope, carefully unscrewing its lens, made her want to pull him to his feet and run with him out of the room.

'Why don't you call me when you leave here and I'll set off for La Mas d'Antigne and meet you there.'

'Perfect,' said Sam, not looking up from the Aeroscope.

'Bye, Ella,' called Carey.

Something in her voice made Ella look back one last time, still feeling that she was missing something important, but now giving up on what it could be.

She found out what it was about half an hour later, when her phone rang. She was standing in her underwear, in her hotel room, surrounded by the contents of her wardrobe, just minutes after she'd had a call from Sam to say he'd left the hay barn.

'Hello?'

'Ella!'

It was Hayden, heaving a noisy sigh of relief at the sound of her voice.

'Hello, Hayden.'

'Thank God I caught you.'

'Are you okay?'

'Yes, yes, I think so. Gone over what we did today and everybody's very pleased. Wilf Ronson – lighting designer, you must have met him? No, I suppose Rosalind has handled that side of things – anyway, he's absolutely terrific. It was he who insisted that we wait for the five o'clock light. I thought it wouldn't make enough difference, being inside, but seeing what we've got, he was clearly right – he says the light this evening was the best he's ever worked with.'

'Pleased to hear it.'

'So. All in all, yes, a very good day.'

'Excellent.' She wanted him to go. She stood in front of her mirror and held the phone against her lip and added a coat of lip-gloss, then smacked her lips together.

'Excellent,' echoed Hayden.

'Was that all?'

'Actually, no. Something else too, that I wanted to ask you about. Um, tell me, if you don't mind, what you know about Rory, and Carey, in the hay barn, with the Aeroscope.'

She didn't want to admit to it. Had she been irresponsible to leave them there together?

'Are they in a new edition of Cluedo?'

'A pornographic version if what I've just seen is anything to go by.' Now Hayden's voice was rising in volume. 'Wait a bit longer and we'll probably have the murder too.'

She didn't want to know. She didn't need him to tell her what he meant. She wished that he had never confided in her. Because now, having done so, and having seen that she could keep a secret, it seemed that Hayden's default setting was to bring her in every time Rory and Carey did anything that troubled him. Perhaps the thought only needed to cross his mind that they might, before he wanted to call on Ella's support.

She tried to brush it aside.

'So, let them misbehave. No one will know and in any case, it seems Anton enjoys it when they do.'

'Don't be flippant, Ella.'

'But I'm going out! I don't want to know.'

'You left them in the hay barn on their own!'

'They're grown-ups! I'm his make-up artist, not his minder. And in any case, Sam was there. At least he *was*.' Belatedly she caught up with what he'd said first. 'When you say pornographic? You don't mean Sam was there filming them?'

'Meet me at the hay barn. Now, please Ella.'

'Tell me Sam wasn't there.'

'No, of course he wasn't,' snapped Hayden.

'Then I'm sorry, but I can't meet you.' She thought of Sam, gorgeous, reliable Sam, waiting to walk across town with her to La Mas d'Antigne. 'I'm about to go out for supper.'

'Put him off.'

Funny how assertive he could suddenly sound. How it was only Rory who seemed to make him go to pieces.

'No way! Please, Hayden. Don't involve me. You can handle them.'

'*Film me,*' he replied angrily. 'Do you remember that line? Pascale says it to Ambrose. Remember?'

'Of course I do.'

'And, in the script, remember, Ambrose pushes her away.'

'Yes,' said Ella cautiously. 'We went over it all today.'

'But not in the way that Rory wanted. Rory's always argued with me about that scene. He's always felt that, given the opportunity, of course Ambrose would film Pascale. That he wouldn't be able to resist. I've always disagreed. Ambrose was there to film the solders. He wasn't interested in girls like Pascale, prancing around naked, offering themselves to him.'

Her heart sank. 'Rory is making you the film?'

Why did she ask? When she knew the answer already. She supposed she had to hear it even so.

'Yes.'

'Can't you let him? Will anybody know? Does it matter?'

She could take Hayden's concern seriously but still, uppermost in her mind, was the thought of going out, walking through the town in her heels and her new red dress that she'd never had a chance to wear before. For the first time in ages she'd felt excited about the evening ahead and she didn't want to let it go.

'Ella! Anybody could walk in. Jesus, it was such a shock. I left the set about half an hour ago and then I realized I had to go back. It was only a tiny thing – I wanted to check that the set designers had got the window opening properly for when we start shooting tomorrow. It had stuck and I didn't want it to happen again. Thank God I went back.'

'And? What did you see?'

'From outside, all I could see were two figures in the window, but then I opened the door and found them.'

'They weren't learning their lines?'

'If you have to be naked to learn your lines, yes they were. Both of them, by the way, not just Carey. What is the matter with them? They were like a pair of kids. They had a bottle of wine and some cheese and they'd broken open another bale of hay. Carey had a baguette . . .' At the memory of the baguette he had to pause. '. . .Which she was riding around the room. And Rory, Rory had the nerve to tell me – and, by the way, he wasn't the slightest bit embarrassed that I had caught him naked, just offered me a glass of wine – Rory told me that he'd been filming an extra nude scene, that I might like to drop into *To End All War*.'

'Perhaps you might. Perhaps it's good.' For all Hayden's indignant spluttering, she couldn't help but find his description of what he'd found really funny. 'Why does it matter what they get up to? Nobody's seen them. At least it was you who walked in.'

'*But it could have been Anton!*' Hayden suddenly roared,

making her hold her mobile away from her ear. 'And they won't stop and they're making so much noise that sooner or later it *will* be Anton. And Rory promised me that it was over between him and Carey, so why did he tell me that? Why did he say they both understood? Why bother to pretend? I'm his fucking director!' he cried. 'Why does he not take me seriously?'

And that, thought Ella, was the heart of the problem. That was what was eating away at Hayden. It wasn't really what Rory was doing. It was the fact that he couldn't stop him.

'Hayden,' Ella said gently. 'No harm has been done.'

'As I said. What if Anton comes looking for her?'

'Stop being so terrified of him. I presume you persuaded them to pack away the Aeroscope and put their clothes back on?'

'No! They're still there. I think Rory's taken something. I could see it in his eyes. When I left them, he was still running around with the camera, chasing Carey. He wouldn't take any notice of me. I will never ever direct him again. Please help me, Ella.'

But saying that is not good enough! she wanted to cry. You *are* directing him now. And you're good, and your film is good and you should have faith and make him listen to you because it's your job to keep control of your cast. And please, don't bring me into this. I don't have to know any more. I'm just the make-up artist. I don't want to know.

'Give me ten minutes,' she said instead.

She called Sam, in a rush, explained that she would meet him at the restaurant after all, then changed out of her sandals and into trainers, and strode through the town, part irritated, part intrigued at what she would find. By now it was late and the light had nearly all gone. Whatever they had been filming, surely it had to have stopped by now? But, of course, if they were in the barn, running around naked together, whether they were still filming or not was hardly the problem.

She met Hayden at the barn doors, and, without wasting any more time, pulled them open and walked in, then quickly climbed the ladder to the loft. At the top, she looked into the room and was confronted immediately by Carey's perfect bare bottom. She was standing in the middle of the room with her back to the hayloft ladder and neither she nor Rory had heard Ella's ascent.

'Closer, closer,' said Rory, standing stark naked in the furthest corner of the room. He was bent over the Aeroscope and was filming enthusiastically. 'Remember my lens is only three inches long.'

Carey giggled and walked seductively towards him. 'Looks longer than that to me.'

Hayden came up the ladder behind her as Ella stepped into the room. Rory swung the camera at the sound and then, when he saw it was her, stopped filming, slowly brought down the Aeroscope and placed it carefully on the ground.

Fleetingly she took in the beauty of his naked body and the dangerous, wild look in his eyes.

'That's a great dress, but if you want to stay you have to take it off,' he told her. 'No dresses allowed.'

'The light's all gone,' she pointed out gently, calmly. 'No more filming time tonight.' There was a pair of boxer shorts lying on a bale of hay and she picked them up and walked over to him. 'How about putting them on?'

'Am I embarrassing you?' asked Rory, not taking them.

'Of course not. But I think you should get dressed, all the same. Carey should go now.'

'Leave us alone, nanny-goat. Go have dinner with the billy-goat.'

Irritation made her take a step closer.

'Everyone fawns all over you,' she told him. 'Everyone tells you you're wonderful. Well, the truth is you're not. You're the most selfish man alive.'

He didn't flinch. 'Anything else?'

'Oh, I could go on all night, but it won't help Carey when Anton finds out about this. Let her leave, now, with Hayden, and stop messing up her life.'

'Oh, is Hayden here too? Where is he?'

'She's coming with me, Ella,' came Hayden's voice from the doorway. 'Thank you. I'm taking her now.'

Carey came back into Ella's eyeline. She was still naked, beautiful, tall and slim, her wonderful ringleted red hair cascading down her narrow back. She went over to the hay bale and picked up a sleeveless yellow summer dress and pulled it over her head.

'Hayden's right. I should go,' she told Rory. 'We got some great shots, and it was fun.'

She gathered up the dress and blouse that she'd worn as Pascale, then came over to him, reached up and touched his cheek with her finger. 'Get your pants on.'

He kissed her lips. 'I'll miss you.'

'A good way to say goodbye, my darling,' said Carey.

'Take that dress back to wardrobe or Sacha could lose her job,' Ella snapped at her.

Carey turned to her and smiled. 'You look great. Go and get your dinner before Sam goes cold.'

After they'd left, Rory walked towards Ella and held out a hand.

'Listen, it's going to look beautiful and I filmed it with the Aeroscope. Don't you think that's wonderful?'

'Hayden won't even look at it.'

'I won't do another scene for him until he does.'

'It's nothing to do with me. Tell him. Don't threaten me.'

'It's not a threat. I want you to understand what I was doing.'

'Rory, I don't care.' She turned away from him back towards the ladder. 'I've got better things to think about and better places to be than here – and if I don't go now, Sam will give up on me.'

'Wait! Please listen to me. I want to tell you about Sam. He was brilliant. He picked up the Aeroscope, looked at it for just a few minutes and then, it was as if it was the only camera he'd ever known. He had it working so much better than I could ever have done, I was so stupid not to ask him to help me before, and now I've got these perfect close-ups, these wonderful, twenty-second bursts of film, and Hayden's going to love it. I know he'll want to use this film when he sees it.'

'You're being such an idiot, Rory.'

'Don't be so stubborn.'

'Anton could have walked in at any time.'

He came closer, caught her bare shoulder in his hand. 'It was worth it. I want you to help me get Hayden to watch it.'

'You must be joking! You don't think Anton will ever question how it was filmed? Let me go, Rory.'

He pulled her tighter into his arms.

'Promise you'll watch what we've done.'

Then there came another voice, from the top of the ladder.

'I thought I knew what I would find here,' said Anton, stepping carefully in. 'But it certainly was not this. Rory, I heard Ella tell you to let her go.'

Ella's heart leapt at the sound of his voice, and all she could think was Thank God. Thank God that Carey had gone.

'So, you are dressed,' Anton observed, walking closer and circling around Ella curiously. 'But Rory likes to walk about in his pants. Why is that?'

Ella followed Anton's slow gaze as it moved carefully around the room, taking in the wine and the open bales of hay, Rory's clothes scattered about the floor.

'What have I walked into here?'

She watched as he went to the bottle of wine and checked the label. 'Very nice.' He carried the bottle over to a hay bale and sat down, then stretched out a hand for a fallen empty wine glass. 'It looks as if I've missed a party.'

Rory stepped away from Ella. 'You weren't invited,' he said.

'A party for two.' Anton smiled at Ella. 'I'm sorry to interrupt you. I thought Carey would be here.' He poured himself some wine, then set the bottle back on the floor. 'Was she here, Ella?'

She stared into his cold, fish eyes, and her heart jumped in fear. She didn't know what to say. She could only think how scary he was, how Hayden had been right to leave nothing to chance.

'Yes, she was,' said Rory. He turned his back on Anton and walked over to his clothes and stepped into his jeans. 'But I guess you know that already. If you want her, why don't you ring her? Or has she stopped taking your calls?'

'She *was* here?' Anton stood up again.

'We were all here,' said Ella easily. 'Sam, Rory, Carey and me. We were going over Carey's lines.'

Anton blinked slowly and looked down at the dusty floor. Then in a flash of rage he kicked the bottle of wine across the floor of the hay barn.

'What is the matter with you?' Rory yelled.

'You are.'

Rory strode towards him. 'We were working on the Aeroscope,' he shouted furiously. 'I was learning how to use it with Sam. Carey was acting for us. Stop behaving like an arsehole.'

'Fuck off out of my face!'

'Stop frightening Ella.'

Alone in the middle of the room, Ella watched the bottle roll back towards her across the floor as the red wine poured slowly across the pale wooden floorboards. She was so shocked, so scared of Anton, that she couldn't move, couldn't speak.

Anton pushed Rory a step backwards.

'Go away,' Rory shouted at him. 'Leave us alone to make our film.'

'My film, Rory,' Anton spat back. 'My fucking film.'

'Everybody's film.' Finally Ella had found her voice. Next

she made her legs work, walked forwards between Anton and Rory and tried a reassuring hand on each shoulder.

'Everybody's wonderful film, Anton.' She looked up at him. 'It is as Rory says. Carey was practising her lines and at the same time Sam Lucey was using her as a subject for Rory. He was showing Rory how a cameraman might use the Aeroscope. He was here too.'

Then she turned back to Rory, still managing to sound reasonably unruffled. 'Perhaps we could help Anton find Carey? Have you any idea where she could be?'

'If I did know I'd hardly tell him.' Rory turned his back on them, went over to the wine bottle, lying on its side on the floor, and picked it up. 'Give her the lead in *Broken Wing*. You at least owe her that.'

'Perhaps Hayden might know where she is?' Ella suggested to Anton, cutting in before Rory said anything more. 'Would you like me to call him and ask?'

'Of course I wouldn't,' Anton practically spat into her face with venom. 'You think I can't press the buttons on my own fucking phone?'

Instantly Rory was back, pushing past Ella, just inches from Anton's chest.

'Do not speak to her like that.'

'Okay, I'm sorry.'

Ella stared at him in stunned surprise and he nodded shortly back at her. 'He's right. I don't have a problem with you.'

'Nor Carey,' Ella ventured. 'Really, she's done nothing wrong.'

'No? So why did she not tell me she needed to learn her lines?'

Briefly Ella saw the vulnerability in his face and she realized that, for all the suspicion, all the noise and the bluster, Anton really didn't want to believe that anything was going on between Carey and Rory. Yes, of course he might *suspect* she was screwing him, *guess* she was only with him because of the parts he might send her way, but Anton didn't *know* so, and, as long as there was no proof, he could hope.

'I will ask her.' He turned away from them, aiming for the open hatch and the ladder, and it was clear that now, all he could think about was getting away to find her. 'I will call her and I will ask her.' He hesitated for a few seconds more. 'You never explained why you took off your clothes,' he said to Rory. 'But I am sure there is a good explanation for that, also. Of course there is. Clear up the wine or the set will be ruined for tomorrow.'

Ella looked about for something to use and saw Rory's white T-shirt lying on the floor in front of her. She went over to it and picked it up, then took it over to the pool of wine and knelt down with it in her hands.

'I hope she learnt her lines well, Rory, for the sake of Ella and Sam and everybody else working on this film. Carey finds it difficult to lie to me, and if what you've said is not in the end true, I warn you that I will break up this film, scene by little scene. There, you see, a threat and a promise all at the same time.' He turned to Ella and lifted a hand. 'Goodnight, redhead. You make sure your next job takes you far away from him. Don't ever work with him again. That is my advice to you.'

Ten

Ella mopped up the wine with Rory's T-shirt and poured a bottle of water over the stain, then scrubbed at it with some loose hay. Although there was now a dark wet mark, spreading a good couple of feet across the floorboards, she hoped, optimistically, that there'd be little evidence once the boards had had a chance to dry.

'I think I caught it in time,' she said doubtfully, getting back to her feet. She held out his wine-soaked T-shirt between her fingertips. 'But somehow I don't think you will be wearing this again. You'll have to walk bare-chested through the streets of Florent. Do you think I should tip off the fans?'

'You were a good liar. You nearly convinced me.'

'Thank you.' She looked back towards the ladder. 'That was my first taste of him, face to face. Now I can see why Hayden's worried.'

'He can stop worrying now because it's over, Ella. Anton's not going to find out about Carey and me, because, as of tonight, there's nothing to find out about.'

'Good. But you shouldn't have taken the chance in the first place.'

'I couldn't resist her. Carey's gorgeous.'

Ella turned back to him. 'So are lots of girls. Maybe you just had to pick the one going out with Anton.'

'Or maybe not. Maybe it was just about Carey.'

'Then I'm sorry you've had to call it a day. I'm sure some-one else will pop up on your radar very soon.'

'Who could you mean, Ella? Not . . . ? You're not sug-gesting . . .'

'Sweet of you, Rory, but no, I'm not suggesting me.' She dropped his T-shirt into a bin then glanced down at her watch. It was ten past nine. 'Christ, I hope Sam is still waiting for me.'

'No chance,' said Rory. 'Three-quarters of an hour late?' He grinned at her. 'If it was me, I'd give you five minutes.'

She brought out her phone and saw that she had four missed calls, all from Sam. She bit her lip, knowing Rory was waiting for her to call him back, keen to listen in, and pride made her hesitate because, if Sam had given up on her, she certainly didn't want Rory to know.

She dropped her phone back into her pocket. 'I'll see you tomorrow.'

'But I want to know if he's still waiting.'

'Why?'

She walked towards the door.

'Because I'm interested. I want to know how keen he is.'

She smiled at him from the doorway. 'You need to push the bales back to the sides of the room. I'd help, but not in this dress. Can you manage?'

'No,' he said sulkily.

'Then shall I get someone to come and give you a hand? I'll call Poppy.'

He frowned. 'I can do it.'

But would he? She looked back at him, wondering how much he cared about covering his tracks. He stood hands on hips surveying the room, looking sober and rather bad-tempered and part of her felt nervous about leaving him, just a little bit of her; the rest of her was wanting only to get out of the barn and into the woods, to be able to clear her head and set off for La Mas d'Antigne, and, she hoped, to find Sam.

As soon as she was clear of the loft, she called Sam, only to find that his phone went straight to voicemail. She decided to set off for La Mas d'Antigne anyway, thinking that perhaps she'd find him coming to find her and, if she didn't, that she'd call him again. She was just crossing the bridge to Florent when her phone rang.

She glanced at it and saw it was Hayden, thought about it for a couple of seconds, then cut him off. If she hadn't been wanting to reach Sam she'd have turned off her phone.

She crossed the bridge and started to make her way through the town. She climbed the hill and passed L'Oignon, then brought out her phone to try him a second time and it rang in her hand. Hayden.

'Don't cut me off,' he said as soon as she answered.

'Whatever you're wanting to tell me, I don't want to know.'

'Too late.'

'I'm serious. I've had enough of you tonight.'

'Too bad.'

She knew she had to keep on walking. If she stopped, he'd got her.

'I'm hungry and I need something to eat,' she insisted.

'I can fix that.'

'No thank you!'

'I've told Sam you won't make dinner.'

'What!'

She stopped walking.

'Sorry. But this can't wait,' said Hayden.

'Please leave me alone.'

'Where are you?'

'In town.'

'Good. Where exactly?'

'By the bridge,' she lied. 'And whatever it is, tell me about it in the morning. I'm sorry, got to go.'

She put away her phone and carried on, up the street that led to La Mas d'Antigne.

When she saw him, when he came flying around the corner, running for the bridge, jowls flying, hair flying, belly flying, she wasn't even surprised. She stopped in the middle of the street, waiting for him to notice her, and when he did, he stretched out his arms as if to stop her diving past him and came to a sudden, relieved halt in front of her.

'I told Sam you were having dinner with me.'

He glanced up the street, saw a café just in front of them and, with his breath still coming fast, took her hand and pulled her after him.

'What the hell is the matter with you?' She shook his hand away. 'Just tell me what's going on. Why do you have to be so dramatic?'

'Photographs,' he said, over his shoulder, making sure she was following him as he walked on into the restaurant.

'Awful, incriminating photographs. This is it, Ella. It's happening. He'll crush the film . . . Ella . . .' He hesitated, pulling himself together. 'I'm truly sorry. I never meant to involve you. I didn't know it was going to be like this. Come and sit down with me, somewhere quiet, where we can talk. Please?'

She looked at his face. 'What photographs?'

The restaurant was tiny, no more than six tables inside, three of them taken, three empty. A waiter came hurrying over to catch them, and Hayden let him lead them to the nearest empty table and waited for Ella to sit down.

'Do I have to worry you're about to run away?'

'No.'

'Good.' He sat down opposite her. 'Then order some food and I'll tell you what's happened.'

A waiter came over and handed her a handwritten menu. She glanced down the list of food, struggling to translate, and in any case, not taking in the words. 'Just order me anything,' she told Hayden.

'Sam understands I had to see you tonight,' said Hayden. 'He's not pissed off with you. I told him we have something really important to work out.'

'He didn't wonder what it was?'

'Probably.'

'I presume I won't be able to tell him.'

'No. And I am truly sorry to be ruining your evening with Sam and I hope very much that there will be another chance for you soon.'

He called the waiter over and ordered them a bottle of wine and some food, and then, when they were alone again, sat back in his chair and looked at her consideringly.

'I like your hair and I like your dress.'

The way he said it was strange, full of satisfaction.

'Please tell me why you've ruined my date. Not that I don't like you, Hayden, and thank you for noticing my dress, but I didn't actually put it on for you.'

He nodded. 'Cut to the chase.'

She was sure of it. Even just five minutes ago, when they'd sat down, he'd been nervous, jumpy, terribly distracted. Now she could sense the relief, could see the way his body was relaxing into his chair. Was it really something to do with her dress?

A basket of bread had arrived at their table and she took a piece and broke it in two.

Hayden laid his hands on the table in front of them and looked at her.

'When I said I thought I'd sorted Rory, I meant it. But tonight, just after I got back from the hay barn, I had a call and then a visit at the hotel from a friend of mine who works on *Hollywood Whisper*.'

'Rory hates that magazine.'

'I know he does. But that isn't the problem, which magazine it is is irrelevant.'

'What did this guy want?'

'He wanted to tell me about some photographs he's been offered.'

'Of?'

'Carey and Rory.'

'So? What are they doing?'

'Eating ice cream.'

'Oh, wow,' Ella, frowned. 'That sounds really serious.'

'In one of them, Rory is licking ice cream off Carey's nose.'

She laughed. 'Okay. I can see that might make a good photograph.'

'It is a good photograph. The next one, the one where he's kissing ice cream off her mouth, is even better. Looking at it, you might even think they're in love.' He looked at her sharply. 'It's not funny, Ella.'

'I know it's not! But I suppose this was always going to happen – neither of them are very good at being discreet.'

'Ella. This is a disaster!'

'Yup. Very bad. So, why did this guy from *Hollywood Whisper* come to you?'

'Because we've worked together before. Otherwise he might have gone straight to Rory's publicity people and then I'd never even have known until it was too late. He was very friendly. He had no idea what he was showing me. He thought I'd be interested, thought I might like to work with him on them, have Rory do an interview at the same time. Can you imagine? I don't think he even knew who Carey was.'

'Buy them off him.'

Hayden laughed. 'Oh, believe me, if I could I would.'

'So, how did you react? What did you say?'

Hayden looked at her carefully. 'I told him the girl in the pictures was you.'

'You're hopeless!' Ella burst into laughter. 'Couldn't you have thought of anyone else?'

'It was the only thing I could think of to say, and the more I've thought about it afterwards, the more I thank God that that was what I did say. Because it gets us off the hook, doesn't it?'

'No, Hayden!' She leaned in to him. 'I don't look anything like her. For a start she's got wavy hair.'

'Wavy *red* hair.'

'Right, we've both got red hair. And mine's straight and hers is wavy. And she's six foot and I'm five foot five. And she looks like a supermodel.' She started to laugh again. 'I can't believe you told him it was me.'

'It could be you. They're not close-ups. You see the girl's face in profile, that's all. It could be you. Whatever, this guy believed it.'

She shrugged. 'Why wouldn't he? He's never met me.' She broke off another piece of bread, ate it and then took a long swallow of wine. 'So, I suppose that bought you a little time, but it's not going to solve your problem. He's still got photographs of Carey and Rory. When they're printed nobody else is going to think they're of me.'

'Yes, they are.'

His eyes narrowed and he went very still, and looking back at him, Ella suddenly felt uncomfortable. It was much too late, she should have seen it sooner, but she realized, belatedly, how disarming Hayden was, how clever, how all the bluster and the protestations that he couldn't cope with Rory weren't true at all. All along, Hayden had been playing Rory as best he could, exercising damage limitation, and he'd done it very well. He'd known that he couldn't break him free from Carey straight away, he'd probably known from the moment he'd first heard they were together that something like this moment might come. And he'd clearly had a plan for it, and suddenly, she realized, it had involved her, right from the start. From the moment he'd first come to her trailer, he'd been positioning her to help him.

He scraped back his chair and studied her calmly.

'You're going to pretend to be his new girlfriend.'

She coughed loudly. 'I am not.'

'Yes.'

'That's such a crazy idea. Who would believe it? You think *Hollywood Whisper* would? Come on.'

'I agree you'd have to get to work on yourself.' He folded his arms, sure he was right. 'But take your hair out of the pony-tail, and wear a pretty dress like that and anyone would believe it. It was the first thing I thought when I saw you tonight.'

'You expect me to be flattered?'

'I'm telling you how we can extricate ourselves from a very delicate situation.'

'We?' She leaned closer into him. 'This situation does not involve me.'

'Yes it does. I need you. You are the only person who can help me and you care about this film as much as I do. And you'd do it brilliantly.'

'Now tell me Plan B. Plan A is terrible.'

He pulled his chair forwards and leaned in to her. 'Ella, this is Plan B. And you have to do it and you have to make it work and you have to keep it secret, too. Those photographs will be printed and everybody must think they're of Rory and his new girlfriend, his make-up artist, how romantic is that? For Anton, there must be no doubt. Two, three dates with Rory, a couple of days, that's all I'm asking you to give me – then you can quietly split up again.'

'Dates?' she said. 'Did you say dates?'

'Okay, a date. Two dates at the most. How else will any-body know that you are a couple?'

'I couldn't go on a date with Rory. We'd have nothing to talk about.'

'You think I care what you say to each other?'

'Can you imagine persuading Rory that this is a good idea?'

'He'd be easier to persuade than you. It doesn't matter to him what people think of him.'

'Rory's a film star. He can afford not to care.' Her stomach lurched at the thought of Sam, and what he would think, suddenly seeing her out on a date with Rory. 'And yes,' she agreed, 'I do care what my friends think of me, what Sam thinks. It matters to me if I'm misunderstood. Sam and I are at the very beginning. Perhaps it's the beginning of nothing, but it could be something and if I do this for you, or for the film, or for Rory, however you spin it to me, I'll never know whether Sam and I might have worked.'

'But of course you will! He's a lovely guy, he'll under-stand. When it's all over, you can even tell him why. Two dates, that's all I need you to agree to. It's not for very long. But yes, while you're together, everybody, and that includes everybody on set, must believe that it's true.'

'But there's not just Sam, there's Poppy too! There is no way I couldn't tell her. It would be even harder than saying nothing to Sam. We trust each other with everything. She would never forgive me.' Ella shook her head. 'Even when I told her the truth, afterwards, she'd be so hurt.'

For a few moments, he let the silence rest.

'I know that there's little point in trying to bribe you, but I might as well try. What if I give you that break you've been waiting for and make you head of hair and make-up on my next film? I know you're good enough. I wouldn't be shooting myself in the foot.'

'Nice try,' she laughed. 'But no thanks. I like having Rosalind beside me. I want her there for at least another film yet. You've got it the wrong way around. If you'd tried taking her *away* from me, that might have worked.'

He smiled. 'Something told me that you'd say that and I respect you for it. I don't think you're right, you are easily good enough, and easily ready, and Rosalind knows it too. If I got you as head of hair and make-up on another film of mine, you'd be doing me the favour.' He sighed. 'But okay, so the bribery won't work . . .' He drummed his fingers on the table in front of him. 'I suppose the only other argument I have is the one that you said yourself, when we were first talking about Rory. The one that says, let's think what is lost if Anton pulls the plug. It's not only the waste of everybody's talent and hard work, all those hours and days and weeks and months we've all spent on *To End All War* so far, but it's also the sad truth that nobody ever gets to hear about Ambrose March.'

'Who would have thought I'd have my own argument turned back on me?'

'The truth is I care passionately about this film and I know you do too.'

'I wouldn't be here if I didn't.'

'No. But perhaps you might be thinking, why? Perhaps you might argue that this is just another film about the First World War and don't we know enough already?'

'And if I did think that, what would you say?'

'That we can never know enough.'

'Sure. I agree with that.'

'You know, it's really hard to argue convincingly when you're making me sound so insincere.'

'Try me.'

'If you'll listen.'

She nodded.

'Okay, when I was sent an early script for *To End All War*, it wasn't even Ambrose himself that made me want to do it, although, of course, I think he's the best kind of hero. It was much more because of when he lived, what he lived through. It's nearly a hundred years since the First World War began, and I worry that our desire to think about it afresh has begun to fade.' He stopped, concerned that she was just waiting for him to get to the end, but Ella was listening. 'And I worry, sometimes, that most of us fall back on these phrases, places, words we know so well. We say it was "The War to End All War" and "We will remember them." We have those terrible words, trenches, bayonets, mustard gas, and we know battle names: Ypres, Passchendaele, Gallipoli. And we have numbers. We say twenty thousand British soldiers died on the first day of the Somme. We know some names: Kitchener, General Haig, Wilfred Owen, Rupert Brooke, and we mean it when we say we must never forget. But as another decade passes, perhaps it becomes harder to remember the details or to learn about those people we didn't know before, wonderful, brave men and women who aren't already part of the folklore, men like Ambrose March, and women like Helen Dove. So, I say we need films like

To End All War to help us remember when we say we must never forget, because through films like ours, we learn, for the first time, about men and women like them.'

'Well said.' She looked away, frowning because he was right and she'd found his words rather moving, and *To End All War* did matter to her, and, truth be told, she could feel herself wanting to help him. 'Emotional blackmail is a very cheap tactic.'

He opened his hands to her across the table. 'Ella. It's all I have left.'

'But, following your argument, what you're really saying, is, if *To End All War* happened to be about a Swedish porn star, rather than a First World War cameraman, you wouldn't be asking me to do this now. And, to that,' she raised her glass, 'I say, bollocks, Hayden. Because we both know that whatever this film was about, you'd care about it just as much. It's your job. It's what we expect of you. It's very lucky for you, that this time your film is about something important, something that has got under my skin.'

He laughed but she didn't laugh with him. She couldn't, thinking about what he'd just asked her to do, trying to weigh up what it would mean to her, to lie. If she could only have told everyone on set what she was doing, she'd have agreed straight away, but she couldn't. She'd have to deceive, deceive Sam, and that would mean saying goodbye to him again, when she'd barely said hello. The thought of having to pretend that she liked Rory instead, the thought of having to allow them all to believe that she and Rory could possibly be a couple, seemed appalling. Her brain raced. Was there any way she could hint to Sam and Poppy that her and Rory's relationship was all a façade and still at the same time do what Hayden was asking of her? She knew she couldn't. If she cared enough about the film, she would have to stick her neck out on the chopping board. She would have to face Sam's hurt, Rosalind's disbelief, Poppy's scorn, and the thought of all those people and what they would think of her made her freeze. And yet . . . and yet she knew what she had to say.

She took a deep breath.

'Yes. I'm not even sure why, but okay, I'm going to say yes,' she went on rapidly, 'presuming that you persuade Rory to go along with it too. And yes, a part of me is doing it because I care about your film, but a bit more of me likes the idea of putting Rory on the spot, of Rory having to pretend he's in love with me. Anton just caught me and Rory in the hay barn – Rory with no clothes on – so perhaps it won't be so hard to convince him we're together. But now, I want to know exactly what you want me to do.'

'Right,' he smiled, full of relief and excitement. 'Thank you, darling, thank you. Okay, what to do. Remember, this is all a little scene for Anton. Anton must see Rory with his lovely new girlfriend ASAP. First I want you papped, possibly the day after tomorrow. I would like you to be photographed coming out of La Sauterelle.'

She winced.

'Trust me.' Hayden grabbed her hand. 'I'm a film director.'

'That is such a terrible line.'

'Sorry. What I mean is that they're lazy. Tell them where to be, and what time, point them towards their subject, give them their story and they'll snap away. So, I want you to walk out of La Sauterelle on your way to the set and I'll tip them off that you're going to be there. And then, when *Hollywood Whisper* prints the photographs of Carey, everybody on set will be talking about you, everybody will believe she is you.'

'I can hardly wait.'

'Then, it might need one more date. And for that, I'm thinking somewhere fun. Somewhere that would make this whole charade just that little bit more bearable for you. Perhaps you and Rory might spend the day together? How about a private jet to St Tropez?'

She laughed. 'You are so obvious, Hayden. You think the words "private" and "jet" will swing it for me?'

'It would work on me.'

A waitress arrived at their table, with plates of chips and bowls of moules marinière.

'Taking a bit of a risk,' she told him, picking one up in her fingers. 'They look so gross, you might have ruined the whole conversation ordering these.'

'But they're a speciality of the house,' he said, and this time gave her a genuine affectionate smile. 'And you're a girl after my own heart. I knew you'd like them.'

She did. She ate, pulling apart the shells and dipping the chips into the broth, hardly believing that she'd been so easily persuaded. And Hayden hardly ate a thing but, throughout the rest of their supper, was unable to keep the smile of relief off his face.

Eleven

'Can I come too?'

'Rory, I'm only going to the end of the trailer.'

He sighed a deep heavy sigh and caught her hand. 'Darling, I'll miss you. Don't be long.'

'Stop it.' She leaned over him and whispered into his ear. 'Sometimes, you're a really bad actor.'

He looked to the left and right of him. Next to him was Liberty, but she had pointedly unravelled her iPod and plugged herself in as soon as she'd sat down. And to his right, two actors who were playing doctors in the field hospital sat waiting for Jemima and Minnie to begin work on them, and were clearly deaf to whatever Rory had to say.

'I need to get used to us.' He put his hands up and pulled her down towards him. 'I can't imagine going out with you. I'm finding it really difficult.'

'So am I,' she whispered back. 'But I don't think you need to pretend here in the trailer. Nobody's taking any notice of you anyway.'

'Thank Christ for that. Lovely Ella,' he said loudly. 'You make the world seem right again.'

She rolled her chair towards him.

'Stop fooling around.'

'But it's funny. I like it. When do I get to kiss you?'

'Never.'

'I'll have to.'

'I hope not.'

'Oh, I hope not too. You are so not my type.' He paused. 'How's Sam?'

'Sam's out of bounds. You don't ask about Sam.'

'So, he's taken the news badly, has he?'

'Sam's fine.'

Rory was so decidedly chirpy, so insensitive, with hardly a care of what he'd led her into, no sign of sympathy for her at all. But she couldn't say so, she knew that she had to keep him sweet if she wanted him to behave.

'Did you see him last night?'

She leaned over him closely, gently touching under his eyes with her fingertip. 'Look up,' she told him, watching to see how much the shadows faded. 'Now, down again.'

He did as he was told and she tipped him back in his chair, dropped two pads soaked in witch hazel over his eyes and hoped that, temporarily at least, she'd been able to switch him off.

'Have you talked to Sam?' he asked again from beneath the pads.

She bent over him again. 'Rory, please shut up. Rosalind's coming.'

'Then tell me quickly. I don't want to get in the way of the two of . . .'

She moved fast, picking up a cloth soaked in Face It, and

laid it over his face. 'Shh,' she told him, feeling him flinch beneath her hands.

Rosalind came over to the other side of Liberty, and if she was surprised to see what Ella was doing to Rory, she gave no sign. Beneath the cold, wet cloth, Rory twitched in silent protest and Ella laid her hands down on top of his face, pressing the cloth tight across his mouth. 'Hush, keep still,' she insisted.

The truth was she hadn't told Sam anything, and even though she suspected it wasn't going to be possible, she was hoping that she never would have to, that somehow, although she and Rory were aiming for everyone to know about them, the news would pass Sam by, until afterwards, when she and Rory were allowed to quietly split up again, when she could, perhaps, tell Sam something of the truth.

Tentatively, she lifted the cloth off Rory's face.

'Wait until he sees our pictures,' Rory said immediately.

'I'll put this back on again if you don't shut up.'

Rosalind gave no sign of hearing her. She was bent over Liberty, carefully applying black liquid eyeliner to the corners of her eyes.

Ella lifted the eye pads off Rory's eyes. 'I hate the thought of what Sam will think,' she told him quietly.

'What about me?' he laughed. Quickly he took hold of her hand. 'What about what the whole world will think of me?'

She let her hand rest in his, knowing that he had taken it for Rosalind's benefit, and although Rosalind had given no sign, Ella knew that she'd noticed.

'Am I so bad for your image?' she said, weakly.

He lifted her hand and held it to his cheek. 'You're a disaster.'

'What do you mean? Too intelligent? Too classy?'

'Too serious and scruffy, and with so little sense of humour.'

'Who'd have anything but a bad sense of humour, having to go out with you?'

She pulled her hand away, unable to bear it any longer, and touched her white skirt.

'And, by the way, you have no idea what you're talking about. I am wearing a stylish combination of Marni and Topshop. And my sandals are from the Smiths, which is a shoe designer so cutting edge none of your usual girlfriends would even have heard of them.'

At that Rosalind looked over to her with a sharp look.

'My girlfriends usually wear less clothes,' Rory whispered.

'Exactly. You're bad for my image, too.'

She heard the trailer door open, then Poppy's voice.

In full view of Poppy and Rosalind, Rory slipped his arm around Ella's shoulders and pulled her down towards him.

'Act,' he insisted, whispering it into her ear. 'Imagine you enjoy being this close to me.'

'But I don't,' she whispered back. 'And now you're making me look very unprofessional and Rosalind will hate it.'

Ella pulled away from him and stood up again. She could hardly bear to look at either of them. She waited for Poppy to walk past her down the trailer to talk to Jemima and then quickly gathered together her brushes to begin work on Rory's face. Seconds later, she felt rather than heard Rosalind come up behind her.

'Ella, I'd like a quick word.'

Ella turned to face her and saw the look of hostility on Rosalind's face. She motioned to Ella to follow her up the trailer, and led the way, past Poppy and up to the back of the trailer, where she turned.

'What about my trailer rules? What's going on?'

'It's nothing. You know how he likes to flirt. It's just Rory.'

It wasn't what she was supposed to say. She'd agreed with Hayden that if anyone asked if they were together, she would not deny it. After all, this was what was supposed to happen, she was supposed to encourage the gossip, let it spread like wildfire, all around the set, ensuring that Anton would eventually hear it too. But here, now, in the face of Rosalind's disdain, she just couldn't see it through.

'Only yesterday I heard about you and Sam. The wardrobe department was practically on fire with the news.'

Ella nodded.

'So, which one is it? Rory or Sam?'

Ella stared back at her, holding her nerve. 'Couldn't it be both of them?'

Rosalind gave a chilly laugh. 'No, Ella. That's certainly not your style.'

'Why do I have to go public on my private life?'

'I'm not asking you to go public. I'm asking that you keep *me* in the loop.'

'Why? Because it's messy? Messy when the make-up artist falls for the leading man?'

'Yes, if she then cries all over the make-up when she finds out he's also shagging the wardrobe assistant. Yes, if it ends up getting in the way of us all doing our job. Yes, if it means Rory thinks he can pull you on top of him in the trailer. Minnie and Jemima don't want to see that, Ella, and neither do I. That's why I have trailer rules.'

'Is he shagging the wardrobe assistant?'

'Rory or Sam?'

'Either of them.'

'How do I know?'

Ella shrugged. 'Because you just said that the wardrobe department is on fire with the news of me and Sam. Or was that me and Rory? I take it you'd prefer me to be with Sam because he's crew, after all, like me, rather than the star of the film. Obviously you wouldn't want me forgetting my place.'

Rosalind frowned. 'You know I've never thought like that.'

'You clearly have! *And* you think I'm the kind of flakey, hopeless girl who'd cry into the make-up! Thank you for that, too, Rosalind.'

'No, I didn't . . .' Again Rosalind seemed wrong-footed by Ella's vocal self-defence. 'When I said that, I wasn't thinking specifically about you.'

'Good. Because as far as I remember, the trailer rules are that our private lives must never spill over into our professional ones. And you can be absolutely certain that mine won't.' She looked back down the trailer, to Rory, waiting for her, tipped back in his chair. 'And, having said that, I think I should get back to work.'

'If you don't want to talk to me, then yes, get back to work. But don't ever think I initiated this conversation because I wanted to interfere, or because I'm your boss, or because

I care about the bloody make-up. It was only because I thought perhaps I could help.'

'I can't talk about Rory.'

Rosalind must have seen some of the anguish in Ella's face.

'Oh Ella, what have you done?' Now Rosalind reached out for her, as if she wanted to hug her, but then thought better of it and stopped awkwardly. 'You always come across so fierce and sure of yourself, and I know you're not and right now, I can sense you're in a pickle and it breaks my heart. I don't want you hurt by either of those two rogues. But if you don't want to talk to me then don't. As you say. It's your private life.'

Ella nodded. 'I think I have everything under control.'

'Thank God for that.'

'I mean it, Rosalind.'

She knew she sounded confident, certain about it, and she wished, desperately, that she didn't have to be that person, that she could confide in Rosalind, because Rosalind would be wise. She would be able to step back and see it from a perspective Ella seemed incapable of finding.

'I'm surprised you call Sam a rogue.'

'Then you must have been working in this trailer with your ears shut,' said Rosalind sharply. 'Half the girls on this set are in love with Sam.'

'Of course. But doesn't that just mean they've got good taste? It doesn't mean he's bad news.'

'I've worked with him on four films, so I know what I'm talking about. Just because he's not noisy about it, doesn't mean he's not a rogue.'

'You mean you've had girls crying into the make-up over *him*?'

Rosalind looked down the trailer. 'I know Jemima did. And I expect Minnie's shed a tear at some point too.'

'How do I not know that?'

'And then, don't let me get started on the wardrobe girls.'

Ella started to laugh. 'Oh, shut up, Rosalind. You're making this up.'

Rosalind raised a well-plucked eyebrow. 'Am I?'

'If you're talking wardrobe girls, I know Sacha's never been involved with Sam.'

'How do you know? Perhaps she's the only one to have kept it quiet.'

'Because she talked to me. Rosalind, I do feel so sorry for Sacha.'

'Oh, so do I. I want to bring her into the trailer for a makeover. Tidy up those eyebrows and brush away that appalling blue eyeshadow. But we can't always do what we want to Ella, can we? Perhaps you should think about that?'

It was pique, that was all, Ella thought, slowly following Rosalind back down the trailer towards Rory. Rosalind was getting her own back because Ella hadn't told her what was going on. So she had to make out that Sam was a notorious womanizer and she, Ella, half asleep not to have noticed, when it was ridiculous to think that Sam was that kind of a guy. And if he was, did she care? No. Because she wasn't falling in love with him, she was having fun, that was all.

Poppy, she noticed, had meanwhile left the trailer again. She forced herself to think nothing of it, even though Poppy would usually have taken the trouble to catch her attention to say goodbye.

She and Hayden had planned . . . No, Hayden had planned, and she had agreed, that the last day filming in the hay barn should pass exactly as normal, and that Rory and Ella would make no obvious gestures of affection towards each other, but would allow anyone who was looking to see they were getting on well. Then, and this was the bit that Ella found difficult to imagine going through with, she had agreed that she would meet Rory that evening at La Sauterelle, walk with him through the town, have dinner in Le Grand Surprise, in full view of anybody who cared to look, and that she would then return to La Sauterelle to stay the night in his suite – which, she had been reassured by Hayden, had two bedrooms. And, at 5.45 a.m. – luckily for Ella, no earlier than she was used to getting up – she was to slip out of the main entrance of La Sauterelle, to find that several photographers were waiting for her . . .

The afternoon's filming passed without incident and, when it was called a wrap, she left the set quickly without seeking out Poppy or talking to anybody. As soon as she could, she returned to her room in Le Sport and took out her washbag, a book and a script she thought Rory might be interested to read, written by a friend of hers. Trying not to think about what lay ahead, she chose clothes for the next day and bundled everything together, into her bag, then threw it over her shoulder and walked with it quickly, out of her hotel, across the town, and up the hill to La Sauterelle.

She had passed the entrance several times before but had never been inside until now. As she cautiously bent beneath a beautiful purple bourgainvillea and walked through the doorway, on into a breathtaking main hall, she wished she'd stopped in Florent to buy something new, or at least stopped at Le Sport to change, if only to spare herself from this walk of shame to the reception desk. Too late. As it was, she was wearing a pale blue, very crumpled linen sundress and silver Birkenstocks that had definitely seen better days.

She walked the length of the limestone floor to the reception desk at the far end of the hall and stopped beside an orange velvet sofa. Sitting behind the desk was a beautiful woman in a pristine white dress, with immaculate glossy black hair tied back in a pony-tail. She had her head bent but at the sound of Ella's footsteps she looked up. Ella felt every one of the five seconds it took for the woman to size her up and decide that Ella was not, and never would be, a guest of La Sauterelle.

'Can I help you?' she asked eventually, with utmost politeness and no hint of a smile.

Ella was aware of the heat in her face, the way her breath was still coming fast after her speedy walk through the town.

'I would like to leave something for Rory Defoe.'

The receptionist immediately looked suspicious and when Ella lifted her overnight bag off her shoulder and laid it on the reception desk between them, suspicion turned into open hostility.

They both stared at it. Ella had to admit that it was a grubby, frayed and rather uninspiring bag. Once white, now grey, printed with large blowsy roses, it was a bag she had always previously thought of with affection. But now it was definitely letting her down.

'You say Rory Defoe wants zees bag?'

'I know he does.'

The woman stretched quickly for her telephone and tapped in some numbers, then, while she was waiting, stared back at Ella with haughty contempt.

'And what is your name?'

'It's Ella Buchan.'

'Ah, Mr Defoe,' said the woman, cradling the phone against her cheek, and unable to stop the little flutter of pleasure as she uttered his name. 'I am so sorry to bother you, but I have Ella Buchan? She has just arrived wiz a bag for you? She – ah . . .' The woman stopped abruptly, blinked with surprise, hesitated for a few moments, then replaced the phone in its cradle.

Oh, Rory, you cut her off, Ella thought gleefully. Thank you.

'Shall I leave it here with you?' said Ella. 'Or would he rather I took it up to him?'

The receptionist looked back at her coldly. 'I will send the bag up to his room.'

'Thank you,' she smiled at her. 'See you later.'

Back at Le Sport, she swung shut her bedroom door, then went to her cupboard and brought out the dress that she'd thought about wearing for dinner with Rory that evening, laying it on the bed in front of her. Was it up to its role? Wearing it, would she look anything like the groomed, glamorous, movie-star's girlfriend she was supposed to be? When Hayden had first asked her to do this, she had to admit that a tiny part of her had liked the idea of living out the fantasy. She'd pictured herself stepping elegantly from a taxi, in huge shades, to a thousand flashing press bulbs. Now, she looked down at the chipped polish on her toenails and knew that she should get to work on herself fast. But the dress, she thought, looking down at it again, might pass the test. It was very pretty, V-necked and knee-length, and made from a printed green and white stretchy silk, with a cobalt blue silk frill around the knee. She'd bought it with Poppy on a rare day off early in filming, when they'd caught the train together and had shopped and sunbathed the day away, down at the coast.

Behind her, there came a knocking on the door.

'Open up!'

It was Poppy. She hadn't seen her since the day before. Heart bumping, she went to the door.

'Hello,' Poppy said, striding in and looking suspiciously around the room.

'Who were you expecting?' asked Ella, laughing uneasily.

Poppy didn't answer. Instead she walked across the tiny bedroom and dropped to her knees in front of the mini-bar. One of the first things they'd done upon taking their rooms was remove all the mini-bar bottles into an empty drawer, and replace them with much larger, much cheaper bottles of their own, from the supermarket in Florent. If the maids had noticed, they hadn't complained.

'Vodka and tonic, please,' said Ella, sitting down on the side of the bed and facing her.

Poppy poured them both a drink, handed one to Ella, then pushed herself back against the wall and stretched out her long bare legs in front of her. Poppy would have been good at being the girlfriend, Ella thought. She'd have taken the role in her stride.

Poppy put her glass on the floor beside her. 'So, how was dinner with Sam?'

'I didn't go out with Sam.'

'No. I know you didn't. Just wondered what you'd say if I asked.'

'Why would I lie?'

'I don't know.'

'I didn't make it out to supper with Sam because Rory and Carey were rehearsing a scene in the hay barn and I had to stay and help them.'

Even as she made the excuse, she knew that she was giving herself away, that by not retaliating to the sharpness of Poppy's tongue, she was admitting she'd something to hide.

'And by the time it had finished, and I'd got back here to change, it was too late,' she shrugged, awkwardly stumbling on. 'I started to get ready and then, I was standing in front of the mirror, and I realized I couldn't face going out again.'

'So you called Sam and told him that, did you?'

'No, I . . .'

'I know you didn't,' Poppy interrupted, before Ella could finish, 'because Sam came around to my room trying to find you. I think he said he waited for half an hour. I don't think he much liked being stood up.'

'I thought Hayden had told him,' said Ella.

'Hayden? Why the hell should Hayden have to tell him?

Look, Ella, if you don't like him, just let him know. Lots of other girls do. Sacha's distraught at the thought of you and Sam together. If you're not interested, let her know.'

'I do like him.'

'Then when are you going to start showing it?'

She saw the hostile look in Poppy's eye and finally felt indignation, defiance, anger even.

'To who? To you or to Sam? Since when did I have to explain anything to you? And how do you know what I've said to Sam?'

Just like Rosalind, Poppy seemed to hesitate under the challenge. 'Fair point,' she conceded. 'But you didn't have Sacha sitting on your bed, talking to you until two in the morning.'

'No. Instead I had Rory, dancing around the hay barn with no clothes on. By the time I'd sorted him out, it was too late to see Sam.'

'No!' Poppy's eyes widened. 'He didn't?'

'Yes, he did. So stop giving me a hard time. Admit it. You're only pissed off because you think I'm keeping a secret from you, because you can't bloody stand it if you think something's going on that you don't know about.'

'Yeah,' Poppy agreed. 'That's true. Because I thought we were friends and friends talk and they trust each other. You should have told me about Rory.'

'I'm telling you now.' Ella downed the last of her drink.

'Then I'm sorry,' Poppy stood up, full of contrition and went over to Ella and took hold of her hand. 'I am. Forgive me for being such a cow?'

Ella smiled uneasily back at her. 'Of course I do.'

'So? What next? Are we going out tonight?'

What could she say to that? She looked into Poppy's bright blue eyes and thought how now was the time to tell her that she was going out on a date with Rory that night, but she couldn't bring herself to do it, not without being able to tell her why.

'Poppy,' she began.

'What?' Poppy brought her knees up to her chin. 'What's the problem?'

'I'm going out tonight.'

Poppy looked over to the bed and her eyes rested on the dress, lying there, waiting to be worn.

'That's good! Why do you say it like that? You're worried that I'm going to give you a hard time about leaving me in L'Oignon all on my own with Sacha? Of course I'm not. Look,' she went on in a rush. 'Don't worry about her. She's got to let him go. Go out, have fun, get to know each other. You never know, you might find you don't like him after all. But . . . I must say,' she paused, looked again at the dress lying on the bed, 'it's saying something if you think Sam's worth the special dress.'

If Poppy saw – and she had to have done – the awkwardness on Ella's face, this time she decided to ignore it. Instead she pushed herself back to her feet and returned to the mini-bar. 'Do you want another drink?'

'No.' Ella shook her head. She couldn't have another drink with Poppy, because she needed to get Poppy out of the room so that she could change and get to La Sauterelle before Rory went AWOL.

'No problem.' Poppy stood up and walked to the door. 'I don't either.'

At the doorway, Poppy hesitated again, looking small and sad. Then she gave Ella a rueful smile. And Ella could feel the distance growing ever wider between them with every second that she didn't reply.

'I'll leave you to it. Give you time to get ready.'

'Thanks.' She couldn't speak, couldn't say any more, because anything she did say would be to mislead Poppy even more, and the thought of that was worse than not saying anything.

Just one date, she told herself, that's all I'm going to do. Let Hayden organize his pressmen, let them have their photographs and then let me be free again. And then I promise you, Poppy. As soon as I can, I will find you and I will explain.

This time, in the right clothes, with freshly painted toes and perfect make-up, Ella walked confidently in to the La Sauterelle reception, and, at the sound of her footsteps, loud on the floor, the same receptionist looked up and this time gave her a warm, welcoming smile. Clearly she didn't know she had ever met Ella before.

'Can I help you?'

Ella walked closer.

'Could you tell Rory Defoe that I'm here? It's Ella Buchan.'

At her name, the receptionist did a satisfying double-take.

'Of course,' she smiled, recovering brilliantly. 'Rory said he was expecting a guest. He asked if you would go straight up to his suite. Would you like someone to show you there?'

'No, thank you.'

'Take the lifts. His suite is on the third floor.'

Ella covered up her surprise. She wasn't supposed to go

up, Rory was supposed to come down, meet her in reception and take her out on the town, but, of course, she should have expected him not to. Because since when did Rory ever follow a script when he didn't want to?

She left reception and went to the lifts, passing floor-to-ceiling windows that looked out on to an incredible view of the valley. The lift arrived and she stepped forward, on to a purple suede carpet, and pressed for the third floor, checking herself in the mirror and tucking a piece of hair behind her ear.

When she knocked, he opened his door straight away, dressed in a white T-shirt and a pair of pyjama bottoms.

He looked her up and down. 'Great dress.' He kissed her briefly on the cheek. 'You look very nice.'

'Thank you. Whereas you look very undressed.'

He stepped back to allow her in. 'I wasn't expecting you so soon. I fell asleep.'

He walked her into the most fabulous, enormous room, with beautiful pale gold furniture, and wide oak floorboards covered in thick, soft aquamarine rugs. The room itself must have been about thirty feet long, with the same floor-to-ceiling glass windows looking out across the valley beyond.

'Wow,' she breathed. She walked straight across towards the windows at the far end of the room. 'I've never seen anything like it. It's beautiful.'

'Isn't it? We know the town is perched on the edge of a cliff, but why is it we never get to see it, apart from when we're standing here?'

She turned back to him. 'Show me the bedrooms.'

'Bedroom?'

'Don't joke about it. I know there are two, Hayden told me. Why don't you show me mine?'

'Bedrooms?' He scratched his head as if he was still confused, then led her away from the windows and towards another door and she walked behind him, taking in his broad shoulders beneath the T-shirt, the lean hips and long legs.

He opened the door to an elegant, light-filled room, painted pale aquamarine, with, on one side, emerald green silk curtains tied back to reveal open French windows, leading out to a balcony beyond, and on the other, a whole wall of built-in cupboards. And, in the middle, a huge super-king-size bed, piled with pillows and crumpled white sheets, pulled back as if he'd just got up.

'I was sleeping,' he reminded her. 'I've had a long tiring day.' He frowned. 'Now, about this other bedroom? You sure Hayden said there were two?'

'Yes,' she said calmly. 'He did.'

'Mmm, I wonder where it could be.'

'Rory, you might think you're being really funny but I don't.'

'Sorry,' Rory grinned.

He led her back into the main room, then turned abruptly left and opened another door. She poked her head through. Inside, the floor, walls and every surface was made of limestone. On the left-hand side, behind a clear glass door, was a little sauna, and on the right a steam room.

'Would you like to have a sauna?' he asked politely.

'No thank you,' she answered, equally politely back. 'I'd like to see my bedroom, please.'

He opened another door. 'The kitchen,' he said, with a flourish.

'Oh! For all that cooking you do! And with a dishwasher too. I imagine you make great use of that.'

'What are you implying, Ella? That I can't cook?'

'Can you?'

'No.'

'So, what else have you here? Surely you've requested something really outrageous? There must be a zoo some- where? Or your own private cinema?'

He laughed. 'Yes, there is.'

'Not a zoo!'

'No, a cinema. Not that I asked for it. I request nothing but Jack Daniel's in the fridge. But there is a cinema, through here.' He led her on, out of the main room and into a hallway, and opened yet another door and flicked on a light switch.

She leaned in, and there it was, a tiny private cinema, with a three-quarter size screen and proper curtains, and a row of five squashy leather seats.

'Do you get popcorn?'

'If I want it.'

She smiled back at him, stepping back into the main room. 'What a life.'

'Watch a film if you want.'

She shook her head. 'We're going out, remember.'

They walked back into the main room.

'Can I get you a drink?'

She folded her arms, not saying anything, and waited.

'Ah, yes,' Rory said eventually. 'That other bedroom.'

There was one other door, and now he walked over to it and opened it, stepping back for her to see.

She walked in. It was another lovely room, decorated the same, but smaller than Rory's. In the centre was another huge bed, her overnight bag waiting for her on the counterpane, and beyond the bed there were more long windows, although no balcony for her. Through a doorway in the far corner she could see another bathroom too.

'Perfect.'

'This must be the room Hayden meant. Of course, I've been using it for when there are too many girls to fit into my bed. But don't worry, tonight it's all yours. Although apparently the bed's not quite as comfortable as mine.' He looked at her. 'Sorry. Must be something about that dress, makes me forget who you are.'

She took a step closer to him. 'It's Ella, remember. Ella the nanny-goat. You don't have to flirt with me.'

He laughed. 'I know, I know. And I'm sure Sam the billy-goat is probably stamping jealously around outside.'

She turned away from him, not wanting him to see her smile, because this was the Rory she'd heard about, now running true to form. Here was the incorrigible flirt who couldn't help himself reacting to the fact he'd got a girl, in a pretty, skimpy dress, standing next to a big, soft bed.

'You'd better get dressed or perhaps Le Grand Surprise will turn us away.'

'Ella, I don't want to go out. I know Hayden had it all planned but I've cancelled the booking.' He saw her face and in response flopped down head first on to the bed, her bed. 'Don't make me,' he said with a muffled voice, his face in the pillow, her pillow. 'I can't face going out. I thought we'd stay in and watch DVDs together. Don't you think that would be more fun?'

She stepped forwards and pulled her bag out from under him.

'But it's not about fun. I'm only here so that people can watch us going out.'

'I know. I know.' He didn't turn over. 'But I'm tired.'

She walked towards him, bent down and pinched the back of his bare calf.

'Don't you dare say we're not going out.'

'Ow!'

He turned over, rubbing his leg. 'You really want to?'

'Yes,' she said moving away from him. 'I've made too much effort. I've got dressed, in my most special dress.'

'Which I like, by the way. Did I say that?'

'But it isn't for you. It's for the paparazzi that Hayden will have organized for us. And now you say you don't want to go out.'

'There won't be paparazzi tonight. They'll be there in the morning, watching to see who's spent the night with me. They're there every morning, making notes.'

'You mean they haven't lost count yet?'

'Very funny, Ella.'

'I still think we should go out.'

'Why?' said Rory. 'Why's it so awful to stay here with me? With room service, caviar, champagne, lobster, whatever you want. What else would you be doing? Sitting in that smelly little bar drinking cheap wine with Poppy?'

'It's not smelly. Not that you'd know, never having put your toe through the door.'

He laughed. 'You think I'd walk in there, to that bunch? They're terrifying.'

'Come on.' She held out her hand. 'Get up and get dressed. We must do this properly. Rory, it's the only reason I'm here.'

'Stop telling me that! Why do you have to say it, over and over again?'

'I'm sorry.'

'Hayden should pay you overtime. I know that you'd really prefer to be somewhere else, with someone else. That someone being Sam. Jesus, you don't have to keep reminding me.'

'If I was with Sam at least it wouldn't be a sham.'

'And I'm sorry I've got in the way. I'm sure you and Sam are at the start of a fine romance.'

'Hey!' She touched his arm. 'It's okay. If we are, it's surely not going to hurt being held up for a few days.'

'But if I hadn't sent Hayden into such a spin, it wouldn't have to. God, it's such a ridiculous idea anyway, having you here. Why did I listen to him? Anton's not half as dangerous as Hayden makes out.'

'Perhaps he's even worse.'

Abruptly he climbed back off the bed. 'I never thought you were serious about Sam. Why did I not realize? Christ, now I don't want to do this either. Ella, leave it. Neither of us need this. It's a ridiculous, massive over-reaction. Of course, it must be very inconvenient for you, having to come here tonight to spend the evening, certainly no fun at all,

to be trapped in a hotel room with me. Go home. We'll tell
Hayden it was never going to work.'

'I can't do that.'

'Seriously, you can.'

'Then what does Hayden do instead? Those photographs
in *Hollywood Whisper* have to be explained somehow. No,
Rory. I've said I'll do this and so I will. I don't mind staying
the night. Sure, let's get room service and stay in. I seriously
don't care.'

Now he couldn't look at her. 'I still think you should go,'
he said sulkily.

'Okay, I'll go,' she said sweetly back, changing tack and
wrong-footing him. She looked around the room. 'Where
did I leave my bag?'

'No. Wait, you're right. You can't. Hayden has got press
lined up to take photographs of you, tomorrow morning
at five forty. He has not got anyone lined up to snap us
tonight. Dinner tonight was an extra, the important part is
tomorrow. So I do think you should stay. We don't have to
talk. We could watch a film in the cinema. Do our stuff for
him tomorrow and then let's call it a day.'

She looked seriously back at him. 'Depends what the
film is.'

'Whatever you want to watch.'

'No subtitles. No blood and gore. Something funny?'

He shook his head. 'I'm not feeling like funny.'

'What then? Come on – I'm doing what you wanted, I'm
making the best of being trapped in this hotel room with
you.' She looked around the room again. 'It's not so bad.
I've stayed in worse rooms.'

And the truth was, the part of her that was a coward couldn't help but be relieved at the thought of staying in. Because then, nobody would see them together, and she wouldn't have to explain what she'd been doing, for at least another day.

'Fine. Ring room service and order whatever film you want. They brag about their enormous library, so I'm sure they'll find us something.'

He left her, moving away towards his bedroom.

'Hey!' she called after him. 'How about a Rory Defoe film? I've heard he's quite good. I never saw that one you made last year, *A Little Vendetta*.'

He walked on into his bedroom. 'How vain you must think I am.'

'Vain?' she called back. 'No. Everyone else says you're vain, I just think you're incredibly bad-tempered.'

He reappeared in his doorway. 'And the most selfish man alive? Didn't you say that, once?'

'Did I? Oh, yes, you're definitely that too.'

He held on to the door. 'If I'm a little downbeat, it's only because I don't like knowing you'd rather be somewhere else.'

'Deal with it,' Ella insisted. 'It's the price you have to pay for fooling around with Carey. Oh, come on. It's only one night. And you said it yourself. Let's stay in and have fun and make the most of it.'

'And by the way, I hate watching my own films.'

'So, we'll watch something else!'

He turned back into his bedroom, and she went over to the window again and looked out across the sunset. Behind her, she heard Rory pick up the telephone in his bedroom and as he talked, she looked on, at the sun slowly falling behind the hills, and felt small, and uncertain, and overwhelmed, standing there, in that strange, wonderful room.

When he returned, she saw he'd swapped the pyjama bottoms for a pair of jeans.

She was sitting on a long emerald green sofa, in her beautiful silk dress, with her feet up and her bag on her lap. She looked up and saw him standing there, arms folded.

'I brought you something to read,' she said.

She rummaged in her bag and brought it out and handed it to him.

'Oh, fantastic! A script. Thank you.'

'There's no need to say it like that. A friend of mine wrote it.'

'Even better.' He clutched his head in his hands. 'Ella, don't do this to me. Please not a script.'

'Why not?' She took it back. 'It might be good.'

'Do you have you any idea how many scripts people ask me to read?'

'*People*? How dare you think of me as *people*?'

'I don't want to look at a script, even yours.'

'Okay, not now. But when you're in the mood, it's good. I think you'd like it.'

'Then leave it with me.'

He left her and went to the kitchen.

'What do you want to drink?'

'Vodka and tonic.'

He came back with a glass for her and an empty glass for him with a bottle of Jack Daniel's under his arm. He passed her her drink, then sat down opposite her on a second sofa, and she watched him pour until his glass was almost full.

'Why don't I tell you about the script?' she tried again. 'Just to make conversation?'

'No thanks.' He took a long swallow.

She took a sip of her vodka and tonic. Of course he would be bombarded by scripts, day and night. Even in the make-up trailer, script anecdotes were commonplace, actors telling how they received them from surgeons as they lay on operating tables, from vicars on wedding days, from teachers at parent-staff meetings; but even so, she wanted him to acknowledge that it was different when *she* gave him a script because she was on the inside, she knew what she was talking about. And what's more, she knew this one was good.

Eventually, after a long silence, he put his glass back on the table.

'Okay. What's it called?'

'*On the Out.* It's a phrase. It means when someone's just been released from prison.'

'Good title. Where's it set?'

She took a deep breath.

'A tower block in Hounslow.'

He bit his lip, then tried to cover up the fact that he was smiling by bending down to refill his glass.

'And who did you say wrote it? A friend of yours?'

'Yes. A friend out of drama school. It's her first script.'

'Even better.'

'It's very good.'

'So you say. And how charming that it's Hounslow. I've just been offered a movie in Brazil. I wonder which one I should do.'

'The one in Hounslow. Do something more challenging for a change.'

'You don't think *To End All War* is challenging?'

'Of course I do, but this couldn't be more different, and you haven't even looked at it.'

'I don't need to because I know I'm never going to spend a day of my life in Hounslow.'

She didn't let go. 'I think it might show you off to a different audience.'

'Ella?' He said, laughing at her. 'Stick to the make-up.'

She had to look down at her hands so he couldn't see the hurt in her face, but in any case, he wouldn't have noticed. He went over to the remote and flicked on the television, dismissing her, then sat down on the long sofa and put his feet up.

She got up and picked up the remote and turned the television off again.

'That was very mean,' she said, standing over him. 'Okay, maybe it was ridiculous to think you'd be interested in this script, but you didn't have to be so rude.'

'You know what? I've got a script that I'd like you to read, too.'

'You honestly think I want to? After what you've just said?'

She sat down again, slipped off her sandals and brought her legs up on to the sofa opposite him, crossing her bare feet elegantly at the ankles, making sure that her dress was smoothed down below her knees. Then she rummaged back in her bag and defiantly brought out her knitting. Clearly, it was the only way to get through the evening.

'Excuse me,' said Rory, looking at her in astonishment. 'But what do you think you are doing?'

'I don't want to talk to you.'

There was a gentle knock on the door and Rory got up, walked over, and opened it. Four men and two trolleys trundled into the room.

Keeping her place on her needles, Ella watched silently from the sofa as a table was rolled into the centre of the room and plates of lobsters and prawns, tiny dishes of new potatoes, green salads, asparagus tips with pots of foaming hollandaise sauce, great fat cheeses, grapes, a tower of meringues and an enormous chocolate cake, were all laid out before them.

'Thank you,' she said to them all, from her place on the sofa.

Silently the four men bowed as one and left the room.

When they had gone, Rory returned and sat down beside her.

'Look. If I said I'd look at your script, we both know I'd be doing it just to shut you up. And I vowed, years ago, that I was not going to do that any more. Life's too short to read scripts I know I'll never want, and I wouldn't insult your intelligence by pretending that I might. Whereas my script has got legs. I know who I want to direct it and I know who I want to star in it.' He rose to his feet, went over to the table of food, picked up a plate and placed on it prawns, hollandaise, some asparagus and three meringues. 'But you're not listening, are you?'

She ignored him and was able to knit several more rows before he spoke again.

'I've been mentoring two teenagers in a youth drama club in Tower Hamlets. I saw them in a play there. This could be their big break.'

She looked up. 'Tower Hamlets? Is that supposed to impress me? Did you insist on bodyguards?'

'So, you think I deserve that, do you? All because I know I don't want to do a script in Hounslow? Jesus, stop sulking, Ella.'

She didn't answer. He sat beside her for a few minutes, and then, when he had finished his food, and she still hadn't got to her feet to get hers, he sighed, took his empty plate back to the table of food, then came and stood over her.

'Okay. You're not sulking and I'm sorry I didn't say it better – about your script.' He waited but she didn't look up.

'Look,' he said. 'I've apologized, and if you're still not going to talk to me, I'm going to bed. Make sure you get an alarm call, yes? You really don't want to miss the press. Not after everything you've put yourself through.'

She didn't respond and a moment later he left the room, walking away and slamming the door to his bedroom.

After he had gone, she got to her feet, prepared herself a plate of food and sat alone, eating it, her resentment of him not dying down, angry with the part she was playing, fidgety at the thought of having to stay there all night, and, overwhelmingly, full of regret at the conversation she'd been forced to have with Poppy.

When she had finished her food, she poured herself a cup

of coffee and a glass of wine and took them to the window, looking out across the now dark sky.

Then, when he still hadn't come out of his bedroom, she took her bag to her own room, shut the door, pulled off her dress and put on a pair of long-sleeved, long-legged pyjamas. It was 9.15. She set her alarm for a quarter to five, washed, and climbed into the soft white bed.

But she hardly slept a wink, jolted throughout the night by strange disturbed dreams, and, at a quarter to five, she was awake to turn off her alarm before it rang.

She switched on her light and dressed again quickly, folding her dress into her bag, and putting on a green silk scoop-necked T-shirt and a short red denim skirt. She brushed her hair and her teeth, then quickly put on make-up, more than usual, enough for the cameras that she dreaded would be waiting for her.

If she'd been on speaking terms with Rory, perhaps she'd have woken him, because now that the moment was upon her, the thought of venturing outside, to a crowd of jostling press, made her terribly nervous. And how much better it would have been, for the sake of their story, to have him with her as she left the hotel. But Hayden, the director of the scene, had insisted that the press would be waiting for her, that she was the story they wanted, and that, this time, she'd look better alone . . .

She finished packing her bag and silently left his suite, took the lift down to the ground floor and re-emerged in the grand main hall.

A security guard gave her a smiling, knowing grin that made her feel smaller than she'd ever felt in her life before.

She passed him and made her way towards the reception desk, grateful to see that it was not the same woman who had greeted her the day before. She passed a man, sitting behind the desk, who didn't raise a glance as she passed him by, and then she walked out, through the open glass doors and into the early morning sunshine.

At the point where the hotel grounds met the street, she could see no one. She walked slowly on, wondered if they were hidden, ready to leap out at her from behind some wall or doorway, with provocative calls and flash-bulbs popping, but there was nobody there. She went on, out on to the road, the deserted, empty road, looked right and left, but there was definitely nobody to see her leave.

She left the street that led to La Sauterelle and began to make her way through the town towards the bridge, then on up the lane, back towards the film set, and gradually as she walked, breathing in the early morning air, feeling the first rays of the sun shine down on her face, she had to admit that actually, even though the whole evening had been a complete waste of time, all she felt was relief. She realized she liked being anonymous, liked knowing that nobody would judge her after all, would pick apart her clothes, her face, her friends, and, more to the point, nobody would know she'd spent the night in Rory's room either. And perhaps, with another day to think about it, Hayden might change his mind, and perhaps the charade could be over.

Twelve

When Ella let herself into the trailer that morning, she immediately picked up that they all knew where she'd spent the night.

Liberty was already sitting in her chair, Rosalind on her left-hand side, darkening Liberty's eyebrows with a pencil, Liberty's personal assistant sitting on her right, manicuring her nails. When Ella walked in, with a smile and her usual hello, Rosalind gave her a cold stare; meanwhile, Minnie and Jemima both looked as though they might burst for not speaking. By contrast, Liberty kept her eyes shut and did not react at all.

She guessed that Rosalind would soon find her chance, but, after a few more awkward minutes, it was Liberty who spoke first.

'I've just had a text from Rory,' she announced to the trailer at large, laying her extraordinarily expensive limited-edition mobile phone on the table in front her. 'It says: *Tell Ella she left her phone in my room.*' She looked over to Ella. 'Darling, what a good idea! Everyone knows the best way of getting back inside a bedroom is to make sure you leave something behind.'

Rosalind frowned. 'I imagine she'll be welcome back to Rory's room any time. Isn't that right, Ella?'

'I'm sure he'll bring the phone in with him.'

Ella could feel the blush creeping up her face. She went over to her chair and her stretch of workspace and started to bring out all the things that she'd need to make Rory up that morning. Then, when she had finished, she walked the length of the trailer, past Minnie and Jemima, to the fridge to find a can of Coke. What was she supposed to do? Laugh it off? Giggle stupidly? Admit to them all it was true?

Seeing where she was going, Rosalind left Liberty's side and came striding down the trailer to meet her at the fridge.

'Now what's going on?' Rosalind demanded in a hoarse whisper. 'I thought you told me I didn't have to worry? I thought you'd promised to keep me in the loop?'

Ella pushed herself back to her feet. 'Why is it such a big deal?'

'Trailer rules,' Rosalind hissed. 'You keep me in the loop.'

'But I thought we'd talked about this. I won't be crying into the make-up. And, for the record, I won't be sitting on his lap either. We won't behave any differently to how we've always done.'

'So it's true? You did spend the night in his room?'

'Yes, I did.'

'Why, Ella? Why couldn't you have told me it was on the cards? You must have known it when we talked before.'

'It took me by surprise.'

'Are you serious about him?'

'Maybe.'

'You're sleeping with him?'

'That's none of your business.'

'And what about Sam?'

'For God's sake, why is everybody so obsessed about me and Sam? Nothing ever began between me and him.'

'Ah, but I don't think Sam realizes that. Sam doesn't know anything about this stupid fling of yours.'

'He doesn't?' said Ella, unable to hide the relief in her voice.

'But you had better tell him this morning, or I will. Because gossip like this will be all around the set before you even step outside.'

Ella looked up. 'I'll tell him,' she said, in a low voice. 'Please don't do it for me.'

Rosalind looked back at her, her face full of confusion. This was Ella, her protégée, her apprentice. Ella whom she thought she'd known so well.

'This is so out of character,' Rosalind sighed at last. 'I can't help thinking something's wrong.'

Ella sidestepped her words. 'I will talk to Sam as soon as I can. It's still only seven thirty. It's not as if I've left it all day.'

'You do realize that Rory is not the man for you?'

'How do you know? You've hardly even met him. All the times he's been in the trailer, you've been out with Liberty. And in any case, you're telling me, in all the times you've worked on set, that you've never got involved with one of your actors? I don't believe it. I know you have, hundreds of times.'

'If I did I was always discreet and I never hurt anyone.'

'And so will I be! And neither have I.'

'So you keep telling me.'

'Who told you, Rosalind? It only began last night. How come everybody knows so soon?'

'Hayden told me.' Rosalind's eye travelled back down the trailer, taking in Minnie and Jemima studiously working on their actors, and then her eye fell on Liberty's assistant, still working busily on Liberty's nails. 'Damn that girl,' she breathed, instantly distracted. 'If she dares do a French manicure, I'll strangle them both, I really will.' She looked back to Ella. 'Liberty's meant to be a VAD nurse, for God's sake. Exactly when does she suppose she'd have time for a manicure? But will Liberty listen to me?' She shook her head. 'I told Anna to make them very short and to use no polish at all. She'd better have listened.'

Was this Rosalind's way of calling a truce between them? Ella wasn't sure.

'Rory will be arriving any minute,' Ella told her. 'And you'll see, when he does, that there's really no need to worry about him and me.'

'Good. It had better be so.' Again, Rosalind's eagle eye moved along the trailer, from Minnie, to Jemima, to Liberty's PA. 'I hardly need tell you that we have the most horrendous long day – and night – filming in the field hospital ahead of us. Watch out for Liberty, because clearly she's spitting with jealousy. She won't be wanting to make life easy for you.' She gave Ella a narrow-eyed stare. 'You do know you might have quite a difficult time on set today? And that you'll deserve every bit of it?'

'It'll be worth it.'

'Will it just? You surprise me. Okay. Let's go. Minnie!' Rosalind suddenly called down the trailer. 'Less of that matt-block. And I thought we'd agreed Porcelain not Vanilla.'

Ella knew that everyone in the trailer was waiting to see how Rory would greet her, but when, five minutes later, he opened the trailer door and walked in, he cast barely a glance in her direction. Instead he bent first to Liberty and kissed her smooth white cheek.

'Morning, baby. Here's to our first day.'

As he'd barely spoken to her since their argument over *Hollywood Whisper*, Liberty understandably looked first surprised, and then delighted.

'Morning you too.' She grabbed his fingers. 'Good to see you too.'

He gently disentangled himself and settled down next to her in his chair. Poppy came to stand behind him, Rosalind to her left. Ella caught his eye in the glass in front of them.

'Morning, Rory,' she said brightly.

He stared back at her without a hint of recognition. 'Do I know you?'

Beside him Liberty giggled delightedly.

'Do I sense a lover's tiff *already*?'

Rory turned to Liberty, feigning surprise. 'What could you possibly mean?'

'Everybody knows about you two, Rory. You don't have to pretend it's not true.'

'Knows what?' asked Rory innocently.

'You and Ella,' said Liberty, leaning in to him and whispering, 'spending the night together. I understand. I've done it myself. Take your pleasure where you can.'

'Me and Ella?' said Rory, loudly and incredulously. 'You must be joking. I wouldn't go near her. She's a *civilian*.'

'Oh wow! Aren't you so mean!' said Liberty, laughing with glee. 'What do you make of that, Ella?'

'He's trying to protect me, that's all.' Ella smoothed back Rory's hair and kissed his forehead gently. 'Very sweet, my darling, but quite unnecessary. I want everyone to know about us.'

At that Rory slipped his hand behind her neck and pulled her closer, until her mouth met his.

'Very good,' he whispered, his lips brushing against hers, his breath sweet against her face.

'Urgh,' said Liberty, turning away in obvious disappointment. 'Don't do that beside me, ever again, or I shall have to complain.'

Ella stood upright again, cheeks aflame, resisting the urge to touch her mouth with her hand. Beside her she could feel Rosalind's burning stare.

'You see, she's irresistible,' said Rory, catching Rosalind's eye in the mirror. 'I'm sorry. I couldn't resist.'

That morning's shooting would be the first time that Rory would act on the hospital set, and the schedule for the day was the longest Ella had ever worked, taking in almost eight hours of filming throughout the day, before a break between four and seven p.m. followed by a long night shoot beginning at seven and finishing some time after midnight. In return, the whole of the next day was a rest day.

Field Hospital 29, the backdrop to so much of Ambrose's most powerful footage, had once been a large and impressive church. In reality it was no longer standing – as depicted in *To End All War*, it had taken a direct hit in 1916 and afterwards was never rebuilt – but it had been re-created for the film by the set designers, within a mile of its original location, and with absolute attention to detail.

Now, as with the hay barn set, it looked completely authentic, even though much of the weathered stonework was a mixture of polyurethane and plastic. Set into its walls was a specially commissioned stained-glass window that cast a beautiful, iridescent light upon the scenes of continual devastation that unfolded below it. In a final spectacular scene, the church would be shelled and, loud above the noise of gunfire, the window would explode, raining its shards of coloured glass down upon the hapless doctors and nurses and wounded soldiers below.

On his first day, Ambrose March had arrived at the field hospital expecting to stay for just one night. He had come to find Hawkins, having heard about his injury on the day he'd filmed the motorbike despatch rider, but, once there, literally within minutes of arriving, he had witnessed enough bravery, stoicism, heartbreak, overwhelming waste of life, to know that through this little hospital he could say everything he wanted to about the war.

When they were ready, they left the make-up trailer as one and walked together, in the sunshine, down towards the set for the first time. Liberty and Rory were in front, Rosalind and Ella following behind them with Minnie and Jemima, and as they reached the brow of the hill and could look down, and see it all – the church, with its hospital tents attached to one side, the mass of cameras, arc lights and cranes, the crew all spread out before them, all of them ready to begin their work – Ella felt tears burn in her eyes. She blinked them hurriedly away, not wanting anyone to see how moved she was, least of all Liberty, who was strolling down the hillside in her beautiful nurse's uniform, with its bold, bright red cross, a runner scampering along beside her, shading her with a huge white parasol.

Ella had seen Liberty in costume before, so she should have been prepared for how convincing the other nurses would look, but now, seeing them all milling around on set, a shelled and blasted but still beautiful church, five VADs, six junior nurses, two sisters and two matrons, waiting to begin filming, she caught her breath. They were moving delicately in their identical, immaculate ankle-length grey dresses, tightly belted, with long white aprons, also marked with the red cross on them, their starched white collars, cuffs, caps, their black shoes and stockings. Spread among them were twenty or thirty soldiers in their khaki battle-dress, some of them standing, others sitting in chairs, their prosthetic wounds preventing them from moving about even though filming had not yet begun, and again she felt tears come to her eyes. Because, despite the paraphernalia of the cameras and arc lights and snaking cables and the crew, dressed in T-shirts and shorts, still the set looked like a real hospital about to be overwhelmed with fresh casualties in a real war.

Following the script, Ambrose would enter through the main church door and would be taken on a tour by one of the doctors, Dr Kinsman, an ally of Ambrose's, keen that he should see and record everything. Within half an hour of his arrival would come the sound of the ambulances, bells ringing out the warning of their approach, and the hospital would go from a scene of order and organization to one temporarily overwhelmed with wounded and dying men.

From the script, Ella knew that Ambrose had had no idea of what he was about to encounter: the air suddenly full of bells, shouts of warning, calls and cries, as ever more wounded men were brought in, some walking, others waiting outside on stretchers, lying in their stiff uniforms, caked with mud and dried blood, their great boots on their feet, the inside of the hospital filling with steam and sweat.

Inside, he would encounter – and film – men. Men everywhere, lying on the floor on stretchers. Men hurriedly stepped over by nurses, running to get to the open doors and to the ambulances, and to yet more men. Men who could not breathe lying down, propped up on their stretchers against the church walls, trying to stay alive.

Because there were so many extras and other actors involved in the scenes, an air-conditioned marquee had been set up on the edge of the set for hair and make-up. Rosalind, in charge of Liberty, had been using it every day, and now she took Ella across to it for the first time.

Inside were the usual bright lights and smell of hairspray, long lines of tables and chairs and twenty or so extras being worked on by a posse of make-up artists, most of whom Ella knew by sight though not all by name. As the four of them approached and Liberty moved, like a graceful benevolent queen, to her appointed table and chair, sat down, then beckoned Rory to sit beside her, not one of the other artists stopped what they were doing. Yet Ella felt unbearably self-conscious, as if every single one of them was staring at her, wondering if what they'd heard about the star and his make-up artist was true.

As she had already made him up in the trailer, Rory needed only the barest of touches now, and so, after she had stiffened his moustache, added a little more pomade to his hair and another swirl of setting powder to his face, she pulled up a chair, with her back to Liberty, and sat down beside him.

'Let me check your moustache again,' she told him, under her breath.

He touched it. 'Why?'

'Something to do. Otherwise people might talk.' She picked up a pair of scissors off the table in front of her. 'Oh, yes, I forgot. They're supposed to talk, aren't they?'

'What's up, little Umbrella?'

'I don't understand why you're behaving like this. Are we in it together or not? If it's just some stupid idea of Hayden's that we can forget about again, tell me. Because nobody looking at us now would ever think we were close.'

He yawned. 'I'm surprised you can face the thought of any more of me.'

'I don't feel any different to how I felt last night. If we're going to fake it, let's do it well.' She carefully clipped a millimetre off one side of his moustache. 'When I left this morning, there was nobody there to see me. I called Hayden and he couldn't believe it. I think he's worried I'm just not interesting enough.'

'We'll have to do more to attract their attention.'

'I know,' she whispered urgently. 'But that's what I'm

saying. Nobody believes you. I suppose – what am I saying? – I suppose you're going to have to be more affectionate.'

'I couldn't be sure what your reaction would be but it wouldn't be so hard.'

He took her hand and studied her long pale fingers and short pink nails, then brought her hand up to his cheek and held it there.

'Watch your face,' she cried, unable to stop herself.

'Five minutes,' called a runner from the entrance to the marquee.

Ella stepped back to let Rory stand up and immediately Liberty reached across the space and leaned in towards him.

'Baby, I think you should escort me on set.'

And instead of turning to Ella, taking Ella's arm, leaving the marquee at Ella's side, showing the world it was Ella he wanted to be with, Rory clearly agreed. He put out his hand to Liberty and helped her to her feet; and then, without even acknowledging Ella again, led Liberty out of the marquee and on to the set, to Hayden's applause.

Left on her own, feeling very alone, Ella went to the doorway and watched the camera operators, lighting technicians, set designers, all the crew moving swiftly about the set, as they made their final preparations before shooting began. Then the same runner came past her a second time and shouted a two-minute call and she knew she should go to Rory and check him one final time.

She was standing on the edge of the set when she saw that Poppy was just a few feet away, speaking on her mobile. As she caught Ella's eye, Poppy clapped shut the phone and stared back at her.

Ella couldn't bear it. She walked forward to meet her and reached to touch her arm.

'Hi,' she said awkwardly.

'Hi,' Poppy said stonily.

'It's all looking wonderful, isn't it?'

'If you say so.'

'Please, Poppy. Don't be angry with me.'

'I'm not. I'm angry with me.'

'What do you mean?'

'For being taken in, for thinking that we were such good friends I could trust you with anything in the world and you'd do the same for me.'

Ella looked back at her, her eyes suddenly filling with tears. 'You can and I do feel that. I know I can trust you.'

'Clearly not true.'

'I made a promise not to tell you about Rory.'

'But you shouldn't have done,' Poppy snapped back in disgust. 'Everybody else knows about you and him, so why couldn't I? Because Rory likes to hold on to his private life and you thought I'd spill the beans? Is that it? You didn't think you could trust me? You don't think I'm discreet? No.' She stopped. 'Forgive me. I don't want to hear the bullshit answer.'

'You know what?' said Ella. 'I got you wrong too. I thought you were the sort of friend who wouldn't judge me, who'd give me the benefit of the doubt. Anything you throw at me, about leaping to conclusions, applies to you too. But, like you said, let's not waste our time saying so. I'm not going to stand here, begging for your forgiveness, because you're not worth it either.'

'He's such trouble,' she heard Poppy say quietly. 'Can't you see he's causing this?'

Ella walked away from her, turned her back to the church and set off towards the hill that led to the unit base. She'd gone less than fifty yards when from the corner of her eye she saw that the next one to confront her would be Sacha, now carving a determined route towards her.

'Poppy and I, Poppy and I,' Sacha started loudly, standing square on, and folding her arms across her chest, 'we simply cannot believe it's true. I know you don't like telling *me* anything about your love life, but I thought Poppy was your friend.'

'I don't want to talk about it, Sacha.'

'Now or never? Do you mean if I catch you later, you might tell me then?'

'There's nothing to say.'

'I've been talking to Sam.'

Sam. At his name Ella stopped.

'Look at your face. If you still care, what are you doing with Rory?'

'Perhaps it's not so bad for you if I'm with Rory?'

'Oh absolutely. I hope you are. And if you are, could you do me a favour and go and find Sam? He'd like to know too. Perhaps you could tell him?'

'All Sam and I ever had was a plan for a date that didn't happen. I've not misled him. But you're right. Enough of this. I have to go and see him.'

She looked back down to the set and saw him immediately, his arm around his camera, talking to Hayden.

'*Is* it true, Ella?' Sacha asked quietly. 'About you and Rory?'

'Yes,' Ella said firmly.

'So when we talked, that day after you made him up for the first time, had it already begun?'

'Why does it matter?'

'Because . . . Maybe you'll think I'm an idiot for caring, but . . .' She rubbed her hand against her hot pink cheeks. 'I'd like to think you know you can trust me. I'm not sure you do.'

How kind and sweet she was, Ella thought, and tears burnt in her eyes. Seeing them, Sacha stepped tentatively forward, then pulled her into a hug.

'Don't cry about Rory or Sam. Neither of them deserves it.'

'It's true.'

'But be careful with Rory, please. You know when we joked about him? We weren't really joking, were we? There was a reason for what we said. Don't let him hurt you, Ella.'

She saw Sam and Hayden pause in their conversation and both look up the hill towards her and Sacha. Sacha followed her gaze, involuntarily softening at the sight of Sam.

'Go and tell him. It's a good time, you've got twenty minutes before filming re-starts.' Sacha stepped back, inviting her forward. 'Leave him free for me,' she encouraged. 'Tell him it's over – go on.'

Ella could feel Sacha's eyes willing her forward as she walked towards Sam and Hayden. As she drew close Hayden stepped back and let Sam come forward alone.

'Walk with me,' Sam said, the man of few words.

'Five minutes, Sam,' called Hayden. 'Ella, I want to see you in the next break. Meet me in my trailer.'

Sam looked down at her.

'What's up with him? What have you done? Everybody is asking the same question, Ella. What have you done?'

She walked away with him, up the hill, waiting until they were out of earshot of everybody.

'Should I be pleased for you?' Sam asked, still sounding curious rather than hurt. 'Is this the start of the great film-set love affair?'

She looked down at the dusty ground beneath her feet, feeling the heat of the sun on the back of her head. Sacha's presence silently wishing her on, willing her to say yes.

'No.'

'You didn't spend last night in his hotel room?'

'How does everybody know about that? Yes, I did, but not in his bed.'

'I'm confused. Why would you do that?'

'He had a script he wanted me to see.'

'Of course! That explains!'

'It's true.' She looked up at him. 'Please.'

'Okay.' He stopped, caught her by the shoulders and turned her towards him. 'I accept you went to his room to read a script and ended up staying the night. I believe nothing happened while you were there. But I do object to this awful sense of being rushed along, of being forced to grab you and say things now, way, way before their time, things that might freak you out, that I might want to say weeks from now, when we'd had a chance to get to know each other. But I know that if I don't say them now, I probably won't get another chance.'

'Don't say them!' She waited, feeling the heat in her face, her head aching, thinking again I don't want to hear, and then his big hands closed around her shoulders and held her. She had her back to the cast and the set below, but she knew how it must look. Although they wouldn't be able to hear what Sam was saying, still they'd know from their body language what kind of a conversation it was.

'Let me go,' she whispered.

'Look at me.'

She looked.

'Stop wondering what people think.'

He bent his head and kissed her.

At first it was such a shock that she froze in his arms, but then, as his arms slipped across her back, she dropped her head into the crook of his shoulder and let his big warm body bring her close.

'Ella?' came Rory's voice, out of breath, from very close behind. 'Let him go. We're about to start shooting. You need to come down. My make-up is a complete mess.'

She broke free of Sam and turned to face him.

'And for the record,' Rory went on. 'That kiss was not in our script.'

Sam laughed beside her. 'So it's lucky she's not in the cast, isn't it?'

Rory looked back at him with distaste, and in response Sam pulled Ella closer against his shoulder. 'Ella's a free woman and can kiss who she wants.'

'No. She's with me. And if you hadn't stopped her speaking just then, she'd have had a chance to tell you herself.'

'Are you?' Sam stepped away from Ella and saw in her face the indecision, awkwardness, desire to be anywhere else but there.

'She'll fill you in later,' insisted Rory. 'Right now she's coming with me.'

Ella nodded. 'I must.'

'Okay,' said Sam. 'So find me later. If you want to.'

He walked away from them back down the hillside. Silently Rory and Ella watched him until he joined the rest of the crew, making straight for his camera.

'You see that?' asked Rory. 'He'd always love that camera more than you.'

'It's not funny, Rory. I wish you hadn't interrupted us. We're on a break and your make-up is not a mess.' She studied him critically. 'In fact it looks perfect. Therefore, I had plenty more time to talk to Sam.'

'But you had nothing more to say.'

'What?'

'Because Sam is definitely not your man, whatever you might think at the moment.'

'I like him.'

'That's fine, but what the hell were you doing kissing him? You're supposed to be falling for me.'

'I wasn't kissing him, he was kissing me.'

'Good!' he grinned. 'That's what I hoped. For a moment I couldn't tell. It looked *wrong* but I wasn't sure.'

For some unknown reason she couldn't keep herself from laughing.

'Let Sacha have him. Carey says Sacha's in love with Sam.'

'You don't even know who Sacha is.'

They walked together, back towards the set, matching strides.

'Of course I do. Sacha and Sam have been in and out of

each other's beds for the past two years and she was broken-hearted when she thought you two were together.'

'What!'

'Didn't you know? I thought everybody knew that.'

'No!' she cried. 'Oh God, I had no idea. No wonder she's hurt.'

He shook his head. 'Ella, you're so out of touch.'

'But that makes everything even worse,' Ella groaned. 'Oh God, poor Sacha. I wonder if Poppy knows. Perhaps Sacha told her not to say.'

They were almost back at the set, but at the last moment Rory took her arm and steered her away.

'Walk with me. I want to talk to you.'

She let him lead her on, following a path that wound them away towards some distant trees and fields.

'I'm sorry Poppy's not speaking to you. I'm sure that's hard.'

'It's her choice. I'm not going to keep running after her, apologizing when I've done nothing wrong.'

'We've all been on top of each other for too long.' He laughed. 'Some of us have, in any case. Next week, when you're back in London, perhaps you can call Poppy and Sacha. You might find they've forgotten all about you and me.'

'Hardly.'

'They could, if you tell it right.'

'Can I hear Carey talking now?'

'Okay, I'm repeating something Carey said to me.'

'When would that have been?'

'Why?'

'Because I'm wondering if you're still seeing her?'

He looked down at the ground, and she could see he wasn't sure how honest to be.

'Hayden thinks you were only ever with Carey because she was Anton's girl,' Ella went on. 'But I don't think you'd use somebody like that. When you're with someone, it's going to be because you like them.'

'Don't overestimate me.'

'Is that not true?'

'When I met Carey, I didn't know who she was. I certainly didn't know she was with Anton. When I found out she was Anton's girlfriend, yes, it made me want her. I wanted to steal her off him. I'm sorry if that makes me sound very shallow.'

'And now?'

'I'm not seeing her any more.'

The lighthearted relief Ella felt at that took her by surprise.

'Where did you meet her?'

'Outside a lift,' he said cautiously. 'In a hotel in Los Angeles. Then I met her again inside the lift.'

'How romantic. And then, perhaps, you took her to your hotel room and met her even better?'

'Yes,' he admitted, surprised. 'Are you shocked?'

'You are *so* bad.'

'And then Anton came looking for her and I realized who she was.'

'Is that how it is? Is that what happens? Everywhere you go, girls in lifts, girls in your make-up trailer, girls in bars . . .'

'You know it is. You've seen it with Olga. Girls jumping

into taxis with me when we stop at red lights, girls fooling the hotel staff and waiting for me, in my bed.'

'That's so James Bond. Seriously? Has that happened here, on this film?'

'Sadly not. Not so far, anyway. I'm still hoping you might try it some time. Perhaps Hayden might set it up.'

'So what do you do, with all these inconvenient girls?'

'If they're not so hot, and if the taxi's not moving too fast, usually I'll push them out again. Sometimes, if it's the hotel room, I think what the hell, and keep them.'

'What the hell,' she echoed.

'Sometimes I forget what a normal life is.'

'Don't give me that! You do it because you can. And because you don't meet enough normal girls. Girls who prefer a conversation with someone before they jump into a taxi with them, or into bed, or wherever.'

'Girls like you?'

'Sure.' She blushed. Why had she said that? 'No, don't try the charm on me.'

'Why not?'

'Because it's not real. I don't like it.'

'I'm not trying to be charming,' he said impatiently. 'It's real. I'm trying to be me. Can you not see that?'

She looked back at him in surprise.

'I'm telling you the truth. I'll always tell you the truth, about Carey, about whatever else you want to know. That's what I'm trying to say. So could you please stop being so suspicious of me.'

'Perhaps I could . . . with a little bit of practice.'

He slipped his arm around her shoulders. 'Thank you.'

Much as she wanted to keep walking, keep talking, she knew she had to get him back to the set. With his arm around her shoulders she steered him around in a circle and looked down at the set below them.

'Tell me what happened next with Carey.'

'Anton came looking for her and found her in my bedroom.'

'Oh no!'

'Yes, but Carey was brilliant. A born actress.'

'Even so, that was when you realized she was someone to leave alone.'

'Yup.'

'But you didn't?'

'I liked her.'

She nodded.

'I liked her. I haven't fallen in love with her. It was never serious.'

'For you.'

'Or for her.'

'I think you might be wrong there.'

'I'm not. Carey's in love with the idea of her future. She's looking for her break and she'll get it. She'll hang on with Anton until he gives her the part she wants in *The Broken Wing* and then she'll fly away.'

'So, why's she still hanging around the set now her scenes are finished?'

'Because Anton's here and she stays with him.'

'Not for much longer. She hates him.'

'She'll soon be free. Get the press believing in you and me, and she's off the hook. And if Anton abandons her, Hayden will see her right.'

'I hope so.'

'He knows how much he owes her.'

She looked up at him.

'You sound so cool. Has no one ever come close to getting under your skin?'

'You've said it. I don't meet normal girls.'

'Never been in love?'

'Of course. I was in love with a girl called Emily Peach. I met her when I was twenty and we went out together for two years and then I got a part in a film that meant shooting in India for six months . . . And then I got back, got another part, and went to America, and that took care of another twelve weeks. And when I got back from that one, she told me she'd had enough. She could have come with me, given up her job, but she didn't want to. And I could have turned my back on being an actor, but I didn't want to do that either.'

'It's an impossible life, we know that. And after her? You've had other girlfriends because I've read about them, seen pictures of them, but you're saying no one's got close again?'

'Not so far.' He held her hand closer against him and suddenly stopped walking. 'Ella . . .'

'What?' she whispered, feeling her heart skip a beat, her cheeks start to burn.

'Hayden has tipped off the press that we'll be in Antibes tomorrow. He's booked us on a private jet leaving from an airfield just outside Arras at seven tomorrow morning.'

She laughed in shock, then shook off his arm from around her waist. The thought of what else he might have said, unformed, ridiculous, was left to spin around her head.

He looked at her in concern. 'Are you okay?'

She recovered fast. 'Yes, of course, although we're not finishing shooting until eleven o'clock tonight and tomorrow was supposed to be our day off.'

'I'm sorry. I was hoping the thought of lying on the deck of a super-fast yacht, sipping piña coladas as it skims you around the South of France, perhaps stopping for lunch in a triple-Michelin-starred restaurant, might have seemed like fun?'

'But you're missing out the downside. I'll have to do it with you.' She saw his face fall and instantly felt horrible. 'I'm sorry, Rory. I didn't mean it,' she said hastily. 'I was joking, a bad joke, not funny at all.'

'So it's not such an awful idea? You don't mind?'

'Of course not. I'd be happy to come.'

'Happy? Careful you don't overdo it, Ella.'

'No. I mean it.' She lifted his arm back about her waist. 'Happy to come.'

Later that night, star shells lit the sky, revealing the black zig-zagging scars of the trenches, stretching as far as the eye could see.

From inside the hospital ward came the sound of deep hacking coughs. Wounded soldiers shivered on the floor in their blankets, trenchcoats spread on top of them for extra warmth, and gusts of raw, damp air flowed into the room each time one of the nurses entered or left the makeshift ward.

Ambrose, unable to film in the darkness, sat quietly beside Helen Dove, the two of them watching over a soldier, slowly dying beneath a heavy wrap of bandages.

He watched as Helen put a tin cup to the soldier's mouth, her other hand supporting the back of his head. The man drank weakly, nothing more than a few sips, and, seeing how the movement had exhausted him, Helen slowly laid him back down again, then rose to her feet. Ambrose watched, silently, as she moved on down the ward, stopping beside each bed, sometimes only to move straight on again, other times pausing to say a few words to the soldier lying there.

Then with dawn came the sunlight, and as soon as he could Ambrose returned to his camera, taking it with him as he walked through the church, filming everything that crossed his path. He returned to the three men, still propped up against the church walls, left poignantly, accidentally, between four carved stone angels. One of the soldiers had died in the night, but as yet nobody had had a chance to move him and he was still there, still strapped to his stretcher. Ambrose brought his camera inches from the boy's face, holding the image for long slow seconds, filming how death had turned his skin a marbled white, and then he drew back to reveal the angels on either side, their faces so close to his, his drooping head barely distinguishable from theirs.

He pumped up his camera and moved on, this time catching a soldier, another young boy, who looked up and smiled at Helen Dove with worship in his eyes. And then, as the daylight became bright enough, Ambrose took the Aeroscope out of the church and into the operating tent next door, where he grimly filmed the blood-spattered doctors and then the great heap of amputated legs and arms, piling up in the corner of the room behind them.

Later, after editing, it would be possible to see how, over and over again, his camera began to be drawn most often to Helen Dove. He caught her as she washed her hands in the old stone trough outside the church or quickly tidied her hair beneath her cap. He filmed the grave and beautiful profile of her face as she listened to the Sister talking about the casualties to be expected later in the day, when she bent over a soldier, snuffed out a candle, or held down a man who bared his teeth at her and thrashed around in his sheets in agony.

It was no place to fall in love, the pace of the days and nights so exhausting, the scenes before them so relentless and bloody and appalling, so little time for them to think about each other and even less time to talk, and certainly none at all for them to escape from the church and into the fields beyond. And yet still they did so, talking in hasty snatches, thinking about each other all the time. Even without hearing them speak to each other, even when Hayden relied entirely on Ambrose's footage, it was clear that Ambrose had begun to fall in love with Helen, almost from the first moment that he saw her. And through his camera, it was clear to see the moment when Helen Dove began to respond to him, how, as the days went on, and his camera continued to pause upon her face, sometimes she would now turn to him and smile back shyly, before leaping to her feet and hurriedly, conscientiously, bustling away.

Standing on the edge of the set, Ella watched Ambrose move silently down the aisle of the church to film Helen now. He found her sitting between two beds, holding the hand of a young boy, who was staring back at her with glassy eyes, reciting the Lord's Prayer.

As the cameras continued to roll, slowly, carefully, Sam and the camera crew filmed as Ambrose put down the Aeroscope and came across to sit beside her. Tentatively, he slipped an arm around her shoulders and held her stiffly, and after a moment she let herself fall against him and allowed her cheek to rest against his chest.

'Cut!' called Hayden triumphantly. 'Excellent. We'll take a break.' He turned to include all his crew. 'Ready in half an hour on the second set.'

As soon as he left the set he wasted no time in finding Ella. And having spotted her, on her knees, with her upended make-up pouch spread before her, trying to find a pot of Ghoul White crème base to lend to Minnie, he waved to her to follow him to his trailer.

She bundled together her make-up and followed him in, past the banks of monitors to the little office at the back. He motioned to her to sit down and then, when she did, chucked a magazine on to her lap. It was the new edition of *Hollywood Whisper* and Rory was on the front cover, looking impossibly handsome as he stepped out of a taxi to the flash of a thousand cameras, the headline underneath: 'Who's His New Girl?'

'Look inside,' he told her. 'Page four.'

She turned the pages quickly, stopped at the right place, looked quickly at the photographs, then back up at him.

'It's clearly not me.'

'Everybody else thinks it is. Anton thinks it's hysterical. He was telling me all about catching you in the hay barn together. Says you are far too good for Rory.'

'What did you tell him?'

'That you spent last night in Rory's bedroom. At first he wasn't sure to believe me, but he checked the hotel's CCTV and saw you, so he believes it now. Ha! I knew Anton would do that. That's why I never bothered to call the press.' And now Hayden paused and rubbed his hands with glee. 'So, even better that we've got you out on the sea together tomorrow, plenty more chances to pap you there, Ella.'

'I don't like the sound of being papped.'

Hayden ignored her. 'Rory's got some friends with a boat just off the coast of Antibes. He's called them and it's fine, they're expecting you to join them tomorrow. And this time, don't doubt it, the journalists will be out to meet you.' His eyes widened. 'If not just for Rory and you, then for the other guests on board.'

'Why? Who?' she squeaked in fear. 'Who will they be?'

'Oh, I think he said Orlando might be there, and Shia and Sienna, and maybe Mischa too.'

'You're joking?'

'Yes, Ella. I am,' he laughed, light-hearted with relief. 'Don't worry about it.'

'You mean that I don't have to worry I will be joining a boatload of the most beautiful people on earth, when I'm shooting here until eleven p.m. and you haven't even left me time to wax my legs?'

He looked at her doubtfully. 'You should definitely find the time to do that. Stay up all night if you have to. You must look the part. Don't let me down, girl!'

'So you're not expecting me to spend another night in La Sauterelle?'

'No. You're right. Tonight you need time to prepare

yourself. Take some pretty clothes. You have a bikini here, do you? And some big shades? Come on,' he rubbed her shoulder affectionately. 'You can deal with film stars. You meet them all the time.'

'Yes, but not like this. I can deal with them when I'm armed with a make-up brush, not when I have to make conversation and sunbathe next to them. Oh, God, it's going to be awful.'

'Whoever they are, they'll love you. You'll be fine. And in any case, it doesn't matter what they think, and it doesn't matter what you say to them. All that matters is that one crucial moment when you come back into the marina, at the end of a lovely day, with the wind in your hair, and Rory on your arm, and you look carefree and in love for all my paparazzi friends. They'll love you, Ella, I just know they will.'

'And Rory will tell all the people on the boat that I'm his new girlfriend?'

'Of course. What else would he say?'

'It's not going to work.' She shook her head. 'He never remembers to flirt with me. No one will believe it. I don't think I can do this any more.'

'Of course you can. You're nearly there. I'll have a word with him, remind him he's an actor, and how he's supposed to act. And, in any case, Anton's bought it. He just needs one little piece more evidence and then we'll have him off our backs for ever.'

'And then?'

'Then, in a few more days, filming's over, you and Rory can quietly split up again and everyone will forget all about you. Apart from me. I won't forget what you've done for me, ever.'

Restlessly she got up off her chair, thinking Hayden was way too confident, far too pleased with himself.

'Have you talked to Carey?' she demanded. 'Have you remembered that she might not be feeling so good about this plan of yours? She's gone very quiet and I think that should worry you. She's getting nothing from this, Hayden. Apart from sleeping with Anton, which she clearly finds disgusting.'

'If you're suggesting I give her a part in my next film, I'm not going to. She can't act and the sooner she realizes it the better. Let Anton give her that part in *The Broken Wing*.'

'But you should look after her, after all she's done for you. You don't respect her because she can't act, and she's not some industry honcho, and she's not famous, but still you should. She can open her mouth any time and tell Anton the truth.'

Finally she'd got his attention. 'Does Rory think she will?'

'This is about what *I* think. I think she still cares about him. And the more photographs of us having fun together, the more stories about me and Rory, even though she knows they're not true, the more she might get jealous and start to believe them. And if she does, I think you should watch out.'

Thirteen

Rory and Ella flew by private jet to the South of France and touched down in a small airfield just inland from Antibes. As the plane braked, Ella looked out of the window and saw a waiting crowd of journalists on the other side of the wire fence that ran alongside the runway and thought, with a rush of trepidation, how they'd never believe she and Rory were together. How, as soon as they saw the two of them walk from the plane, they'd just know she wasn't for real. She was lacking the gloss, the poise, the confidence. She imagined them staring at her in disbelief, then downing their cameras in protest and refusing to take a photograph.

She stepped out of the plane and down the flimsy steps to the ground, very grateful for Rory's hand and for the way he kept on her outside as they made their way from the plane towards the airport buildings. She kept her head down, at one point hearing a brief clatter of shutters and a pop of flash bulbs, and then they were inside, and she lifted her head to find they were now in some swanky, empty, private-jet arrivals lounge. A lounge that was never revealed to the long queue of beery, hoi-polloi economy class that

Ella usually found herself a part of, on all those occasions when she didn't happen to be flying in by PJ, with a movie star on her arm.

A smiling security officer was waiting for them and politely asked to see their passports, and then they were whisked on by their pilot, through several more ornately furnished, plushly carpeted rooms, full of fresh flowers and no other passengers, until eventually a pair of smoked glass doors silently opened at their approach to reveal the sunlight outside, and another crowd of press, this time held back from the blacked-out Range Rover that was waiting for them, driver in place, engine running, doors already open. Clearly the airport – or was it Rory's PR – were well-used to the routine, and it was only Ella who was unprepared, doing her best not to look too wide-eyed as they walked out through the doors and towards the car.

'Get inside,' Rory told her quietly, and she leapt in first and he jumped in behind her and then the car was speeding away, so fast that she was thrown back in her seat.

'Wow,' she said, pushing herself forward again and leaning to look out of the window as they passed the crowd of pressmen.

'Don't look unless you want your picture taken.'

'Isn't that the idea?'

He grinned at her. 'Perhaps you might wait until you've put on some lipstick and smoothed down your hair.'

'What?' She touched her hair. 'Why do you say that? What's wrong with my hair?'

'Nothing.'

'Don't say that then! Stop making me so self-conscious.'

'When you look at your photograph in *Heat* or *Grazia* or wherever it is, I'm telling you, you'll wish you'd put on some lipstick. I know these things.'

She sat back again against the cream leather seats, as the car met the main road and smoothly picked up speed, then frowned across at him.

'Who's going to be on this boat, then?'

'Nobody you need to worry about, grumpy goat.'

She smiled reluctantly.

'Friends, two couples,' Rory told her. 'One's an old schoolfriend and his girlfriend. Civvies like you – I thought they'd make you feel at home – and the other two are actors.'

'I can't believe you've kept up with schoolfriends. I can't imagine you went to school, like some normal person.'

He didn't rise. 'What I mean is I think you'll like them. And you never know, they might even like you.'

'Doesn't really matter either way, does it? As long as Hayden gets his photograph.'

'Are you nervous?'

'Of course not.'

'Good, because I wondered . . . When we arrive at the boat, there'll probably be some more press and I think I should kiss you. Do you mind?'

'Kind of you to warn me.'

'I had to. Otherwise you might slap me.'

'What sort of kiss?'

'Lip to lip?'

'But no tongues.'

'Why are you so boring?'

'Rory, I mean it. Anyway, I heard actors never kiss with tongues, so stop acting so surprised.'

'Sure they do!'

'Well, clearly there were tongues when you were kissing Carey in the hay barn but I can't imagine you're ever going to snog Liberty.'

'Absolutely I am. She made it a condition of her contract that I did.'

'What! I thought actors wrote it into their contracts that they didn't have to.'

'I can seriously say nobody has ever had that written down about me.'

She looked away from him, out of the window.

'Aaah,' he said. 'I can see this conversation is getting to you.'

'Not at all.'

'Don't worry about it. I'll be very reserved.'

'I don't care. As long as the cameras think I'm enjoying myself, that's all that matters.'

'Absolutely.' He looked out of the other window.

They turned a corner, and ahead of them she could suddenly see the beautiful, shining, turquoise sea.

'Look!' She couldn't hide her delight. 'After all those weeks in the hills, isn't that the most beautiful sight?'

He stretched back in his seat and smiled at her. 'Sometimes you're so sweet, Ella. I mean it. After all the hard-bitten, stony-faced girls I usually find myself with, it's fun being with you.'

'And that's the nicest nice thing you've ever said to me. Possibly the only nice thing. But don't worry. That'll do.

You don't have to think of anything else for at least a couple of hours. Possibly we'll need another one at lunchtime – do you think you might say one then? Would that give you long enough to come up with something?'

'I see you've brought your knitting?' he said, patting her bag. 'Perhaps leave it in here, at least until we're out at sea. Otherwise people might think that I'm going out with a nutter.'

'Why? Why say that? Just when I was beginning to think I could get through this day quite happily, you go and say something stupid like that.'

'Sorry.' He stretched back in his seat, looking remarkably happy and carefree. 'If I hadn't, I might have kissed you right now, grabbed you and pulled you down on the seat with me. Wouldn't that have been a waste? When there's nobody to see but our driver?' He took her hand. 'Seriously? I like your knitting. Truly I do. It makes me feel safe and warm.'

The Range Rover swept them on along the coast and into the town, then followed the signs for the Marina, finally driving them through a pair of high iron gates and into an area crowded with spectacular boats.

They drove on, past the quays, the boats bobbing gently at their moorings; some of them so big she imagined parties of a hundred guests could easily come aboard, others small enough to take just four or six, but all of them immaculate, shining, glossy white.

Finally the car stopped and their driver jumped out to open their door. She pointed a newly polished toe, in a spindly sandal, down to the ground, then stretched out one long, golden brown leg and dropped her sunglasses over her eyes. From this moment on, she vowed, she was going to be the part, not just act it.

She was wearing her bikini under a pink silk knee-length dress, with a low V at the front, and she felt the sea wind whip at it, slapping it against her thighs, as she stepped completely out of the car. Beside her Rory climbed out too, then walked around to the boot, in bare feet, dressed only in a T-shirt and shorts.

Ahead of her, she could see what had to be their boat, a stunning, shining white yacht about thirty feet long, with a long sunbathing deck in the front and white leather seats and four people standing waving at her and Rory, in welcome.

On shaky legs, clutching Rory's hand, she made her tentative way towards them, wishing she hadn't worn quite such spindly heels, and then, suddenly, she felt him turn her, his arm slipping urgently around her waist. And the next thing she knew, his body was shielding her, his arm in front of her face, as a great surge of people came out of nowhere, crowding around them, cameras snapping, voices shouting.

She could hardly see where she was going. She kept her head bent as cameras were thrust under her chin and lights popped and flashed in her eyes, and instinctively she drew her hand up to push them away. Together, holding tightly to Rory's hand, she ran with him to the boat and someone on board stretched out a hand and helped her climb aboard.

Rory jumped in behind her. 'Go,' he shouted and immediately the engine thrust forward and the boat pulled away from the quay, and finally she could drop the hand that was still holding hers, and lift her sunglasses and look around her, first backwards, towards the marina, where she saw with astonishment that twenty or thirty people were standing along the quay, some of them still taking photographs, even though the boat was now moving even more swiftly away. And then she looked forwards to find four people, two men and two women, laughing at her open mouth, at the shock on her face.

'Welcome aboard,' said a tall, handsome man, his long black hair whipping behind him in the wind. He laughed again. 'You look very shocked, Ella. Has that not happened to you before?'

'No,' she admitted, looking back again, grateful to see that they'd now put a good distance between them and the shore. 'And I don't want it to happen ever again. That was horrible.'

'I'm sorry, darling,' Rory bent towards her and kissed her and she started in surprise.

'What the hell are you . . . ?'

'Shh,' he said laughing, still close. 'Keep still. You told me not to warn you.' And then he kissed her again, his mouth gentle and warm against hers, and instinctively she felt herself responding, for just a few seconds, held against his body before he let her go.

'Take off your shoes. No shoes on board. And then I'll introduce you to everybody.'

On board was Jerome, the tall man with the dark hair who'd first greeted her, and his girlfriend Janey, both American, both of whom Ella felt she should recognize but didn't. And another couple, the man the old schoolfriend of Rory's, his girlfriend, who was called Sophie, probably in her mid-twenties and completely stunning, with waist-length blonde hair and the tiniest nut-brown figure that Ella knew would still have eluded her, even if she'd starved off two stone and taken on a personal trainer for every day of the rest of her life. Rory's schoolfriend, a stocky, hairy, very English Englishman, with the kind of white skin that no amount of sun would ever turn brown, was called Nod. Within half an hour of meeting him, Ella decided that he was perhaps the funniest, nicest man she had ever met.

Their skipper, another impossibly handsome sun-streaked superman, was called Jon. He was English but lived all year round in Antibes, his boat both his investment and his livelihood, taking guests out along the coast throughout the summer, then living off what he earned in the winter.

Once they were clear of the harbour, Jon turned up the engine and the boat skimmed away across the waves, so fast it took Ella's breath away.

For a while they sat together at the back of the boat. Then, when they'd reached the wide open sea, Jon cut the engines. Rory took Ella's hand and guided her along the side of the boat to the bow, then let her go while he went to gather some cushions and make them both a sunbed.

He spread a towel across the cushions.

'Lie here and I'll get you a drink.'

She watched him as he moved, perfectly balanced, to a seat built into the side of the boat, lifted the cushions away and opened it.

'What'll you have?' he asked, dropping his arm down inside. 'Coke? Vodka?'

She smiled. 'I try not to drink Coke after seven in the morning. Fizzy water would be great.'

He threw her an ice-cold bottle then came back to join her, sitting down beside her and pulling off his T-shirt. She dropped her shades back over her eyes and sat for a few moments, supposedly looking vaguely out to sea, but really looking at him, still feeling the imprint of his mouth on hers, the rasp of his moustache on her lip. She looked and thought how gorgeous he was, sitting beside her, oiled and muscled and brown. No wonder half the women in the world thought they were in love with him.

'Hi.' He looked across to her, smiling, his perfect teeth flashing white against his brown skin. Then he lifted her shades so that he could see her eyes. 'Are you okay?'

'Yes,' she smiled back at him, the wind blowing at her hair. 'This is fun.'

She lifted her arms and pulled off her dress, then tucked it under her cushion to stop it flying away and lay back down beside him.

'Like you thought it would be?'

'Yes and no. I'd probably have imagined some huge great big Abramovich yacht, much too big and with too many staff.'

'I wouldn't want that.'

'No. I can see that now. This is exactly the kind of boat, and the kind of day, I'd imagined you'd have.'

'It's more fun when you can feel the waves beneath you.'

'Absolutely. And your friends are far nicer than I thought they'd be. Why did I think you'd have horrible friends?'

He stretched his arms behind his head. 'Admit you've got me wrong.'

'I admit a film set is not the easiest place to be yourself. We both know that.'

She lay on her stomach beside him quietly, her thoughts in a tumble, finding herself struggling to remember anything about him before this day, this moment, lying here beside him now.

'You'll burn,' he said suddenly, sitting up again. 'Hurray! Now I get to put on the suntan lotion.'

She laughed and sat up, pulled her bag towards her and brought out a bottle of oil, then unscrewed the bottle and handed it to him.

'Ella, I mean I get to put it on *you*.'

'No, let me do you. You'll burn too.'

She sat behind him and spread the oil across his shoulders then down his back, feeling the knobs of his spine and the muscles beneath his hot, smooth skin. How funny it was that she should have touched him so many times before, and yet here, now, it could feel so completely different.

When she had finished, she pressed her hands against his spine, then finally let her fingers trail up towards the nape of his neck and into the back of his hair.

'Don't stop!' he murmured.

'No. You're done.'

She put down the bottle beside her.

'Now it's your turn,' he said, immediately picking it up again. 'Lie down, on your stomach.'

She did as he said and waited for what felt like an age, then felt his warm hands touch her back and slide together slowly around her shoulder-blades and on to her shoulders and up and down each of her arms.

She couldn't speak, couldn't move, could think of nothing but what he was doing. One finger, that was all he was touching her with. It had started at the nape of her neck and was slowly, lazily gliding down her spine, before stopping at the line of her bikini bottoms.

Did he know what he was doing to her? If she turned over, would she see him laughing at her? It seemed as if he was waiting for her to move and, at that moment, just at that moment, she had to fight the urge to roll over and pull him into her arms. But she didn't do it, just stretched and sighed, and immediately the hand lifted away from her back and she turned her face away from him, even though he couldn't see her eyes beneath the shades.

'You didn't say it was a thriller. You should have done. I love thrillers.'

She saw that he was reading the script she'd tried to give him in La Sauterelle.

'Too late.' She reached across, trying to pull it out of his hands. 'You shouldn't have been so horrible before. You could have had an exclusive. Now I've told Cat, my friend, to show it around.'

'Then un-tell her. You know she couldn't do better than me. When else does a world-famous movie star get to read a first-time script from a girl fresh out of drama school. *Set in Hounslow*.' He laughed. 'I want Mikey and Jess to come in for screen tests. I think it would be perfect for them.'

'Seriously? Not the Tower Hamlets Two?' She sat up, delighted. 'How much have you read?'

'Only the first page.'

'Oh, Rory!'

'But I can tell. It's good. You were right. And those two

kids, they would have to be played by unknowns. Mikey and Jess would love it.'

'But they've done drama club. They've never made a film. How do you know? And you'd have to look after them. Imagine how intimidated they'd be, being on a huge movie set.'

'You haven't met them.' He laughed. 'They don't do intimidated, either of them. I do intimidated when I'm with them.'

'We're dropping anchor,' called Jon a couple of minutes later. 'Have a swim if you want to.'

Ella sat up, to see that they were, perhaps, five hundred metres or so from a rocky beach.

At Jon's words, Rory immediately bounced to his feet, dropping her script into her lap, then ran across the deck, leapt up on to the rail of the boat, teetered for half a second, and dived untidily into the water with a terrific splash.

She looked over the edge and watched him surface.

'Come on,' he called, encouraging her. 'I dare you! Do it too.'

She stood up, pulling her bikini straight and her tummy in, and thought about it for half a second, and then decided that if she thought about it any more she'd never do it. She jumped up on to the rail, wobbling for a moment in terror because she was so high, then dived after him, into the air, feeling the rush and then the plunge, the cold water, going down so deep, then turning, making her way up again, bursting back to the surface to find him just a few feet away from her.

'Wow,' she cried, swimming towards him. 'Just wow. That was amazing. I've never dived from so high before.'

He held out his arms to her. 'You're brilliant, Ella! Do you know that? And clever and brave! So brave.'

She started to paddle towards him, but then she heard a shout of warning from back on the boat and turned to see Jon standing over the rail, waving at them.

'Rory! Ella!' he called again, his voice urgent. 'Get back here. Now! Right now!'

Treading water, she looked back towards the shore and saw three speedboats racing towards them, abreast of each other.

'Shit!' said Rory. 'Come with me. Swim around to the back of the boat and get back in. Quickly, Ella!'

She did as he said, frightened by the urgency in his voice, kicking and swimming as fast as she could. She made it to the back of the boat in a few seconds, then tried and failed to lift her legs high enough to catch the ladder. Behind her she could hear the growl of a motor as an engine cut, and she looked over her shoulder to see that one of the speedboats was now rocking dangerously close towards her, so close that it might hit their boat or mow her down. On board were a couple of men, leaning out across the water, taking pictures, almost close enough to touch. She looked up into the camera lens and unfortunately a huge wave chose that moment to slap straight into her open mouth, making her choke and splutter.

'Get away from her,' Rory roared at them furiously. 'Get back. Get back. You're too close.'

One of the men on board cut the engine, while the other shamelessly continued snapping Ella, as, still coughing out seawater, she tried and failed, and tried and failed, to fit her foot into the ladder of the boat until, finally, she felt herself lifted bodily out of the water by Rory and was half thrown, half pushed up into the waiting hands of Jerome. Seconds later Rory had climbed up behind her and immediately Jon accelerated away.

'Fuckers!' shouted Jon, throwing Rory a bottle of beer, their superior engine meaning they immediately left the press boat behind. 'But now they know you're here, they're not going to let you go again. We can try and make the restaurant for lunch, but I don't think you'll have much fun if you go ashore.'

Rory glanced sympathetically across to Ella. 'If this is Hayden's doing, he's gone too far.'

'And just imagine the photographs they got of me,' said Ella, knowing there'd definitely been a moment when she'd lost her bikini bottoms halfway down her legs. 'It'll be a double-page spread. *Bottoms Up!* That's what they'll say . . . That's what they saw.'

They looked very serious as they thought about what she'd said, and then, one by one, beginning with Nod, they began to smile. And then, as they remembered the way she'd done the splits trying to reach the boat, her salty hair plastered across her face, seawater up her nose, before being shoved unceremoniously upwards by Rory, the smiles got worse. And seeing what was happening, Ella stared stonily back at each of them, one by one, until finally her lips began to twitch too, and she gave in and began to laugh. At that, suddenly Rory stopped laughing and came across the boat to Ella, with a strange, soft look in his eye, and she found herself being pulled roughly against him, wrapped in his arms, and felt him kiss the top of her wet head.

So, instead of going ashore, they ate lunch from cold boxes on the boat, and spent the rest of the afternoon cruising the coastline, occasionally stopping to swim, but never for long, moving on whenever it looked as if another boat was about to come too close. And then, at about four o'clock, they decided that it was time to go in to shore.

'Now,' said Rory to Ella, out of earshot of the others. 'We have to give those bastards a photograph to print. If I kiss you this time, do you think you could stop yourself pulling away?'

'Of course.' Did she sound much too eager? 'As I said before, just don't tell me when.'

He waited until they'd pulled up at the quay, having clocked that three or four pressmen were there waiting for them. He held off until the other four had left the boat and escaped to the safety of their car, and for Jon to disappear back into the cabin of his boat, and then, finally, he jumped off the boat and on to the quay, and held out his hand to Ella, and she climbed out after him and let him take her in his arms, pressing her head close against his shoulder.

'Ella Buchan?' someone called to her. 'Ella, Ella, give us a smile.'

Rory pulled her closer against him and kissed her briefly on the cheek. 'In a moment,' he told her. 'Do what they say.'

He led her along the quayside and towards his car.

'Had a good day, have you?' someone else called. 'Give us a picture and we'll leave you alone. Love the moustache, Rory.'

'Smile at them now,' he told her.

Ella stopped and looked at them all and smiled shyly, and immediately came the grasshopper clicking of a hundred camera shutters.

'Well done.' He kissed her again, slowly on the lips, and touched her face softly with his finger. 'You're my girl now. You do know that, don't you?' And again the cameras pressed.

He turned to face them. 'This is Ella Buchan and she is my make-up artist on *To End All War*. And yes, thank you, we've just had a good fun day out together. Right, guys, that's enough. Leave us alone now.'

And they did. Having got their photographs, the men stepped back and Ella and Rory passed between them and on towards their car. At their approach the driver got out, opened the boot, dropped their bags in, then opened a back door to let them climb inside.

'Go ahead,' Rory told him. 'We'll be just one moment more.'

The driver turned his back on them and stepped back into his car and therefore missed the kiss that would appear, the next morning, on the front page of magazines and news-papers around the world: *Rory and new love, Ella Buchan, full of joy as they return from a sun-kissed day upon the sea and talk about their love.*

Although Ella hadn't spotted it, Rory had known there was a camera still waiting for them, hidden behind a lav-ender hedge, and he turned Ella towards it and kissed her again, first tentatively and then, as she pulled him closer, full of passion. And Ella, not acting at all, because she hadn't known that there was anybody there to see, kissed him back, feeling as if she might faint in his arms, wishing that they could stay like this for ever, and never go back to Florent, and to how he used to be.

As the car pulled away Rory sat back in his seat and spread back his arms.

'Let's not go back.'

'What?'

He laughed at the shock on her face. 'I mean it. I'll call Hayden and tell him we're not coming back until the morning.'

'But why? We have to. Where would we go?' Her eyes widened. 'Seriously? You think we could do that?'

'Of course we can. We can do whatever we want. Remember, Hayden's asked for this, Ella. We're doing him the favour.'

'What about the schedules? Poppy will go crazy. She'll be so angry with me.'

But Poppy was already angry with her, and the schedule would survive. And in any case, she knew she wanted to stay. Just being beside him filled her with a wild kind of hope, of abandonment, exhilaration. Of course she knew that they were acting out roles. Of course she knew they were only there at all because of Hayden and Anton and Carey. And, of course she knew not to trust him, knew she had to remember that he was famously charming, and was surely only playing his part with her now. And yet, despite all that, she knew that she was being hooked, and that the longer she stayed with him now, the harder it would become to disentangle herself again afterwards.

He flipped open his phone and called Liza Nash, his PA,

told her what he wanted, and to call the driver once she'd found the right kind of place for them; and, about five miles later, instead of turning back to the airport, the car slowed down and made a U-turn, following the road back along the coast.

Half an hour later, as the evening sunlight turned the sky a deep pinky red, they turned off the coast road and began to climb into the hills, then finally they turned up a narrow lane that wound between tall cypress trees, until they reached a pair of beautiful wrought-iron gates, open to a gravel drive, and at the top a grand stone farmhouse, low and square, built of old Provençal stone. Warm yellow light pooled on to the gravel drive, and at the sound of their wheels the front door opened and a smiling, balding, middle-aged man in a black suit came striding out to greet them, beaming with smiles.

Their driver opened the door for them.

'Shoes?' Ella asked him.

'I didn't bring any,' Rory admitted, stepping out of the car.

'Rory Defoe and Ella Buchan, what a very great pleasure it is to welcome you here tonight.'

'The Hôtel d'Or,' said Rory, treading painfully on the gravel, as their driver sprang open the boot of the car and brought out her bag. 'The Hôtel d'Or has a three-star dinner. I thought we'd make up for having to miss lunch.'

Ella followed the black-suited man into the hotel, Rory hobbling beside her, then across a pale grey limestone floor, and up a wide staircase to the first floor.

'When your secretary called us this evening I was so

delighted that I could tell her we had this space for you.' He turned back to them both, grinning merrily. 'It would have broken my heart to have had you to stay and not to have been able to give you our very best room.'

Room, noticed Ella, not rooms.

But as in La Sauterelle, Rory was not expected to rough it in the kind of twelve foot by twelve shoebox she'd been given at Le Sport. Their room was beautiful, looking out across the valley towards the navy blue sea, with a sumptuous bathroom and a huge four-poster bed.

Bed, thought Ella, looking around the room and seeing no sign of a door that might lead through to a second bedroom.

'It's perfect,' Ella said, imagining how it would be to climb into bed beside Rory. 'I can't believe we're here.'

With a happy smile the manager returned to the doorway.

'Dinner can be at any time. I wonder if you'd thought when you might like to eat?'

'Ella?' asked Rory.

'I'm starving,' she told them both. 'Any time soon.'

'Then please do come down to join us whenever you are ready. Aahh,' the manager stepped back from the doorway as a waiter appeared, holding an ice bucket with a bottle of champagne and two glasses. 'As I said, you are so very welcome at the Hôtel d'Or.'

Once they had been left alone together, Rory opened the bottle and poured Ella a glass.

'Would you like a bath, or a shower before we have dinner?'

She looked back at him steadily. 'I don't think so.'

'Would you like me to book you a second bedroom?'

285

'I have to admit, I'm feeling a little strange, being here with you now. I've only just realized how odd it is.'

'We'll get you a second room.'

'No,' she shook her head. 'Of course I don't mind. That bed's big enough for six and I'm sure you've brought your pyjamas.' She hesitated, smiling. 'You mean you haven't?'

'I'll tell you why I thought we should do this, Ella.'

'Why?'

She waited for him to explain.

I got caught up in the moment, back in the car with you. It's been such a wonderful day and I realized I wasn't ready for it to end, because usually, on set, we're always on our guard, aren't we, you and me? Everybody watching everybody, all the time. And now after this day together, I've seen how it could be. And I don't want to go back to Florent until I'd had a chance to tell you. You're amazing, Ella, you're wonderful. I never saw it until now. I never thought I could feel this way . . .

'We can tip the press off that we're here,' Rory said instead. 'It wasn't enough, having those photographers down at the harbour. They need more of a story, certainly Anton needs more of a story if we're going to convince him.'

'Oh,' she said quietly. 'Whatever you think. That's fine.'

'Look, I know you're keen to put all this behind you. Don't argue, Ella, I know you are. Christ, I want this over too.'

She nodded. 'Of course you do.'

'Then you can stop pretending, and start running after Sam again.'

'I expect that's what I'll do.'

'So, let's get this second little photo-call over and done with tonight or tomorrow morning – as soon as the photographers can get here anyway – and then there'll be no need for any more acting. You'll be free. Imagine that, we can go back to being as horrible to each other as we were before.'

'That'll be great,' she agreed, her mouth so dry with disappointment that she could barely swallow.

'But we won't be doing that, Umbrella, will we? Because we know each other better now.'

'You're right.' She nodded. 'No need to be horrible now.'

Just civil, and friendly and remote. She could hardly bear the thought.

'So how do you go about this?' she managed to say. 'How do you tip off the press?'

'Usually I'd call my PR, but obviously Hayden will have to work it this time. I'll get Liza to give him the address of where we are. I very much doubt the Hôtel d'Or will let anyone in, but they'll be here when we leave in the morning, I'm sure.'

'Good thing we've kept just the one room then. Otherwise it wouldn't look so convincing.'

'You don't need to sound so unenthusiastic, Ella. You know I'm not going to jump on you.'

But I would like you to jump on me, she wanted to tell him, but didn't. And, silly me, up until a minute ago, I thought that you might have been about to. Oh, I know that we're only here for Hayden. And I know I said all that stuff about not jumping straight into bed with girls you hardly know, but I hoped you'd forgotten that. And I know that every single girl on set took the trouble to come up to me and warn me not to fall for you, but somehow, I think I have done, even so, like a stone. How stupid is that?

Back downstairs they found themselves being led out on to a beautiful terrace, Rory so used to the stares from all the other guests that it wouldn't have occurred to him that some of it was surely due to his shorts and bare feet. He was such a super-star that of course everybody would stare whatever he wore.

In the dusky light the terrace was lit with twinkling lights strung from tree to tree, and the air was sweet with the scent of lavender, and warm and still. For a moment all Ella could do was to breathe it in and slowly look about her, taking in her surroundings like she hadn't done for weeks – Poppy and Sacha, Hayden and Anton, the Rory she'd known in Florent, all of them so far away it was as if they no longer existed, the only reality her and Rory sitting down opposite each other now, both of them different people, starting again.

She'd said she was hungry, but the truth was, when her starter was put down before her, Ella found she could hardly bear to lift her fork to her mouth. The thought of food was suddenly impossible.

'I'm sorry,' she told Rory, looking sadly down at her plate. 'I can't eat it.'

'Why not?'

If he only knew the wild acrobatics going on in her stomach, all the pleasure and the pain of sitting there opposite him, he wouldn't need to ask.

'I don't know. Ate too much on the boat I guess.'

In answer he pushed away his own plate and she looked back at him in surprise. 'Is something wrong?'

'No,' he said simply. 'But I can't eat anything either.'

'Please try,' she begged. 'They won't care about me, but the chef will be so sad that you don't like his food.'

'Okay.' He cut a small piece of beautiful pink lamb and slowly placed it in his mouth.

'Good,' Ella smiled at him. 'Now another one.'

'I can't.'

'Any other time ...' She cleared her throat. 'Any other time and I'm sure this would be so delicious.'

He took her hand across the table and held it tightly.

'The truth is I can't eat with you sitting here opposite me like this,' he said in a rush. 'Perhaps in ten years' time, if I've seen you for every single one of those days and then we come back here, then I might be able to eat their food.'

She stared back at him, so shocked she felt as if she couldn't breathe. 'Rory, please. What do you mean?' She said it desperately, aware that she was gripping on to his hand, and it felt as if time was slowing, the darkness of the evening closing around them, the sounds of the other guests, the tinkle of their laughter, moving further and further away. Oh my God, she thought, feeling as if she was falling into his wide, dark eyes. Oh my God.

'Ella, I'm sorry.' He leaned forwards, his voice thick with emotion. 'Please can we get out of here?'

'Of course.' She pushed herself to her feet and again he took her hand and she felt her feet float across the stone floor as he led her away from the terrace and the other guests.

Ahead of them there was the swimming pool, inky black in the evening light. They walked towards it hand in hand, and he sat down at its edge and dropped his feet into the water, wincing at the cold.

She took off her sandals and did the same, sitting close beside him and letting the water slip, silky cool, between her toes. Then he put both arms around her and pulled her close against the warm hard line of his body.

'This is much better, don't you think?'

She nodded, not trusting herself to speak, wondering at the feel of him, so close beside her, thinking that if this was it, if this was as close as she ever got to him, how at least she'd have this moment to remember. But even as she thought that, there was the terrible despair that it might be all she'd ever have.

He stared out across the pool.

'I wanted to say thank you for being so wonderful.'

No, not that. Please don't tell me that that is what you meant.

'It was easy.'

'Maybe today, but I know it hasn't always been. On-set-Rory can be a difficult bastard.'

'Sometimes he can be.' She threaded her fingers through his. 'But usually he's got a good reason.'

He pulled her closer still. 'And I wanted to say how great you are at your job, too. Never had such an even complexion in my life.'

She laughed drily. 'Then thank you for that.'

'But most of all . . .'

'Yes?'

'I wanted to say how being with you, being your bloke for the past few days, has been more fun . . .' He stopped, frowned. 'It's been better than I could ever have imagined.'

'It doesn't have to be over,' she heard herself whisper.

'Oh, but it does,' Rory said firmly, still holding her close but saying it just the same. 'After tomorrow, we're back on course. The film's almost finished, Hayden's got his story.'

'Yup,' she whispered miserably. 'Of course.'

He was letting her down, gently, full of understanding, full of affection and tenderness, but letting her down all the same.

Abruptly he rolled away from her, lifting his feet out of the water and standing up, then he held out a hand to pull her to her feet.

'Come on, my darling. I think it's time we went to bed.'

In their bedroom, she lay in their bed, her back turned away from him, and listened to him moving about above her, going to the bathroom, the sound of him washing and brushing his teeth, then the click of the bathroom door as he closed it shut, and then she felt the dip of the bed as he climbed in beside her and she found that she was unable to stop herself turning to meet him. In the darkness, she caught the scent of toothpaste on his breath as he reached forwards to kiss her goodnight, the briefest of brushes of lips against hers, before he immediately rolled over on to the other side of the bed and left her alone.

Back in Florent, they arrived at the entrance to La Sauterelle to find another wall of press waiting for them.

'This is crazy,' Rory insisted. 'Hayden's gone mad.'

Instinctively he tried to shield her face, but she stopped him.

'No,' she said, nervous of what she was saying but wanting to see it through. 'I want them to see me. This is what we agreed. We did it this morning, and we'll do it again now, and then surely it will be enough for everyone and it can be over.'

She walked as fast as she could beside him in her spindly high heels, ignoring the shouts and pleas to wait, but letting them see her face and snap her picture, all the way to the door of La Sauterelle, where the hotel security guards stepped forward to let her and Rory through, and keep the others back.

Inside his room, she felt as if she could breathe again for the first time. She unbuckled her sandals and threw them across the floor, then walked across the deep pile of the rugs in her bare feet. She could hear the silence behind her, not just in the stillness of the room after the frenzy of outside, but in Rory too.

'What's wrong?' she asked, turning back to him. 'We've done it. Don't be sad now.'

'Over for you.'

'I'm sorry. I know it's not the same for you. I know this is what happens to you every day. I'm lucky that I can walk away.'

'That's not what I meant.'

'Does this happen every time you're with someone new?'

He nodded.

'So, keep a lower profile. Stop giving them so much to write about, stop watching the pole-dancers in Kiev and stay in a bit more with your popcorn and your DVDs.'

He gave her a rueful smile. 'I've never watched a pole-dancer.'

She flopped down on the sofa. 'So, Hayden said he wants you to stay here? Why can't you go on set?'

'I can do, in a couple of hours. But because we stayed over last night, Poppy had to rewrite the schedule and apparently it will be less disruptive to everybody if I stay away now. But you can go. Seriously, if you want to, there's no need for you to wait here with me now.'

'No reason apart from the fact that there are about a hundred cameras waiting for me outside and Poppy about to eat me alive when I go back on set? And if you're not needed, I'm not needed either.'

He smiled back at her. 'Then stay here with me. Look, I'll call Poppy, see what she says. See how badly she's missing you.'

'No,' she said in alarm. 'Don't do that. She's so mad at me, you'll only make it worse.'

But Rory had already made the call.

'Poppy,' he said. 'Yes, thank you. A very good day away.' He paused. 'Yes, I think we both needed it, very much so. It was . . . Yes . . . Fantastic.' He waited again. 'How much do you want Ella on set this morning?' He paused. 'That much? Oh. I hope you're not going to do that. That would be very unfair. Okay, I'll keep her for a couple of hours more and then she's all yours. Okay. I'll tell her. Twelve o'clock, that's fine.'

He put down the phone.

'I'd avoid her for as long as you can. I think she needs to calm down.'

The thought of Poppy, still angry with her, still fuming, filled her with weariness.

'Then I'll stay here, if you don't mind.'

'Of course not. Find us something to watch. Order some

room service. Whatever you want. I'm going to find some
clean clothes.'

He left her and went through to the bathroom, and she
stood up and found the big leather book of Hotel Informa-
tion and flicked through the pages, seeing, as Rory had said,
that they had almost any DVD she could think of. She put
the book down again, thinking she would let him choose,
and wandered around the room, touching the petals on
the creamy roses bunched in a round glass vase upon the
sideboard, then picking up a fat cream envelope with Rory's
name upon it.

'What's this?' she asked him when he returned from the
shower. 'Perhaps it arrived while we were away?'

'No. It's Olga's show reel. I suppose I should pass it on to
Hayden, do her a favour like you said.'

'Why don't we watch it? It might be good.'

'You know that's not likely, Ella. You just want to laugh
at her.'

'I don't! She might be brilliant. You might be able to find
her a part. Rory? Perhaps you should be nicer about her?
She had guts, coming to find you like that. I say let's watch
her show reel.'

'We can't find every headcase like Olga a part in a film.
Okay? Now, I'm going to call room service and get us some
more breakfast, yes? A pot of good English tea and cakes and
scrambled eggs and bacon too? Yes? I wasn't hungry at the
Hôtel d'Or but I'm very hungry now. And then,' he went on,
'when that has arrived, okay, we'll watch Olga's show reel.'

They balanced their plates of scrambled eggs and bacon and
their tea on their knees, sitting side by side in the little cinema.

The curtains unfurled. The screen lightened. And suddenly, there was bright blue sky, but nothing else, and then the camera dipped dramatically and there was Olga, in the bottom right-hand corner, grinning at them both.

'What a good start,' said Rory. 'I've never seen a camera angle like that before.'

'I haf been in menny, menny good films in Kiev,' Olga said, from her corner of the screen. 'My first film was called *Stolych Nykya*.'

Abruptly there came a shot of snow-heavy ground, and tall miserable-looking pine trees, and what looked like a child, wrapped in a sheet, slowly making her way towards the camera. It was so poorly shot that it looked as if it had been filmed on a hand-held camera in the middle of a forest, but then, so did *The Blair Witch Project*.

'In Kiev, it was the beegest-selling love story of all time . . . The movie gross menny menny dollar.'

There was a second cut, this time to a bedroom – could it have been Olga's bedroom? A man and a woman lay upon a bed, perhaps sleeping, perhaps dead.

Beside her Rory twitched. 'Okay.' He made to stand up. 'I've seen enough.'

'No, wait,' insisted Ella. 'We must watch it all.'

'In nineteen ninee-ade,' said Olga, 'I was in movie *My Chariots of Fire*. I theenk you know vis film. I voss the starter,' she giggled. 'Viz the red flag.'

Rory sat up straighter. 'Did I hear that right? What did she say?'

'*My Chariots of Fire*,' Ella repeated.

On the screen appeared a young stocky man. He had

short fat legs and was completely naked. He walked across the screen, then dropped down to his haunches and spat on the palms of his hands, one after another. Then the camera angle widened to show that he was not alone and that there were several other men lining up alongside him.

'Which one's Ian Charleson?' Rory whispered.

Then on to the screen came Olga, dressed like a cheerleader but clearly wearing no knickers, a red flag in her hand. She moved into the centre of the camera and smiled boldly.

'Ready, boys? Are you ready to run?'

The runners began stretching their legs, preparing for the off, shifting position restlessly.

Olga waved her flag and the runners broke forward, running in a pack, all apart from the first man they had seen, the young stocky man, with white hair in a pony-tail, and a familiar look in his eye.

'Play it again. Rewind. I need to see that face again.'

'I know!' Ella cried. 'I'm thinking it too, but don't go back. We have to see what happens next.'

As the body of runners passed Olga and ran out of sight, the pony-tailed man began to saunter towards her, swinging his naked hips.

In response Olga giggled and waved her red flag in the air. 'Stay back. Stay avay.'

'Look at his face,' Ella whispered. 'It's him. Can you believe it?'

The pony-tailed man now reached Olga and tried, half-heartedly, to pull the flag from her hand.

'No,' she cried. 'No. Vie do you not run?' And then she smacked him with it on his bare white bottom. In response he ripped off her frilly cheerleader's skirt and, within a frame, the two of them were tumbling naked together on the ground.

'Ouch!' Ella winced, looked through her fingers. 'That flag just went somewhere it shouldn't have done. This is getting much too explicit.'

Rory laughed. 'You saying you've had enough?'

'Yes and no.' She took her hands away from her face. 'He's not really my idea of a romantic lead but we must see it to the end. We have to know what we've got.'

'Quickly, quickly,' Olga encouraged, up on the screen. 'Soon ze other runners will be returning. They must not know vot we haf done.'

'I need to check this,' said Rory.

He leaned across and took the remote off Ella and sent the pictures flying back again to the first few seconds, and then he held 'Pause', so that the man's face filled the screen in front of them.

'We've got him,' Rory cried, jumping to his feet. 'We've got him! Whatever he says. If he finds out about Carey and me, threatens Hayden, blames you, it doesn't matter any more.' He looked at Ella gleefully. 'All we have to do is show him this and say *You Tube*. And Anton Klubcic, movie mogul, with an ego the size of Kiev, will do exactly what we say.'

'Poor Olga,' said Ella sadly. 'Someone needs to tell her you don't put a porn film in your show reel.'

'Ella, thank God she did. She's done you a monumentally huge favour. Don't you see, it means you're off the hook! You don't have to pretend any more.'

'Of course! Isn't that great,' she said drily. 'Great for both of us.'

'Fantastic,' Rory agreed wholeheartedly. 'But, having said that, we've convinced Anton already. We don't need to use this now. I think we should hold on to this film, save it for the next time he acts like a bully and tries to blow someone up in their tracks, or forces some poor girl like Carey into his bed. Save it for a better time.'

'Whatever you think,' said Ella, remembering only the relief with which it had occurred to him that she wasn't needed any more. The memory of it pressed down between her shoulders like a physical pain, making her want to run out of his room with her head down, out of the hotel, down the streets and back to Le Sport, to where she could close the door, and sit, and think and think about how awful it felt not to have to pretend any more.

Fourteen

An hour later, when she left La Sauterelle for the set, the press were waiting for her. Unprepared, she found herself running down the streets of Florent to get away, hesitating only to push their lenses out of her face, only getting clear of them when she reached the boundaries of the set and the security guards were able to help her in and keep them out.

Outside her trailer, waiting for her, was Poppy.

'I've got a car picking Rory up from the hotel in the next ten minutes,' she said coldly. 'He's on set at one fifteen.'

'Thanks.'

Ella looked back at her steadily, already so miserable even Poppy couldn't hurt her now. 'When are you going to stop being so angry?'

Poppy blinked slowly. 'I'm angry with myself.'

'You probably don't believe it but I do miss how we were.'

'Why? Because you're sad now and you want someone to help you? You certainly look terrible.'

'I missed you when I was happy too.'

'Ells, I missed you too. But we can't ignore the fact that one, you didn't trust me. And two, you lied to me. And three, why create the myth that you liked Sam? And while we're at it, four, why treat him so badly?'

'It wasn't a myth.'

'But you forgot all about him! Just as soon as Rory gave you the nod.'

'Did I?' Ella asked. 'Is that how it was?'

'Well, wasn't it? Tell me! That's what I mean. Talk to me. If I'm getting it wrong, start putting me right.'

'Okay. I'll tell you that the famous film star has run true to form and has now dumped his lowly make-up artist.'

Poppy looked back at her curiously. 'You're really upset!'

'Yes,' Ella shouted back at her. 'I am!'

'You're in love with him?'

'Don't ask me that.'

'Why not? There's nothing more important.'

'Yes,' said Ella.

'Oh, Jesus,' said Poppy.

'But it means nothing because we're over. Over, even though we never began.'

'And Sam?'

'Sam and I never even started but it wasn't my fault. And I'm happy for Sacha, I really am. I wouldn't want it any different.'

'Hayden did say to tell you that you can talk to me now.'

'He did? Okay, then prepare yourself, because you're going to see you owe me one big apology.'

'Do I? If I say sorry, will you forgive me?'

'Possibly.'

'Oh Ells, I'm so sorry. Whatever you're going to say, I'm sure you're right and I'm in the wrong, because I always am.' She reached forward and hugged her. 'You say you've lost Rory but perhaps you are wrong about that, and what the hell?' She hugged her tighter. 'Think of it this way, even if you've lost him, at least you've got me back.'

Inside the trailer, Rosalind handed her a stack of magazines.

'You should look at these.'

Ella took them, sat down with them on her lap and brushed through them quickly, seeing her face and Rory's on the front of nearly every one.

'They're as accurate as usual,' Rosalind said. 'Read what they say inside.'

She picked up the first one, turned to the right page.

'Ella Buchan trained in the burns unit of a major London teaching hospital,' she read aloud, then looked up at Rosalind. 'Did I?'

'They got you right in *Star Dust*. Read that one.'

Ella shuffled through the magazines until she'd found it, moved to the right page and read on.

'Unknown make-up artist, Ella Buchan, snares our favourite man.'

'It wasn't quite like that, you know,' said Ella, quietly.

'I agree. You're certainly not "Unknown".'

'I didn't mean it like that.' She turned to another magazine and read aloud.

'Flame-haired Ella Buchan once earned thousands of pounds a night as a lap dancer in a bar in Tottenham Court Road.' She looked up at Rosalind. 'I wish.'

Rosalind moved to the window of the trailer. 'And in *Secrets of the Stars*, they say that you did the make-up for a troupe of transvestites, before being spotted by your boss

Rosalind Lane, which, as far as I know, is the only line of truth in the lot of them.'

'They've written me up so fast. I had no idea it could be like this. And I am a nobody – imagine what it's like to be Rory and have this happen all the time.'

'It'll settle down again, once they've got used to you. It's because you are new. You're new news, it won't be the same in a few weeks' time.'

'Rosalind,' Ella stopped. 'There's not going to be any *few weeks' time*. It's over already. It's over before it even began. And in the interest of keeping you in the loop, I think you should know that.'

'I'm sorry to hear it.' Rosalind turned back to her. 'You look very sad.'

Ella shook her head, biting her lip, again finding she was having to fight not to cry. 'It was never about anything more than a bit of fun. We all knew that.'

Rosalind touched her ear uncomfortably. 'Ella, I'm sure he's the last thing on your mind, but I hope you're not thinking you can now have another shot at Sam?'

'You're right. He really is the last man on my mind.'

'I'm so glad, because I have to tell you that Sacha spent last night in bed with Sam. They first got together three and a half years ago, and I have to say – I hope it's not hurtful to hear it, I don't think it will be – that I'm delighted that finally they are back together now.'

'I'm very pleased for her too.'

Rosalind smiled. 'May I also say that I have no doubt that this happy change in her fortunes was entirely due to the make-up lesson I gave her last night.'

Despite the misery enveloping her, Ella found herself raising a little smile. 'You mean you persuaded her to ditch the Peacock Blue?'

'I did. And we agreed to tone down the clothes, too. She's moving on to Shabby Chic. Myself, I have my doubts. In my mind, once a pink-polka-dot-hot-pants kind of a girl, always a pink-polka-dot-hot-pants kind of a girl.'

Ella laughed. 'You know I'd never have gone near Sam if I'd known about him and Sacha?'

'Of course. But Ella?' Rosalind leaned forward to her. 'Are you okay? What happened when you went away with Rory?'

Ella bowed her head.

'You think you're in love with him?'

'But how could I be?' Ella muttered miserably. 'How could it happen in just a couple of days?'

'Oh, darling,' Rosalind cried, and pulled her forward into her arms. 'How terrible for you, poor Ella. Because you do know, my darling, that there is absolutely no point thinking such thoughts about Rory. He's a film star, and film stars are the most unreliable, arrogant sods that ever walked the earth. You don't want to fall in love with one because it will only make you terribly sad, far more sad than you even are now. I know because it happened to me. I was in love with someone for twenty years, I followed him all over the world, and I gave him the best years of my life. Why do you think I've never lived with anybody, never got married? So don't, don't, darling, don't fall for Rory.'

Ella bent her head and started to cry. 'But that doesn't mean it would be the same for me. Look at Dustin Hoffman, didn't he marry his make-up artist? I'm sure there are loads more examples of faithful film stars and really happy make-up artists. Don't tell me it can never work.'

'But you know this life. You know what it means, new films, scooting about the world on location for months on end. It's an appalling lifestyle.'

Ella looked up at her, tears swimming in her eyes. 'I could do his make-up. I could go with him everywhere.'

'Yes, you could,' Rosalind conceded, 'and you certainly know Rory better than I do. And Ella, what I can say in your favour is that you're a good judge of character and if you've fallen in love with him, than maybe that's a sign that I've got him wrong.'

'But it's not the lifestyle that's the problem.' Ella could feel her bottom lip start to quiver violently. 'The problem is Rory. This was always a sham. He doesn't really like me at all.'

'What do you mean? Of course he does.'

'No,' said Ella. 'He doesn't. Or he does *like me*, but that's all. You'll see once we go outside. It's over now. It was never anything more than a sham.' If she was allowed to tell Poppy, why shouldn't she tell Rosalind? 'We set up the press, we were never together.'

Rosalind breathed in sharply, her face suddenly clearing. 'Oh, my God, of course. Haven't I been so stupid? I've been trying and trying to work this out, and of course, Hayden put you up to this. This was about Carey, wasn't it? I knew they were close. What happened? Did some journalist get photographs of them, something like that?'

'Exactly like that. I don't think it matters to tell you now, as long as you don't go marching round to Anton.'

Rosalind nodded grimly. 'So Hayden found an exit from

a very sticky situation. But he's made a mistake using you. I'm not going to let him get away with hurting you.'

'He didn't hurt me. I hurt myself. I didn't have to fall for Rory. That was never meant to happen.'

Rosalind gave her a long, considered stare. 'What a very good and loyal friend to this film you've been.' She reached forward and pulled Ella into her arms again, hugging her tightly. 'I'm sorry. Sorry I didn't see it right from the start. If I had, you might have let me help you. He is a complete devil to have persuaded you to do this and not to let you tell anyone.' Her eyes widened. 'Please tell me you didn't sleep with Rory? Hayden is completely shameless. I wouldn't put it past him asking you to do that too.'

'Of course I didn't, I'm a good girl.' Ella looked back at her, smiling through the tears. 'But I wish I had.'

Rosalind laughed. 'You never know. You might still.'

Ella couldn't bring herself to agree. 'He'll be here in a moment. I think Hayden has told him he's done enough. I don't think he feels he needs to be with me any more.'

At that moment the trailer door opened and Carey leaned in.

'Hey,' she said to Ella. 'Is it true that Hayden's given you the thumbs up to call it a day?'

'It's still a secret!' Ella cried. 'Shut up!'

'And in any case, Hayden certainly hasn't said *call it a day*,' said Rory, coming up the steps behind Carey. 'As I was just telling you, Carey.'

He glanced up into the trailer, took in Rosalind and Ella and thought better of saying whatever else he was about to say in front of them.

He took Carey by the arm and led her back down the steps.

'Wait,' said Ella running after them, unable to bear him leaving again so soon. 'What's wrong?'

Rory turned back to her. 'Carey is suggesting that as Hayden's got his pictures, and Anton's off our backs, she and I can pick up from where we left off. And I am telling her it's not an option.'

Carey looked stonily back at him. 'What you're saying is you don't want to. Go on, admit it.'

'I don't want to,' agreed Rory.

Carey's face fell. 'But you always said you would.'

'No.' He shook his head. 'I never said that.'

'Everybody's a winner but me,' Carey said bitterly. 'The film's off the hook, Hayden's happy. How dare you and Hayden abandon me! How dare you hardly bother to speak to me, leave me with him, having to lie in his bed night after night and feel his disgusting hands all over me without even a thought.'

'You're right, Carey,' Ella stepped in. 'I don't blame you for feeling angry. You want that part in the *Broken Wing*? I'll go and have a word with Anton. He's coming on set this morning. I saw it on the schedule.'

Carey looked back at her, astonished.

'What could you say to Anton?'

'Something good, trust me.' Ella saw the look of concern on Rory's face. 'It has to be me,' she insisted. 'Trust me, it's time. And he hates you and he doesn't seem to mind me. It's better I talk to him.'

'But what are you going to say?' Carey asked incredulously.

She turned away and quickly keyed in Hayden's number.

'My turn to tell you what to do,' she told Hayden as soon as he picked up. 'And I'm telling you this. If Anton is not already in your trailer, he'll surely be arriving any moment and I want you to make sure you're out. So sprint away if you have to. I want to talk to him. And trust me, Hayden, it's better that I do.'

She saw Anton outside Hayden's trailer, standing there, clearly waiting for him, his face red and ugly with anger. She arrived hurriedly at his side.

'Do you mind if we have a word?'

'I'm waiting for our cunt of a director. Talk to me out here.'

'I think you'd prefer it if we went inside.'

'Why? What have you got to say? Are you telling me you know about this film too? Of course you do. You were there with them, that night in the hay barn. You were there when they made it. This piece of shit. Of course you knew what they were up to.' Suddenly he lunged for her, caught her shoulder and pulled her up close to his face. 'Who else has seen this? Who else knows?'

When he let her go again he seemed surprised that she didn't immediately make off across the film set, but instead stayed where she was, standing her ground.

'I don't know,' Ella said, looking back at him coolly, 'but you need to forget about it right now, because we're about to go on set to shoot the most important scene in the whole of this film, and I haven't yet made up our leading man.'

Anton opened his mouth and took a deep furious breath.

'No!' She cut across him. 'None of that. None of your *Rory Defoe won't ever work again* crap. Because it's not going to help you any more. Nobody's double-crossed you, Anton. What has Carey done to you that you didn't do to her? You both used each other. And Carey's the one who's paid the price, not you. And because of your ridiculous rages, Hayden had to use me too, to protect his film. Why did he think he needed to do that? You put him in that position. You storm around, you rage, you lose control, so people can't be honest with you. I know what you're wanting to do now. You want to march on set and tell everybody that the film is over, finished, and what will that gain? The only truth here is Ambrose. And Ambrose lied too. He betrayed his wife. But you don't hate him, you love him. He is the one you must protect now. He's the one that has pulled us all together. That's why we've been here. Everything else is incidental.

'He fell in love. And he made a good film. And he lost the love of his life. Perhaps that's like you? Who do you think you lost? Carey? Liberty? Were you in love with her? Of course not. You weren't in love with either of them. You just want to let them rot when you think they're beating you. Stop, stop doing that. Let Rory and Carey take their chance if that is what they want to do, be gracious, give her that part in *The Broken Wing*, or a better one, and pay for her acting classes or something, it's the least you can do. We're only talking about your pride. Care about the film, not them. Give it every chance, support it now. It won't succeed without you.'

She'd got into her stride and was not stopping now, not when she'd got him, listening silently, his eyes never leaving her face.

'And stop using your position to get the girls,' she rushed on, 'because you'll never get one worth having if you don't. And another thing, if Rory's little film is good, let Hayden use it.'

'He was making fun of me with that film. I was not supposed to see it. Unfortunately for Rory, a friend on set made sure that I did.'

'I heard you had spies on set, but I never believed it was true.'

He stared back at her. 'Believe it.'

She knew he'd been listening and perhaps he'd taken some of her words to heart, but she also knew that it wasn't enough.

'In that case,' she went on. 'Perhaps a spy told you that a girl called Olga came to visit Rory in the trailer a few days ago. Olga Valena, you might remember her.'

At her name his eyes darted nervously to her face.

'Did you hear about her? She was sweet. She wanted a part in a film, left us her show reel, that kind of thing. You know, she made such a funny mistake – she included a porn film. Someone should tell her it's not the done thing.'

'Where is it?'

'Safe, up on a shelf in a library, marked *The Klubcic Show Reel*, and it'll stay there just as long as you look after Carey, don't threaten Rory and give *To End All War* all the support it deserves.'

Fifteen

The next morning, make-up had a 5 a.m. start. Before Rory arrived in the trailer at 6.30, Ella had already worked for an hour and a half in the marquee down by the field hospital, helping Rosalind and the rest of the team of artists prepare the huge number of extras needed for filming that morning.

With her brushes and sponges, bases, powders and concealers, Ella had first worked on the wounds, each time carefully checking against her notes for the level of impact, whether it was a sniper's bullet or a random shell, checking for whether the extra was supposed to be alive or dead, with or without bruising. Next, she'd sculpted facial wounds, painting on layers of sweat and dirt, then she'd turned to the gelatine prosthetics, and finally to the several wigs and hairpieces, knotting facial hair and applying moustaches, and it was only when the five-minute call was shouted into the marquee and the extras rose to their feet to leave that she realized how she'd been running on adrenalin, had not thought even to snatch a can of Coke, in the whole time she'd been there.

She returned to the trailer just ten minutes before Rory,

and had barely had time to lay out what she would need before he climbed the trailer steps and came in; and she sat on her stool and waited for him to sit down in front of her, almost for the final time. Around her was the usual bustle of the trailer: the radio playing, Minnie and Jemima laughing together, but everywhere, the unspoken, sad acknowledgement that this was almost the last day, almost the end of the show. In a couple more days it would be the wrap party, which she imagined would be an ordeal that she would disappear from as soon as possible, and then everybody would leave, the sets would start to come down, and many of them would not see each other again until the first of the screenings later on in the year.

Rosalind and Liberty had already left for the set. Much as Ella missed having Rosalind beside her, part of her was grateful for it too, for the silence, the chance to wallow in uninterrupted silence, for the fact that Rosalind's absence meant that there was now a definite gap between her and Jemima, and therefore no need for Ella to take part in the conversation that flowed up and down the trailer. The last thing she wanted to do that morning was talk to anyone.

Rory sat down in front of her.

'Hello,' she said automatically, then sat down on her chair beside him to look at his face and belatedly took in that he looked terrible, his skin white, huge dark shadows beneath his eyes. 'What's the matter? What have you done?'

'No sleep, I guess.' He laughed shortly, not meeting her eye.

She went to the back of the trailer, boiled a kettle and poured some of the water into a shallow bowl. Then she took one of her bottles of Face It and dropped it into the bowl to warm it up.

Next she soaked large cotton wool eye pads in the warmed lotion, tipped him back in his chair and brought them carefully to his eyes, laying the pads gently down. She sat quietly watching him, then leaned closer and slipped her fingers into his thick dark hair and began gently to comb it back from his forehead.

'Bye!' called Minnie from the front of the trailer, making her jump and spin round.

Jemima and two actresses playing nurses were standing behind her.

'We're going down to the set, but, just to warn you, Jemima will be back in a moment with an army captain. He's got some kind of trouble with his moustache.'

Then the trailer door slammed shut, leaving them alone.

'Lie still,' Ella told Rory. 'Rest for a moment.'

She sat quietly, looking down at his face, studying the neat curve of his ears, the softness of the skin just at the point where the eye pads rested against his cheekbones, the flare of his nose and the beautiful outline of his lips.

I will survive without you, she thought, looking down at him. I did so before, so why shouldn't I again?

'That night,' he said suddenly. 'The first night when you stayed at La Sauterelle. Why was I such a bastard?'

She lifted an eye pad. 'I don't know, but it doesn't matter now.'

'It does. I can't stop thinking about it. I'm sorry.'

'Don't worry. You'll forget soon enough. You'll be off to Brazil next week, or wherever it is you're filming next.'

'Ella?' He interrupted her suddenly. 'Why were you crying with Rosalind? I came in but you didn't notice and you were crying.'

'Because I found the cameras so horrible. I'd never get used to them. Thank God I'm yesterday's news.'

She took the pads out of his hands, dropped them into the bin and came back to sit beside him, first bringing out moisturizer, toner, and then the base foundation and sponging it against his face and throat, smoothing out his skin tone, even though one side of his face was about to be plastered in soot and dirt.

'Stop, just for a moment.'

She stopped, putting her hands down in her lap.

'I wondered if you might have been crying about me?'

He said it so quietly, sympathetically even, that she felt fresh tears immediately fill her eyes. This was the consequence of no sleep, she thought, abruptly pushing back her chair, standing up and walking away from him, so that he couldn't see.

'Don't, Rory,' she begged. 'Please.'

'But I want to know.'

'You can't. You'll make me cry again.'

'Ella.'

'People are about to walk in,' she insisted. 'Please, don't do this now.'

'Just tell me.'

Jemima returned, stomping up the steps at just the right moment with the army captain behind her, and with them there in the trailer, it was impossible to talk; Ella didn't have to say another word and could work quickly and silently, until finally she'd finished and could stand up to stretch her aching back.

'One cameraman, ready to go.'

Rory pushed himself free of the table and stood up from his chair, not waiting for her to help him undo the gown that had protected his uniform from her make-up.

'I don't think I can wait until the end of the day. I have to talk to you now.'

In answer she picked up his hand and held it to her lips and kissed it.

He breathed out a long trembling breath. 'Ella!'

'Later,' she insisted. 'We can't talk now.'

'Background sound,' called the First AD.

'Rolling sound.'

'Background action!'

Ambrose walked forward, face on towards the cameras, his face white and grim, his eyes wild, covered in soot and dust. In his arms was Helen Dove, her eyes closed, her cheek resting against his chest, blood pouring from a wound on her head, running down her neck, soaking the long white sleeve of her blouse.

'Find the doctor, please!' Ambrose cried, fighting off the frantic nurses who were rushing towards him to help. He swung round to another, tears running down his cheeks. 'We must help her. Please, please, save her!'

But as he spoke, high above the sound of his voice, and the whistle of shells, and the cries of men, came another sound, first from far away, but growing louder with each second, a muffled ever-growing roar that seemed to come from high above them, and then for just a moment the whole church seemed to fall silent before suddenly, with an ear-splitting crash, the stained-glass window exploded high above them, and as the myriad pieces of coloured glass fell in a rainbow down upon them, so too did the beams and rafters of the church, crashing and crushing, toppling down upon the patients and nurses, the doctors, and Ambrose too.

The final scene filmed that morning was of Dr Kinsman, climbing carefully through the dust and the rubble, to the Aeroscope. He picked it up and carried it carefully out of the bombed-out ruins of the church into the early morning sunshine.

Sixteen

Ambrose was lying in the middle of a long row of beds and bandaged men. For once the ward was spotless and peaceful, the nurses moving quietly, the white sheets clean and crisp. On either side of him, soldiers lay sleeping. Sitting beside Ambrose, on a wooden stool, was a woman, a hospital letter-writer.

'Action background sound,' called the First AD.

'Action Eleanor.'

The letter-writer leaned forwards to Ambrose.

'The name is Robert, you say?'

'Yes, *Dear Robert*, that is how I should like to start.'

'*Dear Robert*,' she wrote down dutifully.

'*I trust that if you have this letter safely in your hand, then these latest five reels of film are safely with you also. I hope so, as they are the last we will have for some time.*'

Ambrose stopped. He swallowed, closed his eyes, and his heavily bandaged arm twitched against the cotton bedsheet.

The letter-writer, a pretty young woman with shiny brown hair drawn back in a chignon, wearing an ankle-length navy dress and sensible black shoes, wrote steadily. When she had finished she looked up at him again, eagerly, her large dark eyes full of sympathy, waiting to see if he could go on.

Ambrose continued. *'The truth is that I hate the prospect of going home even more than the thought of staying here. I know that I can never return to Alice and my life back in Doncaster.'*

The letter-writer gasped in shock. 'You can't write that!'

But Ambrose ignored her, full of resolution. *'Once I have been transported out of this field hospital that I am writing to you from now, I will be sent back on a hospital ship to England and I have requested a convalescence in Scotland.* Write it!' he insisted as the letter-writer hesitated, her pen trembling in her hand.

'Cut!' called Hayden, his voice demolishing the intensity of the atmosphere, causing several people to raise their heads to him in surprise and annoyance. 'Sorry, guys. I know. That was brilliant. This will be very quick.'

Wasting no time, he moved to join Rory at his hospital bed. He bent to speak to him, and Ella thought she saw Hayden's face break into a brief smile before he patted Rory briefly on the cheek and then, looking serious again, strode back to his place at the edge of the set and nodded to the First AD that they were ready to resume filming.

'Action Rory,' called the First AD.

'I will be sent back on a hospital ship to England and I have requested a convalescence in Scotland,' Rory repeated, then waited as, reluctantly, the letter-writer began to write.

He went on. *'Robert, I have nobody else to ask but you, so forgive me if I put you in an impossible position, asking you to do this for me now.'*

Again the letter-writer stopped. Her eyes had taken on a tearful, wide-eyed stare.

'Write it down,' Ambrose insisted. 'I have to ask Robert to do this. I want my wife to know not to visit me. If I write to her she will not believe it, but Robert will convince her because he knows the truth.'

'You have been a brave man. Are you sure you . . . you have to do this now?'

'If Alice sees me like this – lying in a hospital bed, without my hand – I know that she will convince herself that I will return to her. She will probably persuade the hospital to let her bring me home. And I won't go. I do not love her. I never loved her.'

The letter-writer leant towards him. 'When a man is contemplating leaving his wife, the least he can do is tell her himself, not leave it to a man she hardly knows.'

'Robert is a good friend to both of us. And once I am well, I will travel back to Doncaster and I will tell her how I am not finished yet with this war. But now I need to write to Robert and he has to pass on to her that I am safe.'

The letter-writer bowed her head and Ambrose fell back against his pillows in exasperation.

'If I could write it myself I would.'

'Cut,' called Hayden. He turned slowly about the room, taking them all in. 'This is great, guys, it's working really well and it's looking fantastic.'

Ella – like most of the rest of the crew – was finding the scene unbearably sad. Perhaps it was the state she was in herself, but she could hardly look at Rory, lying there in that narrow bed in that great long room. And knowing that the story was true, and that Alice did indeed get a visit from Robert, and consequently never saw Ambrose again, made the scene all the sadder, because what had Alice ever done wrong but love him? How devastating it must have been for her, Ella thought, to hear that Rory – no, not Rory, Ambrose – to hear that Ambrose couldn't even bring himself to say goodbye to her.

Ella had her script in her hand, and she turned to the back of it, knowing that there was a paragraph there which would be added to the end of the film in the edit, just before the credits rolled, detailing what happened to Ambrose later. In all the times she'd read the script, she'd never read the final words before, but she did now.

Ambrose March never did return home to Doncaster and to his wife, Alice. After the death of VAD nurse Helen Dove in 1915 and the loss of his hand, he returned to England to convalesce and then, as soon as he could, he went back to the war, first to the Western Front and then in 1918 to Gallipoli.

His footage of Field Hospital 29, and the battles witnessed in the countryside surrounding it, were not shown until after his death, but they are now respected as the most outstanding filmed sequences of the First World War ever shot on a moving camera. Ambrose March died in 1951 at the age of sixty-one.

She looked back at the set, to Rory lying there among his pillows, and thought how far away he seemed, how he would be leaving the next day, to go straight to another film, another location, another country, and she felt as if he had already gone, leaving just Ambrose behind.

Around her, Ella could feel the restlessness that always built before Action was called, and she realized, for the first time in her working life, that she'd forgotten to do her job and run on to the set to check Rory's face. And, also for the first time ever, that she didn't care.

'Roll sound,' called the First AD.

'Action Eleanor.'

'Tell me what you want me to write next,' the letter-writer instructed Ambrose. She waited, pen poised.

'*Robert,*' Ambrose went on, '*I know that without Helen Dove there will never again be joy in my life. Perhaps these words might even be making you smile, to think of someone as cold-hearted as me falling so deeply in love, but it happened, and without her I now see no point to my world. She made me a better man than I can be alone. She was so full of passion and wisdom. I loved her so much.*'

'Keep rolling,' called Hayden breathlessly.

The letter-writer paused to wipe away her tears, then continued writing and, as she did so, Ambrose pushed himself up in the bed and brought his shattered, bandaged arm across himself and held it carefully in his lap.

Rory looked across to Ella.

'*Perhaps I always loved her, even from the first moment that I saw her, standing in the window of her trailer.*'

Immediately the letter-writer stopped, her pen held mid-air.

'The window of *her trailer*?' she repeated, confused.

Ella felt her heart stumble.

'Keep rolling,' called Hayden.

'Yes,' said Rory, 'the window of her trailer. That's when I first saw her. I looked at her as she came through the door and stood at the top of her trailer steps, trying to stop me from going in, and she was the most beautiful girl I'd ever seen in my life. And the thought that she had a man inside made me feel as if I would faint with jealousy. I felt that, all before we'd even said a word to each other.'

Poppy and Sacha let out a great whoop of delight, and the letter-writer looked over to Hayden, confusion all over her face.

'Keep rolling,' Hayden called again to the cameras. 'Don't stop.'

Ella had moved – no, floated – to the edge of the set. She didn't want to move again in case that made him stop speaking.

'And ever since then, I have only wanted to be at her side. She makes me laugh. She has, although she doesn't know it yet, very nearly made me cry.'

'Hurray!' called Poppy.

Rory ignored her, his eyes only on Ella. 'She doesn't take any of my messing around. She makes me a better man too. I want to woo her with flowers and romantic dinners and diamonds, but I know she probably would say no.' He smiled at her. 'Yes? Perhaps she'd say yes to the diamonds?'

'Action Ella!' called Hayden.

She shook her head.

'Yes to the flowers?' asked Rory, holding out his hand.

'For God's sake. Action Ella! Go on, get out there!' called Hayden for a second time.

She walked to the very edge of the set. Ahead of her the white lights were still blazing, the cameras still rolling.

She walked on, into the heat of the lights all around her, the dazzle, the silence, everyone staring, and saw, ahead, Rory waiting for her. She walked over to his hospital bed and he opened his arms to her and drew her towards him, on to the bed, and kissed her.

'I love you,' he whispered, so that only she could hear. 'I

321

love you very much and I want to be with you for ever. And if you don't want this life any more, I don't either. I'll write scripts. I'll live in Hounslow, if that is where you want to be.'

'I never wanted to live in Hounslow,' said Ella, laughing, burying her face against his shoulder, then kissing his neck, his cheek, his lips.

'All I mean is that wherever you want to go, I want to be there too.'

'Me too. Everywhere,' she breathed. 'Anywhere, I don't care. Rome, and Singapore . . .'

'I was thinking *On the Out* might be better if we moved it out of London.'

She giggled. 'Don't you think we could skip the work chat, just now?'

'Work chat?' He kissed her gently on the lips. 'You think this is work chat? This isn't work chat, this is love chat.' He tightened his arms around her. 'You do know, I only agreed to Hayden's stupid plan to get close to you. How could anyone have resisted an offer like that?'

'Mmm,' she laughed, kissing him again. 'I think some little part of me must have thought the same. I liked our days away from them all.'

'Me too, my darling, me too.' His arms tightened around her. 'The hardest thing I ever did was share a bed with you and stay away. But I thought I had to. I thought that was how an honourable man would behave. And now that I know I can be dishonourable, you do know that I'll never let you go?'

'I'd stay here for ever,' she whispered, kissing him again, then burying her face in his neck. 'But perhaps the crew might start to get restless.'

Kiss Like You Mean It

With Rory's arms around her, she glanced over to Hayden; she caught his eye and he grinned back at her happily.

'Cut,' he called, laughing and walking towards them. 'It's a wrap.'

Acknowledgements

A great big thank you to Olivia Lloyd (second assistant director) and Jenny Shircore (hair and make-up designer), who allowed me to watch them at work on the set of *The Young Victoria*. I learnt so much and they were both so kind and welcoming. I'm not sure Jenny would approve of all Ella's methods, and I should be clear that any strange techniques, odd choices of colour or bizarre use of equipment are nothing to do with Jenny. Many thanks too to Emily Blunt, Rupert Friend and Rachael Stirling for allowing me to sit in the make-up trailer and watch and listen as they were made-up.

Thank you, too, to my HGF for sorting out the Corporals from the Lance Bombardiers and for telling me some of the history of the Shropshire Division of the Royal Horse Artillery, and to all my lovely family and friends for their patience and good advice as I talked (and talked) through the glitches. Especially thank you to Josie – Jo, it's a cliché but so true, once again, I couldn't have done it without you – and of course all my love and thanks to Ant, Tom and Jack too.

Finally, a big thank you to Imogen Taylor, for all her editorial care and good advice and to her team at Pan Macmillan. And to Araminta Whitley, who is still the best agent in town. I'm very lucky to have her looking after me.

extracts reading groups
books competitions books new
discounts extracts extracts discounts
competitions events
books new
competitions
events books
extracts
new titles reading groups
interviews
reading groups events extracts extracts
discounts
new books events
events new
discounts extracts discounts
www.panmacmillan.com
extracts events reading groups
competitions books extracts new
books reading groups